COURT

of

VENOM

COURT

of

VENOM

by Kristin Burchell

OOLIGAN PRESS ✳ PORTLAND, OR

Court of Venom
© 2022 Kristin Burchell

ISBN13: 978–1–947845–32–9

Ooligan Press
Portland State University
Post Office Box 751, Portland, Oregon 97207
503.725.9748
ooligan@ooliganpress.pdx.edu
www.ooliganpress.pdx.edu

Library of Congress Cataloging-in-Publication Data
Names: Burchell, Kristin, 1972- author.
Title: Court of venom / by Kristin Burchell.
Description: Portland, Oregon : Ooligan Press, [2022]
Series: Ooligan Press Library Writers Project Collection
Identifiers: LCCN 2021052329 (print) | LCCN 2021052330 (ebook)
ISBN 9781947845329 (trade paperback) | ISBN 9781947845336 (ebook)
Subjects: LCGFT: Fantasy fiction. | Novels. | Classification: LCC PS3602.
U734 C68 2022 (print) | LCC PS3602.U734 (ebook)
DDC 813/.6--dc23/eng/20211029
LC record available at https://lccn.loc.gov/2021052329
LC ebook record available at https://lccn.loc.gov/2021052330

Cover design by Amanda Fink
Interior design by Alexandra Magel
Set in Adobe Jenson Pro and Nobel

References to website URLs were accurate at the time of writing. Neither the author nor Ooligan Press is responsible for URLs that have changed or expired since the manuscript was prepared.

Printed in the United States of America

Library Writers Project

Ooligan Press and Multnomah County Library have created a unique partnership celebrating the Portland area's local authors. Each fall since 2015, Multnomah County Library has solicited submissions of self-published works of fiction by local authors to be added to its Library Writers Project ebook collection. Multnomah County Library and Ooligan Press have partnered to bring these previously ebook-only works to print. *Court of Venom* is the fourth in an annual series of Library Writers Project books to be published by Ooligan Press. To learn more about the Library Writers Project, visit https://multcolib.org/library-writers-project.

Ooligan Press Library Writers Project Collection
Court of Venom by Kristin Burchell (2022)
Finding the Vein by Jennifer Hanlon Wilde (2021)
Iditarod Nights by Cindy Hiday (2020)
The Gifts We Keep by Katie Grindeland (2019)

Acknowledgments

First of all, thank you to the amazing team at Ooligan Press. I am especially grateful to Bailey Potter for her enthusiastic support; to Erica Wright for her insights that helped improve the plot; to Rachel Howe for her expertise in editing; and to Wren Haines, who came up with so many exciting ideas for marketing *Court of Venom*—especially the Zodiac!

I couldn't have done this without my writing partners: Kerry, Kim, and Pam. They read so many versions of this novel over the years but always assured me that they never got tired of it (truthfully or not). They cheered Badriya on through all the stages of her development.

Thank you to Kady Ferris and the Multnomah County Library for choosing *Court of Venom* for the Library Writers Project out of so many other wonderful novels.

Clark County Writers: Tina, Nancy, Maia, Gretchen, Lori, Delia, and Melinda—thanks for the support and advice during our monthly meetings.

Mom and Dad, thank you for always believing in me; and Brent and Tricia, I am grateful for all your support.

Finally, thank you to Shane for cheering me on and giving me space to be creative, and for many, many pep talks. To Max and Mimi, who inspire me to do my best every day. And of course Lady, for the countless walks that inspired new ideas and for being a fantastic support dog.

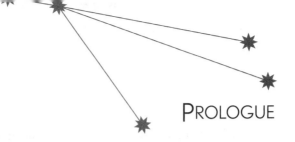

The court sat transfixed as Mina's voice filled the Dining Hall. Tears welled in the eyes of even the most jaded as she sang of regret and lost love. My eyes burned too, but I hadn't been able to cry since the day the King followed me into the garden.

The end of the song would come soon, and then I would look for my chance to poison her.

I wondered what Mother would say. She never meant for our magic to hurt anyone—to kill anyone.

And yet it had.

I planned to mix something that would only hurt Mina's vocal cords: she would have a sore throat and her voice would be raw and gravelly for a few days. I hoped she would take it as the warning it was meant to be.

But the anger I felt must have made its way into the drink. The liquid was perhaps a bit more amber than it should have been, the smell more bitter.

The song died away and she curtsied to thunderous applause. There were calls for an encore and I held my breath. But she gave a graceful wave and swept from the stage.

The spell of her voice still hung in the air as I approached her. "I'm sorry for how I've acted," I told her, my voice as repentant as I could make it. "I know your throat gets sore after a performance, especially one as breathtaking as that. I've mixed you a tincture to help. Please take it." I offered her the glass.

Her eyes narrowed. "Did you spit in this, little orphan?"

I forced myself to smile, though it must have been more of a grimace. "Of course not." I lowered my eyes. "I really am sorry for how I've acted."

She studied me for a long moment, and I held my breath. "I accept your apology," she said at last, and began to drink.

She was truly arrogant if she couldn't sense the resentment, fear, and anger in the drink. If she only knew the truth about the King's death, she wouldn't be so amused.

For a moment I thought about knocking the glass from her hand and warning her, but I waited until she drained the liquid before I turned and rushed from the Hall, the poison dripping from my fingertips.

Later that night there was a knock at my door so soft it might have been a scratch. I was not surprised to see Mina on the other side.

She pulled down the scarf, revealing the lower half of her face where the poison had burned her flesh. Her chin and the skin around her mouth was left blistered and wrinkled. "You should have killed me," she said through her ruined lips in a voice that was barely a whisper.

"You're lucky," I told her. "She wanted me to kill you."

She slipped away without answering.

I closed the door and sank onto my bed, eying the vials of poison on the table. Surely Solena would consider my debt paid now.

But I should have known better.

CHAPTER ONE

The desert wind slinks into Aran from the west, winding its way through the pathways, turning corners, and catching people unaware. Nights like this end in fights and tears. My mother jumped from the Wall into the Lost on a night like this, her body swallowed by the sand and her soul held ransom for silver.

Tonight many will remember things they'd rather forget, deeds that are best left in the past. Some will dread terrible events lurking in their futures if they aren't vigilant enough, or lucky enough, to stop them. Dark plans will take root in the minds of others, things they would never consider on any other night.

The chime of tambors in the Dining Hall is louder than usual. Drums beat like a heart and laughter echoes off the walls. The wistful melody of the lute holds a warning but it is lost in the sounds of merriment.

We sit on soft cushions around a low table, our goblets filled with sweet wine and our plates overflowing with spicy fish. Queen Solena presides at our center, her eyes glittering and her ebony hair shining. Our honored guest, the Duke of Dorros, sits to her right. He drinks deeply from his wine, his eyes fixed on her.

I sit on her left, per her request; either so she can more easily ridicule me or so she can whisper a command she doesn't want others to hear.

"What do you think of the fish, Diya?" Solena asks. "It was so kind of the Duke to bring it for us, don't you think?"

That's not my name. The words boil in my mind but I don't speak them. What would be the point? Instead, I make a show of raising my glass to her. A smile twists her mouth as she mirrors my gesture and takes a small sip of wine. She taps the table with her long nails, painted the color of rubies. One, two, three. The order will come soon.

I take a drink from the glass to wash down a piece of fish that is stuck in my throat. I am mindful not to drink too deeply—the wine could affect me in unexpected ways. Solena watches as I set down the glass, her smile widening. "Delicious," I manage.

"Vile, you mean," Petra breathes from beside me, so quietly that only I can hear. She is one of Solena's ladies, and nearly my friend, if such a thing were permitted here.

The Duke's round belly bumps the table and everyone's drink sloshes from their goblets. Petra curses beneath her breath. Oblivious, the Duke tilts his head back and drains his glass, then belches and slams the goblet onto the table. Everyone's hands dart to their drinks before they spill again.

In the shadows behind the Duke stands a Witch. She wears trousers and a loose white shirt, but it is the coins woven into her red hair that give her away. Her skin is smooth and unmarred, and her gray eyes gleam intently. She could be anywhere from twenty to fifty years old. To Solena's court the sharpness of her cheekbones speaks to hunger; the color of her skin to exposure to the sun; the searing color of her eyes to the demons in the Lost, to the threats that lie just beyond the walls of Aran. No one wants to be reminded of those.

Following my gaze, the Duke grimaces. "Terrifying, isn't she?" he says. "But I had to hire her to guide us across the Lost. She charged one hundred silvers."

Solena murmurs a sympathetic response, and even Petra can't suppress a shudder. The Witch's face doesn't change.

"What wonderful hospitality, My Lady Solena," the Duke continues. "You and your sister are delightful hostesses." My stomach churns as his eyes sweep over me.

"Oh, we aren't related," Solena says. "We hardly look alike, do we?" She widens her eyes in dramatic horror. Her court exchanges smirks, but no one dares laugh aloud in front of me, not if they want their potions and tonics.

She is right though; we don't look alike. Her hair is dark and smooth, thanks to the tonics I use to wash it, while mine is wavy and coarse. Her face is oval and her cheekbones defined, while mine is shaped like a heart, as my mother used to say. Her eyes are dark and watchful like a cat's. Mine are watchful, too, but they are round.

"I didn't mean to offend you, My Lady," the Duke says quickly. "She is sitting at your side, is all."

"My father adopted her," Solena explains. This story is a favorite of hers and she does not want to be interrupted. "Her mother was a dancer." She lowers her voice as if the word means something contemptible. "My father took Diya in out of the kindness of his heart after her mother died."

"Diya," the Duke muses. My skin crawls as he regards me over the lip of his glass. "What an interesting name. Is it a type of bird?"

"It's a beetle, actually. It digs in dung until it finds a living creature." Solena delivers the inevitable barb. "Then it burrows into their flesh and slowly poisons them." The Duke gives an uncertain laugh. Under the table Petra's knee bumps mine, perhaps by accident, or maybe she can see that my hand has tightened around my glass and my teeth are clenched and she wants to remind me of the pleasure Solena would gain should I betray my feelings.

Letting out a breath, I force myself to smile as I take another drink. Once again Solena raises her glass to me with a mocking smile.

The truth is, the King treated me as his own because he loved my mother more than he loved his wife, Solena's mother. Now all three are dead because of it.

"My name is Badriya," I say, but the Duke is already speaking.

"You are lucky to have one another. It must be difficult to rule a kingdom when you are so young." Solena's eyes narrow as he moves closer to her. She taps her nails against the table again. One, two, three. Yes, she will want him dead soon. I glance at the Witch but her face is like stone.

"I am glad you are enjoying yourself," Solena says. "I hear you are a daring gambler. Perhaps a game of chance?"

"I am daring indeed." He snakes his arm around her waist. Petra sucks in her breath and Solena's bodyguard takes a step forward, but she gives him a slight shake of her head.

The Duke leans forward, his lips at her ear. "I would enjoy some time alone with you."

"Perhaps after some dancing and more wine." She rises, the Duke's arm sliding from her waist, and we all stand with her. Petra drains her glass as Solena signals to the musicians. They end their plaintive song and strike up a livelier one, the drums beating an infectious rhythm and the tambor jingling. A young man in the Duke's entourage draws me into a dance. For a moment I can't resist pretending like I am an ordinary eighteen-year-old enjoying a flirtation with a stranger. He smiles at me and I smile in return. The music swirls around us.

Over his shoulder, I catch Solena's gaze and pull away from him. His hand brushes my arm as I side-step his reach. As much as I would like to stay, it is for his own safety that I depart.

I can feel the eyes of the past Kings and Queens staring down at me as I wind through the crowd of couples dancing. Each is honored with an effigy carved into the wall of the Dining Hall, so that they can forever watch their courts dining and carousing without them. There is the First King, Medacus, who made the bargain that founded Aran, and beside him stands his Queen, her expression grieving at the price she was asked to pay.

Other Kings and Queens wearing expressions varying from arrogance to joy to solemnity stand in a row, until one reaches the last King: Solena's father. He smiles kindly over his subjects, and even in death the sight makes me shiver. His eyes seem to follow me as I struggle through the crowd.

On one side of the Third King stands a sculpture of his wife, the Queen, Solena's mother. Her expression is serene as it never was in life. On his other side is an odd space where a statue of my mother once stood. As soon as the King died, Solena ordered it to be removed. The space is now covered with a great stone urn.

I have nearly reached the door when I catch a glimpse of wide eyes peering out from behind a silk hanging like a crocodile's. The cloth drops back into place. With a sigh, I walk over and pull it aside as Solena's younger sister, Najma, shrinks away.

"This is hardly dignified. Do I need to remind you that you're a princess?" I ask.

"Don't tell," she begs. "Please?"

My scolding dies on my tongue as I study her. At first I hated her because she was Solena's sister. Then I noticed the way she watched Solena and the other courtiers hungrily, waiting to be noticed, to be invited, as I once had. As I still sometimes do.

"I'm old enough to be here," Najma persists. "I'm thirteen! You've got to convince Solena. Please?"

With a grimace I join her, letting the hanging fall around us, our backs against the warm stone wall. The fabric is light enough that we can faintly see what is happening in the Hall. The Duke is swaying, his eyes unfocused, and Solena is just out of his reach. A smile is frozen on her face. Petra dances nearby with one of the Duke's men, a tuberose blossom tucked behind her ear. Girls in Aran are told that the scent of the tuberose might cause us to act recklessly, but Petra always wears one. She tilts her head back and laughs, always merry, no matter how tense the moment might be. I almost consider her a friend. Almost.

The young man I had danced with is now swaying with Yadira, Solena's favorite lady-in-waiting. He gazes at her hungrily, though she hardly seems to notice, smiling with her eyes closed as if she is in the middle of a pleasant dream. I hope she didn't take too much of the Stardust I had given her.

"What is the matter with Yadira lately?" Najma wonders.

"Bed," I tell her, and her smile vanishes. I regret the sharpness of my words, but I don't want her to guess the reason for Yadira's behavior. Before I can soften my words, Najma rolls her eyes and storms from behind the cloth. I follow her out of the Hall but she rushes ahead. She crosses the courtyard and races up the steps to the gallery that leads to her chamber. Before I can reach her, she closes the door.

"Good night," I say, but there is no answer from the other side of the door. I know she wishes to wound me—I did the same to my mother—but her coldness hurts more than I would like to admit.

Sighing, I wander across the gallery and look out over the city. Mother and I arrived here six years ago, when I was twelve, and even after all that's happened, there is no denying the beauty of Aran. The buildings are all made of white stone, gleaming in the moonlight. The glass in the windows is tinted light blue so that in the sunlight it turns the color of water. The scent of lilies hangs in the air.

Behind me are the Favorites' Chambers, where those closest to Solena reside. These rooms are the most opulent on the northern side of the city, where it is slightly cooler. Trees grow in a row in front of them, jeweled with oranges. Their scent sweetens the air on even the hottest afternoons. Though I am hardly one of Solena's favorites, I reside here as well. She needs to keep me close. Of course, my chamber is merely a maid's room, adjacent to hers and only a quarter of the size.

The less fortunate live across the courtyard, huddled against the southern side of the Wall. The sun is relentless there, heating the rooms like an oven. The rooms are much smaller and the floors are rough compared to the smooth, polished tile in the northern side of the city. In the mornings the air smells of manure from the horses in the stable a few yards away. Tonight, most of the windows are dark, for the residents here are mostly servants, and nearly all of them are busy entertaining the Duke and his entourage. A few yards away are the Lesser. That's what the Favorites call these quarters.

Despite the name, I am envious of the easy chatter and light laughter among the servants that holds none of the danger of the Favorites. No matter how stealthily I try to approach, their laughter dies away the moment I come close.

A great roar bursts from the open doors of the Gambling Hall across the courtyard. Someone's fortune has either been made or lost. For a moment the music spilling from the Dining Hall is drowned out.

Within Aran's walls there is only revelry and light, but on the other side lies the Lost, lapping at the stones, seething and waiting to devour anyone foolish enough to venture into it. It rolls in every direction toward the horizon, where the sand and the night sky melt together.

Supposedly the Wall was built to guard against the hostile armies of other cities, but few are willing to risk a trek across the wastelands to attack tiny Aran. Everyone here knows its true purpose.

At the center of the city a fountain bubbles with the water that gives Aran its radiance and its citizens unusual youth and beauty. Legend says that it is enchanted. King Medacus built Aran on a bargain he made with a Witch nearly three hundred years ago.

While the contract has been forgotten by most, there are signs that the city's time has run out. The walls are cracked and faded from centuries of relentless sunlight. The grass is brown and sharp against bare feet, and the city's famed horses are finding less and less to eat.

The water that bubbles in the fountain no longer tastes sweet and cold but gritty and warm.

Tonight the paths are empty except for servants hurrying to and from the Dining Hall. Everyone is either laboring in the kitchen, dining, or gambling. I am surprised to hear voices a few yards away. Two women approach, lost in conversation.

"…can't keep his eyes off her," one hisses to the other. They freeze when they see me. Both turn on their heels and scurry in the opposite direction.

One of those women knocked on my door last night. She paid me a sapphire ring in exchange for a cream to ease the shadows beneath her eyes, though only her lover's fidelity could truly do that. Next time she comes I will raise the price.

With a sigh I turn back to the railing and gaze at the sky. The Snake constellation seems to writhe across the sky. Its red eye pins me with its gaze. Though I know it is just a far-off planet that gives the eye its hue, it still makes me shiver. Under the Snake everyone must be watchful or risk being deceived. The Duke has chosen an unlucky time to visit Aran.

On nights like these, when Najma was younger, I would tell her stories to ward off the wind. If she were speaking to me tonight, I would tell her a story about the spirits that dwell in the Lost. I would warn her about the Wind Demons who whisper venom into the ears of the unwary, and the Sand Ghosts who slither just beneath the surface, ready to drag down the unlucky until they suffocate on their own despair. Then there are the Witches who disguise themselves as travelers and appear out of nowhere. But no one questions them because they offer water, food, and companionship—all things one craves in the heart of the Lost. Only when they come to their senses do the victims realize they've traded their souls for a sip of water.

The wind gusts. I should go to my chamber and close the door against it, but that would be useless. Its taunts and whispers would still find their way in. I could light the lamp in my window—surely I am not the only one who feels unsettled. On a night like this, heartsick courtiers will visit in search of balms or potions. Hopefully they will have silver.

The wind's restlessness has infected me, so instead I begin to walk, descending the stairs. The wind follows me as I pass the fountain. I cross the courtyard to the Great Hall, topped with its dome. Beside it is the low stone building with heavy doors that lead to the Crypts. Even over the wind I can hear the whispers and taunts of the dead. To distract myself, I recite the ingredients for the sleeping draught I plan to create and sell for a good price.

Dreamsigh for pleasant dreams. Clearvine for snoring—only a pinch, though or the user is likely to stop breathing altogether. Slumberweed for deafness to loud noises.

I let my breath out as I leave the Dome behind and head for the shop where fine sandals are crafted. Those purchased with pentos are lovely enough, but only the best can be purchased with silvers. Usually only the Favorites are able to buy them, but every once in a while the servants, too, are able to scrape together enough silver to buy a pair. Even now, when the windows and doors are closed, I can smell the deep leather scent from inside. Beside it is the shop where the delicate dresses are sewn with fabric that is light enough that ladies hardly notice the sun, in colors of the morning sky or the sunset.

Tonight I am wearing a frock that floats around my ankles, the color of the sea in Mera. I traded it for a potion for luck, and as much as I hate to admit it, I love the way it is hardly more than a whisper against my skin.

The White Garden grows in a courtyard just north of the fountain. As I pass, I hear the sound of weeping among the lilies and tuberoses. For an instant I see a shimmer among the blossoms and catch the scent of licorice. The wind blows the petals in a sudden storm of white.

"Don't worry, I won't come in," I mutter, then shake my head in disgust. I am speaking to ghosts that are best left alone. I'm just as mad as my mother.

A fistful of slumberweed. A finger of clearvine. A pinch of air root.

A long reflecting pool separates the White Garden from the Gambling Hall. As I approach, another great shout erupts from inside. I continue walking toward the Lesser.

As I come near, a group of young laundresses appear from the room where the city's linens are washed. They are arm in arm, whispering together, one throwing back her head and letting out a loud laugh. Perhaps they are off to meet other servants in the little courtyard tucked away behind the buildings, where I sometimes hear shouts and music that is much louder than those coming from the Dining Hall. They rush off, their stylish sandals slapping against the stones, hushed laughter trailing behind them.

I feel a touch of envy. I want to join them, but I know the party would fall silent if I were to appear, the revelers scuttling away one by one. Instead, I continue past the Lesser to Mother's garden at the western edge of the city.

I come to the willow, its branches forming a thick leafy curtain. Pulling the brambles aside, I fight my way through as twigs grab at my hair. Beyond it lies a thicket of thorns and thistles that emit a bitter fragrance. Mother believed that the enchanted stream ran beneath the garden, for the plants inside, though wild and neglected, had potent and powerful qualities. Now everyone calls it the Cursed Garden, of course, because my mother cared for it.

A scorpion hisses as I push my way inside, but it quickly falls silent. It has grown used to my presence here.

My mother planted the sprigs and roots that she'd brought from Mera among the plants in the dark, cool place, so different from the rest of Aran. She taught me which leaves eased the pain of grief and headaches; which roots slowed one's heart until everyone thought the person was dead, even though they weren't; which berries made a person's breath so light that it was undetectable.

In our chamber, Mother taught me how to smile without showing my teeth and how to cast my eyes down to hide my thoughts. She showed me how to laugh in a way that would make arguments seem unimportant, and how to lift everyone's hearts with a dance. Everyone, that is, except the jealous Queen.

In the garden she taught me how to slide a knife from my sleeve too fast for anyone to see, and how to stand so still and silent in the shadows that no one would notice me. That same knife is now warm against my wrist, buzzing with energy and the secrets she didn't have time to tell me. Or perhaps it is the poison coursing through me that has convinced me of this.

As I do every night, I go to the bramble of thorns that grows in the shadows, the ones that are the color of bruises and old blood. Bitterthorn. As I reach in, the barbs catch at my hair and scratch my wrists, but they can't penetrate the thick scars on my skin. A lucky thing because a wound from these thorns could give me nightmares for three nights.

Buried deep within the brambles are leaves that are covered in thistles. I sigh as I hear the thin fabric of my dress tear. I should have stopped to change into my tunic and pants, but the set that I brought from Mera are too small now, and the dressmakers refuse to sew me another. So I must wear my mother's. Her scent still hangs on them, which is part of the reason I prefer them to the gowns of the Favorites, no matter how soft the fabric.

From the time we arrived, my mother ordered me to chew the bitterthorn and swallow the pulp even though it left the inside of my throat raw. At first I would spit it out, but she only made me eat more. "You must eat a little every day," she said. "Then you will grow immune to the poison. No crying," she ordered as she wiped my eyes. "Even your tears will become poison. Save them for when you need them."

I wonder if she knew how my fate would turn by taking this poison. And now, even though she's gone, I continue to take it each night; I have to, for my own protection.

I pluck several of the leaves, but not too many. Before I can think too much, I bite into them, dreading what's to come. The spikes sting my tongue as the juice flows thickly through my mouth, coating my throat. For an instant it burns as if I've swallowed fire. My breath stops and my eyes water. As I force myself to swallow, the world swims around me. Eyes seem to watch from the thicket of thorns, and the willow tree might have begun to dance.

When the wind blows this way, the past wraps itself around me like a snake, and tonight is no exception. The memories are hazy, as if I've dreamed them. I push them away and cross to the corner where a bush grows with narrow, soft branches, like veins. Clearvine. I dig until at last I am rewarded with the twisted vine that is the same color as the earth, despite its name.

The dreamsigh is even more challenging to coax from the earth. It is a good thing that I am not vain about my nails, as they are broken and permanently stained with earth from this nightly struggle. The slumberweed grows in clumps at the base of the willow and is easy enough to pluck.

Everything that grows here is infused with magic from the enchanted spring, but there is a way to make it stronger, despite the weakening spell. Mother's knife warms in my fingers as I raise the blade. *Magic has its price, Badriya.* I grit my teeth and draw the blade across the soft flesh of my inner arm, choosing a place that isn't already scarred. The cut burns as blood wells from it. Turning my arm over I allow a few drops to fall.

It's not as strong as Mer blood, I think as I watch the soil swallow my blood greedily, but there's still magic in my blood, as there was in my mother's. But how much can I give?

I shake my head to drive away the negative thoughts. I only have to last long enough to pay my mother's ransom, and then I can be away from here and never have to give anything, my blood or otherwise, again. The scorpion hisses from its hidden place.

A song floats over the Wall and the world steadies. The wind carries it like a streamer, twirling it tauntingly overhead and then whisking it away. It is wistful and full of longing, a lullaby my mother sang to me on nights when I shivered with cold and the demons groaned just beneath the surface of the sand.

The song draws me to the Wall, where a narrow set of steps has been cut into the stone. I climb them, my dress whipping around my knees. By the time I reach the top I am out of breath. From here I can see the Lost stretching in all directions. To the north I can just see the faint outline of the mountains; otherwise there is only sand rolling to the horizon.

The sand is silver in the moonlight. The top layer shifts, and every once in a while I catch a glimpse of hands reaching up from the depths. The moon is a scythe poised to fall on the city below.

"The demons are hungry tonight," the Bones note. They hang from the Wall in chains, tatters of clothing hanging from bones that are whitened by years in the sun. They were once the body of the guard who was on duty the night my mother jumped into the Lost. They often speak to me on nights when the wind blows like this.

A swarm of crows fight over what is left of its ribs. Finally, one takes flight, clutching something dry and black. The rest follow, squabbling over the prize.

I imagine my old home in Mera: the sea churning where the sand meets the vermillion sky, the city clinging to the cliffs above it. I close my eyes and try to remember the whisper and hiss of the waves, and for a moment I think that I can. But the wind must be playing tricks on me, for a journey of many days lies between my old home and Aran. The distance between the two is filled with perils that could rise from the sand without warning.

"Someday I'll return," I murmur.

"Are you sure that's what you want?" the Bones ask.

"Of course it is," I snap.

"Of course it is," the Bones croon, and I shake my head to clear it. Though I must take the poison, I can't let the darkness overtake me as it did Mother.

The Snake twists in the night sky—no, it's only a cluster of stars. It must be the bitterthorn affecting my vision.

A few yards from the Wall, the sand stirs. It spins and rises, becoming a silvery shadow. My mother's ghost twirls in the sand as if I've summoned her with my thoughts. Everyone in the city believes that she danced to seduce the King, but I know that she also danced to regain what she'd lost.

Badriya, her voice comes like a whisper. My true name. Or perhaps it is only the wind.

The ache in my throat tightens. Every time I see her it's hard to breathe. "I'm still saving, Mother," I whisper. "I've got eighty silvers." After five years it's almost enough to fulfill my promise to her, to pay the Witch to set her soul free, to bribe them to let me pass across the Lost to Mera, our home, to the person I used to be. But Mother pays me no mind, intent upon her dance.

Behind her, the shadows thicken and another ghost emerges from the darkness: the King. He is tall and broad shouldered, as he was in life, with a beard shading his jaw and hair flowing to his shoulders. He moves toward my mother, his hand extended hopefully. But she dances as though she can't see him, and he can only watch. Just like me.

Hoofbeats pound against the sand and a great dark horse appears, its gold and blue martingale identifying it as the late King's. Another flies at its heels. They gallop toward the ghosts, and then at the last minute, shy away from them, reversing their course despite the shouts of their riders. The horses are bred for speed and strength, the only creatures that can outrun a hungry ghost. And they can see them, as well.

"That's five silvers you owe me," one of the riders shouts to the other as they trot through the great wooden gate.

Five silvers. If only I'd been allowed to learn to ride. The horses and riders pass through the gate, trailing curses and braying. I watch the place where they disappeared, lost in the memory of another rider who vanished long ago.

"Behind you," the Bones warn.

"Lady Diya." I turn to see a young page, favored by Solena for his eyes, which are ringed with thick lashes. I sigh, resigned. I should have known I could not evade the order for long. There are not many places to hide in this city.

He glances past me, over the Wall, but his face shows no sign of surprise. He does not see the King or my mother—they are my particular ghosts. Perhaps he sees his own, perhaps not.

The page holds out a lily from the White Garden. "A token from the Queen." A bead of sweat rolls down his temple. "She says the Duke must…"

Die. I finish the thought for him silently. He thrusts the lily toward me.

It is the sign I feared in the Dining Hall, the one I knew would come. "I cannot accept it," I reply in a low voice.

He swallows. "The Queen says to remind you of the debt you owe and what will happen should you renege."

The Bones clatter against the Wall as a bird settles itself inside the ribcage, gnawing at a splinter of clavicle.

I glance out at the Lost where the black sand meets the horizon. I could make it to Mera. I've saved enough silver to bribe the Witches to grant me safety, but I don't yet have enough to buy my mother's freedom.

"Please," he whispers urgently. If I refuse, he will also face Solena's wrath. Heaving a sigh, I take the lily and he rushes away, disappearing down the stairs.

Turning back to the Lost, I think about what poison to use. Something to turn his blood to powder? To close his throat? To stop his heart?

"I had a heart once," the Bones muse. "Until the birds ate it."

"Quiet, I'm trying to think," I mutter. What will it cost me to poison the Duke? *Magic has its price*, I hear Mother's reminder, though whether it's in my memory or in the present is hard to tell, especially on a night like this.

Eighty silvers. I'm nearly there. I think of Yadira and her vacant eyes. She will be desperate—I can charge her more for the Stardust she craves, then I might have enough.

"This is the last time," I vow aloud.

"You know it's not," the Bones chuckle.

"It is," I insist, thinking of the distant expression on Yadira's face. Perhaps she will be desperate enough to do me a favor.

The Bones rattle gently as a breeze rises. "Someone's coming. From the east." I peer out into the Lost but I see nothing except the ghosts of Mother and the King and curtains of sand.

"You don't have any eyes," I tell the Bones. "How can you see?"

"I see," they reply. I close my eyes and take a breath. Perhaps I should eat less bitterthorn.

The night is deepening, the Snake is brighter, and I haven't yet decided what to do about the Duke. I must hurry if I'm to ready the poison and still prepare for my clients. Turning my back, I descend the stairs to the garden and step through the willow door.

Powder of spoor, I recite. *A drop of belladonna.*

A seamstress, shoulders sagging with exhaustion, pulls her child closer as I pass.

Belladonna—a trace of the poisoner's blood always makes the potion more potent. I recite the words all the way back to my chamber, though I know them by heart.

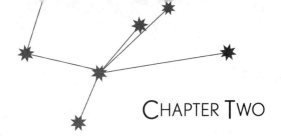

CHAPTER TWO

Inside my chamber I light a candle and sweep it through the room, peering into each corner for any surprises, a habit I've gotten into since finding a dead rat on my pillow years before. I see only my bed, draped in a rich, thick cloth that is worn in places, and the armoire that holds two other dresses, one the color of the moon, the other the color of blood. On the floor of the armoire, folded neatly, are my worn tunic and pants, along with the set that belonged to my mother, which are now stained with various roots, blossoms, and dirt. Alongside them hangs my old cloak, the one that protected me from the damp winds in Mera, but that I hardly need here, except when I don't wish to be seen.

In the corner is the table where I create my potions, piled with blossoms and leaves. Lying next to them is my mother's knife, its blade stained crimson and emerald. A long, jagged crack runs along its handle, which is made of shells from the Turquoise Sea. The blade has grown dull with use, but it holds my mother's blood; it is all that I have left of her. On a shelf above are jars full of different herbs and roots. A poisonous odor fills the room, both sweet and biting at once.

Usually my clients wait until I've lit the lantern on the windowsill before they come to my door, hooded or disguised as servants. Many are the same women who've tormented me since I arrived with my mother, whispering that I should drown myself in the fountain, or better yet, join the demons in the Lost.

Each taunt and whisper used to cut me like a blade, tiny and sharp. I would cry myself to sleep, stifling my sobs into my pillow, my tears full of enough poison to make my eyes feel as though they were on fire.

Now, years later, these women come to me at night. They weep and shake, begging for a potion for youth, for wellness, or something to keep their beloved's eye from wandering. They seek powders to make their eyes dance, creams that stop their skin from aging, and wash to scent their hair and drive those nearby mad for them. At first I refused; then they began offering me their treasure in exchange.

Those with no riches pay with favors: the laundress makes sure my clothes smell of flowers when they are returned. A cook saves the freshest bread and most savory meat for my plate. A seamstress gives me gowns in the loveliest hues.

The wealthier pay with silver when they can, though they usually trade their jewelry. But the cruelest women, those whose insults cut the deepest, must pay twice as much as the others. They narrow their eyes as they offer their payment, but make no comment.

I have a jar of rings and earrings in a coffer, but they are of little use to me. What I really need is silver, but the few people who have it are either reluctant to trade or have already given it to me. The silver that I have collected is wrapped in old scarves and tucked beneath a loose tile under my bed.

I curse when I hear a tap at the door. I should have known the wind would make my clients even hungrier, more desperate. A woman with a scarf draped over her bright hair slips inside as soon as I've opened the door. In a low voice she asks for a tincture for love.

"Your husband seems besotted with you," I tell her as I add a few drops of Fervor to a vial of perfume.

"I want him to love someone else," she replies. "I don't have any silver. Safiya has won it all."

I roll my eyes as I take the ruby earrings she offers. "Good luck," I say as she steals away.

Safiya comes a moment later, seeking her usual charm for good fortune.

"I shouldn't give this to you. You're taking silver from my other clients."

Safiya laughs. "Don't worry, I have plenty for you."

"It's dangerous to be too lucky," I warn her.

"Only if I lose."

"If you win as well," I retort. "Especially too often and against Solena." Many have noticed how Solena's luck has soured lately, as steadily as the oranges on the trees have shriveled and the grass for grazing has dried.

"I'll let her win sometimes. Thank you, Diya," she says, handing me a silver coin.

"That's not my name," I murmur, but she winks as she slips through the door, leaving me with the heavy coin. Eighty-one silvers now.

Safiya has hardly left when Yadira enters like a ghost, the shadows nearly swallowing her. "Do you have it?" she whispers.

When I first arrived she had been among the cruelest of my tormentors, so I had been only too happy to offer her the powder that I knew to be so addictive. I regret it now as I watch her eyes dart around, seeking demons in the darkness. Her mind is like a fragile thread about to snap. But I need her payment to help my mother.

I hold up the little bag, the dust within sparkling in the dim light. She moves toward it so quickly that she stumbles over her slippers. I hold it just out of reach and her eyes narrow.

"Here is your payment," she snarls. She tears a bracelet from her wrist, leaving red welts across her skin.

I stare at the bracelet, dismayed. "It must be silver."

"I don't have any. You've taken it all."

"No I haven't."

"Take this too." She pulls at an emerald ring on her finger. "And this." She jerks at the chain around her neck that holds a ruby pendant. Her hands shake as she holds them out, her mouth trembling.

"Keep your jewels," I tell her.

"What?" The gems quiver in her hands.

"I want a favor instead."

"What must I do?" she asks, her eyes on the Stardust.

"Hardly anything. Only dance."

She frowns. Once she would have scoffed at the idea of dancing for anyone but herself, and she would have laughed at the notion of agreeing to any request of mine.

But now she asks, "With whom?"

"The Duke's bodyguard. You must invite him to your chamber." Her mouth tightens. "Only for dancing," I tell her quickly. "Nothing more. After dinner tomorrow night. Just keep him away from the Duke's room for a few minutes."

When she doesn't speak, I catch her tiny, fragile hand. "Have a little now." I pour a tiny bit of the crystals onto her fingertips.

She raises her hand to her eyes in a flash, pressing the Stardust into them. Tilting her head back, she sighs, the stiffness in her shoulders melting away.

"There will be more when it's finished," I assure her. "It will take only a few minutes, and then I'll have more Stardust for you."

Guilt, sharp as a poisoned knife blade, twists in my gut, but I have to free my mother. As soon as I do, I will never have to poison anyone again. I will ride on the fastest mare for the horizon and the poison will seep from me at last.

When Yadira is gone, I shred the slumberweed and put a fistful into a bowl. I chop the clearvine and add a finger's length, then grind the dreamsigh into a powder. Only a pinch, I remind myself as I drop it in. I mix it all in cold water since I don't have time to heat it. I drink some myself—I need a good night's sleep.

But the concoction doesn't work. I should have known better, immune as I have become to poison. I spend hours lost in a waking dream filled with the sounds of the Bones rattling against the Wall. Suddenly they transform into the Duke; birds peck at his heart as he calls, "Just let me sleep!"

I sit up and drink thirstily from the water on the table next to me. My head pounds. If nothing else, my dream helped me decide that it must be the Duke's heart that fails him.

The darkness has lightened somewhat: it's the perfect hour for gathering stillbreath. It is most potent when it's cut in the moments just before the sun rises, especially when the moon is still faint. I dress in my mother's old tunic and pants, which I wear to gather plants, and wrap myself in my cloak. Taking up my basket and a vial, I step outside.

A young servant scrubs the stones at the foot of the stairs where someone vomited the night before. He gags as I approach, then dips his head before he can see my sympathetic smile.

The Dining Hall is dark and silent, the odor of sour wine and greasy meat so overpowering that I pull my tunic over my nose until I pass.

Though the Favorites' Chambers are still hushed, a racket comes from the Lesser. Goats bleat in their pens, perhaps hoping to be milked. Servants call to one another as pans clatter in the kitchen. The smell of bread wafts from the bakery.

The wind rises, soft and warm, blowing gently from the west as I pass the White Garden. The blossoms have opened in the dark like ghosts, their dangerous scent floating in the air. A cloaked figure moves among the flowers. She glances at me as I pass, her sharp eyes holding mine: the Duke's Witch.

For a long moment we stare at each other. I hardly dare to breathe. Has she guessed my intentions?

Turning away, she draws her hood over her head and glides away among the roses. I hurry on, willing my heart to slow.

I think of the Duke's words at dinner. She cares nothing for him, only for the silver, I tell myself. His entourage will be sure that she is paid, even if it's just to get their own skins back across the Lost, with or without the Duke.

The water in the fountain at the city's center bubbles cheerfully in the dark. A faint odor of rot wafts from it; the spell that has kept it fresh and cool has begun to wear off. Someone's forgotten scarf is draped over its edge. Foolish. It would be too easy for the owner's enemy to sprinkle rash powder into the fabric. Within hours the wearer would either be scarred with welts that would never heal or be plagued with madness.

As I cross to my own garden, the cursed one, night birds chirp from the branches of the willow tree as if greeting the morning. They avoid haunted places, so they don't enter the White Garden.

The sun has nearly risen—I must hurry. Kneeling, I pry up the half-buried stones in the back of the garden and begin scraping the stillbreath from the undersides. It is easy to mistake it for moss, but stillbreath has a faint sheen.

I tip the scrapings into a vial. Sitting back on my heels, I hold it up to the growing light. The stillbreath lies harmless in the glass, but even this small amount is nearly lethal.

Now I must find a way to convince the Duke to take it.

Though the sun has barely risen, it has already scoured away the enchantment of the previous night. Two servants scrub the tiles outside the Gambling Hall; one of them sings the melancholy song that the musicians played the night before. A woman hurries past them along the path, her sandals in her hand. Her dress is wrinkled as though she's slept in it. The kohl around her eyes is smudged, and the rouge on her lips has worn away so that only a thin line remains around the outside. She hardly notices when she jostles into a man carrying a huge pan of bread toward the Dining Hall, lowering her head before darting away toward the Favorites' Chambers.

As I pass the White Garden, I see Petra cutting lilies for Solena's daily bouquet. I can see that she has also cut some tuberoses for herself. Her mouth is set in a grim line, her eyes squinting against the sun. She must have celebrated too enthusiastically the night before. I will mix a tonic to help with her headache. She lifts her chin in greeting as I pass, not daring to call to me in such an open place. It is safer for both of us if no one thinks that we are friends.

At her shoulder the air shimmers, and for an instant I catch a glimpse of a woman, pale and thin with a bottle in her hand, before she disappears, leaving the scent of licorice behind. Petra does not seem to notice.

The Favorites' Chambers are still and quiet as I climb the steps. I tiptoe to my chamber, keeping an eye on the great carved door of Solena's room. Thankfully it stays closed as I slip inside my room. Leaning against my door I let out a great breath.

Unfortunately, the stillbreath alone will not slow his heart enough for people to believe that he is dead. I cross to my table where remnants of the previous night are still scattered across the top. I pull the cork from the vial of stillbreath and take up the knife. It hums as I find a place on my palm where the skin is still soft and unscarred and draw the blade across it. My blood is sluggish and reluctant, but I only need a few drops. I let them fall into the vial and watch as it stains the stillbreath.

Now, how to persuade the Duke to consume this?

It would be most lethal to pass it from my lips to his. The poison would act the fastest this way, and his death would be more merciful. But the idea of touching my lips to his makes me feel nauseous. No, it's better to hide it in wine.

I search for the bottle of wine I'd filched, only to find it half full. I curse under my breath, remembering Petra pouring herself a generous glass the previous day.

I can't risk going out and being seen again, so this will have to be enough. I pour the potion into the neck of the bottle and force it in further with the knife. As I swirl the bottle, I watch the stillbreath dissolve. The wine turns a deeper shade of scarlet, but the Duke will likely not notice.

Now all there is to do is wait. The sun has only just risen, and the hours between now and dinner stretch endlessly. My head aches and my bones are heavy with exhaustion, but I don't want to lie back down and be lost in terrible dreams again.

There's a familiar knock at my door, a playful rhythm. I open it to find Petra, still bleary-eyed but less pale. She waves a basket, and my stomach growls at the scent of bread inside. "You were missed at breakfast!" she sings.

"By who?" I grouse, but I stand aside to let her in.

"By everyone, naturally! We needed your sunny personality to lift the dour mood."

I roll my eyes but can't suppress my smile. "And without me, who could Solena belittle?"

"Oh, there is always someone. Today it was the poor servant girl who stutters."

"Oh, no."

"Don't worry, I told her to go help with the dishes."

"And what did our Queen think of that?" But I already know. No one can be angry with Petra for long, not even Solena.

She doesn't bother to answer, eying the table with distaste. "I was hoping you'd want to play cards. I need to practice before I play Safiya tonight, but clearly we can't play here."

"Do you have any silver?" I ask.

"You know I don't." She holds up the basket. "But I brought bread, and since you missed breakfast I thought you might be willing to wager."

My stomach gurgles. Petra seats herself on the chair and I sit on the bed across from her. "It smells lethal in here," she says, wrinkling her nose. "What have you been doing?"

"You don't want to know," I tell her. "Let's see the wager."

She pulls loaves of bread from the basket: olive, cinnamon, and chocolate along with two oranges. "Wait," she says as I snatch up a loaf of cinnamon bread and tear off a bite. "That was our wager."

"And if you win?" I ask around a mouthful of bread.

She pulls out a deck of cards. "I could use some of that wonderful cream that erases the shadows under my eyes. I couldn't sleep." I think of the man she'd danced with the night before and raise an eyebrow. She smiles and deals the cards. "It looks as though you didn't get any sleep either."

I take another bite of bread and close my eyes as it melts on my tongue. The Bones, the dreams, the poison—they all fade away. I pick up my cards and look at my hand.

"Well?" Petra says, studying her hand. "Don't you want to know the gossip?"

"Of course."

"Well, Queen Solena seems completely repulsed by the Duke."

"Really," I roll my eyes and discard a card, then take another.

"At breakfast this morning he had the worst breath. I couldn't even breathe! You should have seen the expression on our Queen's face! And poor Najma looked as though she wanted to vomit. Our Queen finally let her leave to eat in her chamber."

I imagine Najma chewing stoically and I feel a twist of sympathy for her. She would try to be regal like her sister.

Petra chatters about gossip from the night before, though I am so tired I can hardly follow. Still, I fall gratefully into the gossip: there was an argument among the musicians that led to tears and broken instruments and a disagreement in the kitchen that made everyone who ate the soup feel melancholy.

As I play another card she gives a slight sniff. Her tell.

"Our Queen has been talking about needing to marry," Petra says. "Can you imagine?"

No, I can't. But I've seen the cracks in the fountain and the dying trees. The spell that has protected Aran is fading. Something must be done if the city is to survive, even Solena can see that.

"She sold him a horse," Petra adds. "Her father's favorite."

This news causes me to forget the game and look up. If anything could still hurt Solena, it would be this.

But it's dangerous to feel sympathy for her—I've fallen into that trap before. I play another card and Petra sniffs again. She must be getting close to a Fortune.

"I wonder," she says carefully, "if tonight's meal will agree with the Duke?"

"I fold," I tell her, laying down my cards.

Her face falls. "Ugh, you always know. How?"

I smile, holding out my hand for the bread.

"I am getting a headache from the smell in this room anyway," she says. "That cloak is awful," she adds. Insulting one another is our ritual to help keep misfortune away.

I give her a vial of the salve as she leaves. "Good luck, Badriya," she says softly.

Exhaustion washes over me as soon as the door closes. The bread in my stomach and the comfort of Petra's prattle allow me what the sleeping draught did not: a deep, dreamless sleep.

I wake to the sound of tambors in the Dining Hall and voices raised in song and cheer. The light is warm and soft.

I have slept the day away. The wine bottle sits on the windowsill holding its murky poison. Somehow I must convince the Duke to drink it. The ease I'd felt earlier seeps away and anxiety returns.

I dress in my moon-colored gown and comb and pin my hair so that it does not look so much like a bramble. Then I settle my cloak over my shoulders. It is threadbare and far too heavy for the warm night, but I need it to hide the bottle of wine.

Inside the Dining Hall, the smell of fish and sweets hangs in the air but no food has been served yet. I hear Solena's silvery laugh over the chatter of the court. Najma catches my eye and waves, and I wave back. She doesn't seem angry anymore. I'd love to join her, but Mina is alone, which is rare. I must speak to her now.

Her face, as always, is wrapped in a bright scarf so that only her sharp eyes show. I see the gleam of hatred in them in the instant before she curtsies. As she straightens, the scarf falls away, revealing dark red scars. She raises her chin, the lesions vivid in the candlelight. "What might I do for you, Diya?"

I take the bottle from my cloak. "Queen Solena has requested that you give this to the Duke tonight after dinner. With her compliments."

I try to press the bottle into her hands, but she folds her arms. "Did you not hear me?" I ask, desperation making my voice rough.

"I heard you. But I will not do it."

I glance over at the other musicians. They don't seem to notice our conversation. "You must—Queen Solena requested it."

Mina shakes her head. "No, she didn't. She would have asked me herself." Her eyes gleam shrewdly. "No, she ordered you to do it, but you are too cowardly." She holds my gaze, a smirk playing over her ruined lips. "At least have the courage to take it to him yourself."

I should threaten her, frighten her into obeying my will. It's what Solena would do.

"You'll hang from the Wall," I whisper, like the coward I am.

She leans forward. "You will hang from the Wall long before I will." She holds my gaze for a long moment, then finally turns to join the other musicians.

I slip from the Dining Hall before Solena can call to me. Najma watches me go, and I offer her a quick smile before I slip outside.

So, it must be me. I wait through the long dinner. I pace, I sit, and I pace again.

For youth: chlyme and prideblossom, best left whole.

For confidence: ragolweed with a pinch of salt and a hearty serving of wine.

The music rises and the crowd cheers. The music falls and voices sing along unsteadily. Darkness falls and the stars rise as the air cools.

Why couldn't I take the poison to the Duke myself? My mother would have.

Then she shouldn't have left me here alone, I think savagely.

Outside I hear unsteady footsteps and laughter. At last the diners have begun to leave the Dining Hall.

Opening the door to my chamber, I look down the gallery to the Duke's chamber. His bodyguard is gone. Hopefully Yadira has kept her promise.

I take a breath and square my shoulders. Tucking my knife into my belt where it rests reassuringly, I step into the gallery and slip across the tiles to the Duke's chamber.

Opening the door, I find the Duke sitting on the bed, his mouth slack. His eyes widen slightly, but his senses are dulled by the wine he's already consumed.

"I've brought you something, Your Grace." I must breathe through my mouth; the sour stench of drink and sweat is overwhelming. Petra did not exaggerate. Holding out the bottle, I tell him, "This is much higher quality than the others. I wanted to bring it to you myself."

He reaches for me, but I side-step him, pressing the bottle into his outstretched hand. His fingers curl around it. "Drink," I urge, but he just stares at me.

Will I have to force the liquid down his throat? He is drunk enough, but I don't want to touch him. He finally raises the bottle to his mouth and swallows noisily, liquid running from the corners of his mouth. I can only hope that what he's swallowed is potent enough.

He blinks slowly and I curse under my breath. The effects will not be immediate. "Shall we play a game?" I ask.

After another long moment he nods. "What shall we play?" he asks thickly.

"Do you have any silver?" I ask.

"Silver?" he says. "My dear, more than you can count." He takes another noisy slurp.

"Do you have any cards, Sir?" I ask. Perhaps I can benefit from this night after all.

It's too late. The bottle drops from his hand and clatters to the tile. He falls backward onto the bed, gasping for breath, his eyes wide, and his lips moving wordlessly. *Help*, he mouths.

I force myself to lean in as close as I can stand, wrinkling my nose against the smell. But I can't let him believe he's going to die. "Your heart will slow," I whisper. "Your breath will nearly cease. Everyone will think that you are dead. You will awaken, but not until you are far from here and safe."

He clutches at his chest, and I am not sure he hears me. My stomach turns.

"Your courtiers won't bury you until you reach your palace. But you'll have returned to life before then."

I can't risk staying any longer. Snatching up the bottle, I hurry to the door. Once on the other side, I draw my hood close to my face and move silently back down the gallery to my room.

With any luck, everyone will assume that the Duke overindulged, danced too much, and it all proved to be too much for his heart.

Hopefully Solena will be convinced that the Duke is dead and I will escape the fate of the Bones for another day. Perhaps I have bought myself more time to earn enough silver to free my mother and escape.

The wind rises, catching at my hood. Of all of my victims in Aran, only one has died: Solena's father, the King.

CHAPTER THREE

Once I return to my chamber, I undress and get into bed, burrowing into the linens and silks despite the warmth of the night. Should the Duke be discovered before dawn, I must look as though I'd spent the night asleep and alone. I spend the hours with my eyes squeezed shut.

To have good luck: goldenray, a spoonful stirred into tea. A fingernail of sugar will make the luck sweeter.

To persuade others to your point of view: swayleaf, dried and crumbled, then added to butter. It makes a delicious spread.

To forget: greenbell, gathered when the moon rises.

No matter how many times I repeat these potions in my mind, I can still hear the Duke's terrified gasps.

The only sound is the wind howling at the window. The Duke's staff is either very negligent or they are having trouble recovering from the previous night's revelries.

When at last the light breaks, it brings no comfort. Solena will be waiting to hear that I've done her bidding. I force myself from bed and slowly dress. I comb my hair even though my fingers shake, and weave delicate plaits through it, tucking in a few blue serenity blossoms for calm. I must appear placid, as though this is just another ordinary day.

But I can't face her. Not yet.

I think of hiding in the Cursed Garden—few people would seek me there. Then I hear a light, familiar knock at the door. I open it to find Najma.

She is dressed in a pink gown that is nearly identical to Solena's favorite, a white blossom tucked behind her ear. "Good morning, Little Crocodile!" I hold out my arms.

"I'm too old for this," she tells me, but gives me a brief hug, squeezing her arms around me for an instant before she ducks out of reach. I push away the prick of hurt. There is no time for my fragile feelings, not this morning.

She wrinkles her nose. "It smells in here."

"Does it?" I'd left the window open all night. Perhaps the poison is part of the room now. I step outside and close the door behind me. "Maybe we can have breakfast together."

"Solena wants to see you," she says.

"So early?" I ask. She lifts one shoulder in a shrug, her eyes sliding away. She is not as good as her sister at hiding her feelings. Solena must be having a bad morning.

We walk in silence together toward Solena's chamber, my dread growing with each step. Will the illusion work? Will she see through my trick? Will she be appeased?

"I didn't feel well last night," Najma breaks into my thoughts.

"Oh?" I am only too eager to be distracted. "Was it the fish? We're not used to that here."

"Maybe." She casts a sly grin toward me. "Or maybe it was watching the Duke dance with Solena. He is like a slippery fish himself."

I begin to laugh and she smiles, looking pleased with herself. The thought of leaving Najma behind when I finally return to Mera is like the prick of a knife.

Too soon we arrive outside Solena's chamber.

I hesitate outside the door, unwilling to lose the peace of the morning or Najma's company. The door swings open and Solena's guard, Darien, stands on the other side. He moves outside once we enter, closing the door behind him.

Solena sits at her vanity, wrapped in Petra's favorite silk gown. She'd won it from her in a wager a few nights ago, although we all know Solena would have taken it anyway. "Well?" she asks.

I glance at Najma, who has slipped to her side, her face unreadable. "He indulged too much last night and his heart failed him. He should be gone by evening."

Solena shrugs. "I will miss the fish." Her eyes narrow as she studies me. "My poor, sensitive Diya," she croons. "Are you feeling guilty? Just blame it on the wind or whatever else your mother taught you to ease your conscience."

My head begins to ache. "If there's nothing else you need, I'll be going."

"You can't leave. I need you to apply my cosmetics."

She can't be serious, not this morning.

A smile curls her lips. "I'm waiting."

With a sigh, I cross to where she waits with the creams and powders that I've created lined up on the table.

"You know what this does, don't you?" I take the lid off one of the little jars on the table. Veins cross her white cheeks and wrinkles pull at her mouth. Though she is only a year older than me, she looks much older. The price of magic has taken its toll on her just as it has me.

She doesn't bother to answer. I warn her every day, just as every day I increase the amount of arsenic that I add to the powder and the amount of nightshade that I put in her eyedrops. It only serves to make her more mad. Her heart beats as vigorously as ever, her eyesight sharp.

But then I remember her tear-stained face from years before, and the shouts that I heard from her chamber. *It's your fault this has happened. Who could love an ugly troll like you?* Nothing matters more to her than being beautiful. I feel an unwelcome twist of sympathy as I pour the powder into a silver bowl and add a bit of water. She watches hungrily with her bloodshot eyes as I stir the mixture until it becomes a cream.

She tilts her face upward as I dip my fingertips into the bowl and rub the cream on her face. Her skin feels like tissue paper that might tear away from the bone if I am not careful. The cream will someday make her lose what is left of her sanity—I thought it would have happened by now. She sighs and closes her eyes, her shoulders relaxing.

I paint extra Eyebright in the creases around her eyes to hide the haunted look that countless nightmares have etched there. Ironically, this powder will make her dreams even worse tonight. I paint cream on her lips to make them fresh and full, but it will also make everything she eats taste bitter. Her breathing has slowed and her lips curl in a faint smile.

When I am finished, I wash my hands in the basin, not to protect myself—the poisons hardly have an effect on me—but so they will not harm others. The scars across my hands glisten in the water, some dark red and some pale pink.

I turn to see Najma dipping her fingertips into the cream.

"No!" I leap forward and knock the jar from the table. It falls to the floor with a crack. Najma snatches her hand away, narrowing her eyes. My throat tightens. She already looks so much like Solena.

"That is poison," I tell her. Najma looks to Solena.

"You are probably too young," Solena concedes, and Najma's face falls. "But I expect you to replace the cream you wasted," she says to me.

"I have already repaid you by poisoning the Duke," I remind her. "My Queen," I add with a dip of my head. I wait with my head bowed and my heart pounding.

After a long moment she speaks. "You poisoned him for the debt you owe me. Najma and me." She snakes an arm around our sister, pulling her close. No, she's not "our" sister—she is Solena's sister, not mine. Najma looks between us, uncertain.

My throat tightens at her words. "Very well. I will be sure to mix a new batch. But it's dangerous for Najma to use." I turn to look at Najma. "Being beautiful is not everything—it's not even the most important."

Solena stares thoughtfully at Najma, and for a moment the ghost of her younger self hangs between us again, tears dripping down her face. I feel a flicker of pity for her but the moment quickly ends. "Ugh," Solena groans. "You would say that, wouldn't you? I mean, look at you. Think of your mother's fate. She didn't think beauty was important either."

Her barbs still hurt, no matter how often I hear them. I turn to leave before my expression betrays me. Just as I reach the door Solena says, "Diya, you reek of fish. You'll want to wash, to deflect suspicion." I wrench the door open and storm outside, slamming it on her laughter.

I consider going to the garden so that I can skim bark from the willow to make a lotion that will ease headaches, but my mother's knife hums in my fingertips. I am so agitated that I might slice off my thumb. Besides, anything I gather in my current state will grow sour faster and its effects will be unpredictable.

From the goat pen comes a bleat that quickly falls silent. The preparations for the evening meal have already begun. Heat rises from the stones that line the paths below, but it is not yet unbearable. Children chase each other around the fountain; their mother calls for them as she strides toward the Favorites' Chambers with a basket and fabric draped over her arm.

Why has there been no outcry? Surely the Duke has been discovered by now.

I can't return to my room and hide there like an insect, so I turn to the Dome that rests atop the Hall, with its blue and gold tiles and windows that twinkle like diamonds. Travelers across the Lost can see it for miles. It is like a beacon luring them to cool water, food, and rest. They never suspect that the spell that once made it an oasis is now turning it into a pit of madness. They would be better off turning back and braving the Lost.

A set of narrow stone steps is built into the curve of the Dome that faces the western side of the city. Servants scale the steps often to wash the windows out of sight of the royal buildings so that Solena and the other nobles aren't bothered by them. Today the windows have already been polished, reflecting the cloudless sky.

The air grows hotter as I scale the stairs and look out over the Lost. Just beyond the walls are the remnants of grass where Aran's famed horses roam, or at least what is left of them; now they graze alongside the goats. The grass is brown and crisp, and the goats bleat sadly as they chew on what is left.

As the centuries have passed, the spell that once made Aran prosperous has weakened, retreating until it only holds inside the gates. Fruit trees studded with oranges grow alongside olive trees at the edge of the Cursed Garden, though as time passes fewer and fewer fruits appear among the leaves. Sometimes children from the Lesser will steal an orange or an apple from the trees when the Favorites are inside taking shelter from the heat. If they are spotted by the Favorites, they might be shouted at or even chased, though it is too hot for the pursuit to last for long.

I see Petra, her hair reddish-gold in the sun, strolling past the fruit trees. A child freezes with an arm raised, probably in the act of picking an orange. Usually this would warrant a sharp reprimand from most of the Favorites, but Petra strides over and plucks the fruit, then hands it to the child who clutches it and races away. Though she is too far away to see, I imagine Petra's wry grin as she resumes her journey toward the Dome.

I turn back to my vigil of the Lost.

The name suits it well. It rolls out in every direction, gold and relentless, a layer of sand whispering over its surface. A crooked smile in a tan face flashes across my mind and a laugh ripples through my memory before it is carried off by the wind.

"We missed you at dinner." Petra joins me after several minutes, breathing heavily from the climb, a sheen of sweat across her forehead and her scarf fluttering around her face. The bags under her eyes are gone, so the salve must have worked.

"Did you have any luck at Fortune?"

"No." She grimaces. "I want some of that lucky potion you give Safiya."

"She's naturally very lucky."

Petra makes a rude noise, and I smile despite myself.

"So," she says. "What will happen to the Duke? Will it be his head? His heart?"

I sigh. "His heart."

She bites her lip. "When?"

"It should have happened already."

As if on cue, screams erupt from below. Figures race across the courtyard, pulling on clothes as they run. A gardener looks up from clipping Solena's favorite flowers, then turns away and returns to his task.

I rest my forehead on my arms and close my eyes, the sun beating down on the back of my neck. "His heart will stop." *Or at least seem to.* "The healers will labor over him, but it will be for nothing." The screams are like knives against my ears.

Did I mix the poison correctly? Only a little too much and his heart won't restart, and then I'll have another ghost haunting me from over the Wall.

"I'm sorry, Badriya." At the sound of my true name, tears burn my eyes, but they can't fall anymore. Petra touches her hand to my shoulder. She sits with me until she must see to Solena, to support her in this calamity. I remain atop the Dome.

The Duke's entourage departs just as the sky turns vermillion and the moon fills with amber light. I watch from the Wall as the caravan leaves the city, not quite fleeing but insistent upon not remaining another night. The men cast many looks over their shoulders as they journey into the Lost, the Duke's body enclosed in an elaborate litter.

They hurry past my mother as she dances. One of her scarves brushes against a bodyguard. He shudders and urges his horse forward, though I know he can't see her. The King's gaze never wavers from my mother.

The Duke will wake as dawn breaks, weak, confused, and terrified from nightmares. Everyone will marvel at the miracle. He will live, though he will never again have the strength to flirt with queens, to dance, or even walk very far. His heart, weakened as it is, may still give out within a few years. Still, I have given him the chance to escape Solena's wrath. I have bargained more time for him.

I hope that by the time Solena learns of his marvelous recovery, and by the time he has gathered the strength to take revenge, I will have somehow gained enough silver to escape. I will have to charge the ladies more, but they are desperate enough to pay—I have made sure of that.

I stare out at the Lost, shielding my eyes from the sun as I remember the warning from the Bones. Do I imagine a caravan far out on the horizon?

The King raises his face, his dark eyes locked on mine, and a shiver shoots down my spine despite the warmth of the evening. *He is dead,* I remind myself. *He can't hurt me.*

My eyes sting with tears that refuse to fall. If only I could feel anything, but the years of poison have deadened my heart as surely as they have paralyzed the nerves in Solena's face.

As much as I hate this city, I am glad for the Wall that separates Aran from the Lost and the ghosts within it. Even as I turn away I can feel the King's gaze, just as I did when he lived.

Shadows have pooled at the foot of the stairs and a rustle is my only warning before a figure steps forward. The silver woven into her hair jingles softly as I recognize who she is: the Duke's Witch.

"You have lost me my payment," she says.

"What?" I take a step away from her.

"My payment," she says, moving closer until I can smell the spice on her breath. "The Duke paid me to ensure his safety. Thanks to you, he is not safe." I turn my face away from her unwashed scent.

"What was the payment?" I ask.

"Two hundred silvers."

Two hundred? I swallow. "The Duke is a wealthy man. He will pay you when he wakes."

She snorts. "Of course he won't. He will blame me for this mishap and refuse to pay. So now you must."

"I don't have two hundred silvers." My voice is a panicked squeak.

"But you're earning it, aren't you girl?" Turning her head, she gazes at me with one eye. "You might not have it now, but you will soon enough, especially if you are motivated enough." She studies me. "You have until the Bat rises in the sky. Then I will return for my payment."

The Bat looks even brighter tonight than it did last night, though the Snake still shines the brightest. "That is not enough time."

She shrugs. "Then I will take your mother's soul instead. I'm sure my sister will be happy to turn her over. She owes me, after all." The Witch disappears without another word, leaving me alone with the scorpions.

THEN

I was born in the village of Mera, where my mother spent most of her life. It was cool and green, with the constant rush of the ocean in the background and a mist so soft you didn't notice it until your cheeks felt wet, as if you'd been crying and didn't realize it.

The buildings were made of white stone and tucked among the cliffs. Paths of sand and grass wound their way through the tall, spindly buildings from the highest houses down to the beach. At the top of the highest cliff stood the Lighthouse of Mera, its emerald glass winking in the sunlight by day and sending a formidable beam into the darkness over the ocean at night.

Mother and I lived in a small room on the top floor of a house that belonged to a quiet family. Gulls often cried just outside the window and infiltrated my dreams.

Mother made a living by dancing at weddings, feasts—any celebration. Nearly every night she would put on a dress that flared out from her hips but also hid the scars on her arms. She wrapped herself in bright colored scarves and painted her nails scarlet. I usually accompanied her, hovering at the edges of the crowd until she held out her hands, inviting me to join her. We would twirl beneath the lights together until the faces of the guests became a blur, the music weaving around us like a mantle.

If the music was lively, she would spin and leap with abandon until all of us, even the most hard-hearted, were drawn into the dance with her. If the song was a love ballad, the sway of her hips was so infectious that couples who didn't even know they had feelings for one another would suddenly vow to never part.

The best nights were those when the air went still just before a great green fireball flashed over the ocean followed by a thunderous boom that rattled the windows: the Lights of Mera. They were really only lightning, but for some reason the lightning just exploded over Mera. The villagers whispered that it was the merfolk who lived just beyond the surf, beneath the surface, out of sight of the town; sometimes they liked to remind us that they were here first.

Many would take shelter and cower when the Lights streaked across the sky, but Mother's eyes would shine. "It's good luck to dance under them," she would tell me, and then we would spin with our hands locked as the air echoed with thunder.

She was paid in bags of gold, carafes of wine, or sometimes even jewelry. We were always invited to join the feast after, and I would eat sugary, frosted cake until my teeth ached.

Mother always slept late the next morning, the shutters pulled shut against the bright light and pounding waves. I would go down to the beach while the tide was out and tug blue-tinted seaweed from beneath the surface of the rocks that lined the surf. Sometimes I would hike up the hill behind the village to a meadow where tiny starred blossoms and wide palm leaves grew and gather them by the basketful.

Mother was usually awake by the time I returned. We spent the afternoons grinding, slicing, and mixing what I'd collected into potions and cosmetics: perfumes to hide the smell of doubt; lotions to stop the skin from aging; tinctures to keep away unwanted pregnancies; shampoos to draw others closer or repel unwanted attention.

Sometimes she had to take out her knife and draw it across her arm, a hiss of pain escaping her as the blood dripped into the powders and lotions.

"Let me, Mother," I offered once, but she pushed me away.

"Your blood isn't potent enough," she snapped. Her words stung as sharply as the knife's blade. But I knew why: I didn't have enough Mer blood to be as powerful as she was. I watched as her blood dripped into the seaweed, then I turned and retreated to the steep path that led to the sea.

She came to find me a few minutes later. "It's not a bad thing that your blood isn't poison," she said, her voice hollow and weak. "You're still young, anyway. Perhaps we just haven't seen it yet."

Yet. The word hung between us. The sound of the ocean filled the silence of the town.

She sighed. "I need you to grow strong," she said softly. "But I don't want you to grow up too fast like I did."

Before a dance, Mother would sit in front of the mirror and paint a rouge on her lips that made them fuller. She would drop belladonna into her eyes so that her pupils widened, giving her a look of wonder. "Be careful," she warned. "If you use too much, the rouge might someday numb your lips so you can't speak, and the belladonna could make you go blind."

"Then don't use it!" I protested.

"Darling, I don't plan to live long enough for that to happen to me," she said with a laugh that had a sad edge.

The thought of my mother dying made my chest tighten with panic. "I'm only joking, Badriya," Mother said, taking me into her arms. "Look, I'll paint your nails."

"But I don't want you to die!" I sobbed.

"I am talking about a very, very long time from now," Mother said. "Look, if you stop crying, I'll let you use my special blue polish." I would force myself to stop crying because it was more fun to sit with my mother as she painted my nails and told me stories than it was to think of her dying.

Occasionally she would brush a powder that sparkled like diamonds across her eyelids. Moondust, she called it, but she only used it sparingly. "Too much makes you crave more," she told me. She'd become dreamy, her voice thick and low. "You'll do things, foolish things. Trade your most prized possession, give away your deepest secret. And you'll find it was all for nothing."

Each evening as the light in the sky dimmed, she would lift the lid off of a jar, releasing an odor of bitterness and despair. I dreaded the moment she handed me a shred of leaf or a piece of root from the jar, not only because the thistles stung my tongue, but because of the sharp, sour taste that coated my mouth. In the minute it took for the sensation to clear, the shadows in the room would deepen and the shriek of the gulls at the window would become more sinister. I thought I could hear cries in the rush of the water below.

At her vanity, tears welled in Mother's eyes as she chewed her own leaf. Sometimes I tried to spit mine into my hand, but she nearly always caught me and forced it into my mouth until I swallowed. "Every day, Badriya," she said. "You must take this every day, even if I am not here to remind you."

"Why?" I demanded, my tongue numb.

"If you are already full of poison, then no one can harm you."

"But why would that even happen?" The older I got the more exasperated I became.

"You must trust me, Badriya. Those of us who deal in poisons must always be on our guard."

Rolling my eyes, I turned away, but she was not finished. "The other night at the feast, Polina brought us a plate. You remember?"

Polina, angular and frowning. She was married to a fisherman in the village, Cayo. He had dark hair that fell around his collar and laugh lines around his eyes.

"Do you also remember the nightmare you had?" Mother asked. In my dream the cries of the gulls had turned into relentless screams and I thought someone was drowning in the waves until I woke.

"The dreams could have been much worse—bad enough to drive you mad. But your body is used to much stronger poisons because you've been taking them for years."

I shivered in the cool sunlight that spilled in through the window, the dregs of the nightmare still clawing at me. Polina had seemed kind enough—she always had a smile for me. I wrapped my arms around myself as I realized that even though a smile curled her mouth, her eyes always stayed narrowed.

Mother went back to grinding, a pungent scent filling the room. "And Polina?" I asked with a tremor in my voice that I couldn't hide. "She poisoned the meat?"

"She brought us the meat, didn't she? Remember how she insisted we take it and even watched us eat it?" She nodded toward a pile of blossoms. "Pull the petals from those and shred them. It is a new moon tonight, so it will be dark. We will be busy, and these are most effective when there is no light."

I obeyed even though my thoughts were far away. "And you, Mother? Did you have nightmares?" She didn't answer but began to slice the seaweed, perhaps harder than necessary, as she hummed a melody.

Cayo and Mother often walked together in the evenings, during a break in the dancing, whispers following them like a train. Sometimes they would disappear, just long enough for people to start wondering where they'd gone. But they were only friends, weren't they? Anyway, many of the men seemed entranced by Mother. Nearly everyone did.

Cayo would bring me little gifts. When I was small, they were sweets or a piece of smooth sea glass he'd found on the beach. The latest gift was a large shell, pink and spiked, that curled in on itself. "Put it to your ear," he told me.

By then I was twelve and not easy to impress. "Why would I do that?"

"So you can hear the ocean."

With a sigh I fit the shell to my ear. For a moment there was only silence, and then I heard the low whisper of the ocean, the way it sounded at midday. Suddenly it crashed as if a great storm had rolled in unexpectedly, only to quiet to a rush again.

On nights when there weren't any celebrations, Mother would set a lamp in the window. She would not paint her face, but instead drank strong coffee that filled the room with its fragrance.

When the cries of the gulls had dulled and the only sound was the murmur of the waves, women would come to the door. Usually only one or two came, but on restless nights when the waves crashed against the rocks in advance of a storm or when the clouds obscured the moon there might be half a dozen. They would ask for powders to crush into their husband's ale to enhance or weaken his desire, lozenges to make them thinner, or any of the other potions and tinctures we'd crushed and mixed. In return they would offer coins or jewelry.

Sometimes they would ask for Moondust. When they did, Mother would study them; if they looked too eager, or too sad, or if their hands shook, she would ask for a ridiculous price. "One hundred pounds of silver." If she were in a particularly odd mood, she might ask something like, "Your last-born child."

I would help Mother by gathering the ingredients, starting with the seaweed that had a silver sheen. In order to find it I had to hold my breath and duck under the waves, pulling myself to the bottom of the stones embedded with blood-colored swirls. Then I had to cut it from the rocks with the knife Mother gave me, the one with the blade that could slice through bone, or so she said. The seaweed came away like wet paper, though I imagined I heard a faint cry as I pulled.

When I returned, Mother would use the knife to slice the seaweed into tiny bits that she mixed with a blue powder in a tiny vial. When she found a place on her arm that wasn't already scarred, she would hold her breath and draw the knife across it, tilting it so that the blood dripped into the pile of seaweed and powder that waited below.

Watching the pain and dread on her face, I asked, "Why do you have to cut your arm, Mother?"

"Magic has its price, Badriya," she replied.

Chapter Four

Two days had passed since the Duke's entourage left the city. Last night lightning flashed through the sky, illuminating a demon as it feasted on the bones of some helpless traveler stuck in the Lost. Low rumbles of thunder that sounded like laughter had followed. The storm was nothing compared to the Lights of Mera.

The smell of sulfur lingers in the air. I don't look out the window, knowing that I'll see the Snake in the sky, defying the light.

My knife lies amid a pile of swayleaf petals, their pungent scent filling the air. Whoever comes tonight will be charged double the price.

I worked for a few hours until my hands shook from exhaustion and worry. I'd sliced the petals so badly that I had to throw them away. Blossoms cut incorrectly could lead the wearer into foolish arguments.

I am about to return to my work when the blare of trumpets echoes through the air: someone is approaching from the Lost. Has the Duke returned, ready to make an accusation? An insect skitters to safety underneath my bed; I wish I could join it.

I groan as the door bursts open. "He is here!" Solena hisses from the doorway.

"Who?" I ask. "My Queen," I add.

"My suitor!"

My tired mind sluggishly considers her words. "I thought you hated him. You ordered me to kill him."

She stares at me, her eyes nearly popping from her face. "Not the Duke, you simpleton!"

I push past her, crossing the gallery, and lean out over the rail as the gates swing open. A company of riders on fine white horses enter. One of the men carries a blue and gold banner.

Another caravan? There haven't been any for months and now this one follows the Duke's by mere hours. Why now?

I curse as I think of the Bones' warning that someone approached from the east. I turn to face her. "Another suitor? You really want to go through this again after everything that happened with the Duke?"

She huffs. "Dorros is hardly worth marrying the Duke—no kingdom is worth that. But in case you haven't noticed, Diya, our city is not what it was. Someone must do something, and it must be me."

I feel another unwelcome flicker of sympathy because it's true. A marriage between Solena and a powerful ally would help Aran, and the marriage would have to be to a stranger.

"But Tanera," she continues. "That will give us security and riches." We both look to the fountain and the few oranges that hang from the tree branches.

Once the enchantment fades altogether, what will keep the Lost from swallowing Aran again?

I turn back to Solena. "And apparently the…what is he? A Duke? A Prince? He must be more palatable than the Duke."

"He's Prince Arlo. Besides, Tanera is far wealthier than Dorros and they have a strong military that can protect us."

The military could shield us from the demons and ghosts in the Lost for a short time, but we both know that it won't last.

"When did this agreement come about?" I ask.

"I don't need to tell you everything, do I? You can hardly be trusted."

For a long moment we hold each other's gaze. She looks much older than nineteen. I can see the crone she will become if she survives to old age.

"Diya." A vein bulges out from her temple. I fear she might actually lose her sanity once and for all. "Move your lazy bones."

"All right." I move back into my chamber and pull a wrap over my nightgown, catching my hair loosely in a loop.

"Diya!"

"Coming, My Queen." She rushes ahead of me to the door that connects my room to hers and I follow. Maybe I can finish quickly and get back to my potions.

In her chamber, her guard Darien waits, as stoic as ever. She throws herself on the chair before her mirror. "Hurry," she says. I suspect that her urgency is not all due to vanity: she craves the calm that the powder brings and the confidence the rouge provides.

Each day I add more arsenic and more nightshade in the hope that one morning she will be found in a puddle of her own vomit, just as her mother was. Or that she will cast herself from the Wall, as my mother did. Yet each day she wakes as bitter and biting as ever, her eyesight sharp enough to catch the swiftest glance between courtiers and her steps quick enough to dance with her Favorites. She seems to thrive on the poison, but so does her madness.

Yadira and Petra enter silently. Petra's skin glows against her white gown and gold bangles slide along her wrists. Yadira looks like a phantom in her pale dress. I feel a twinge of guilt, but she hardly deserves my sympathy, nor does she need it. They wait with combs and blooms from the White Garden for Solena's hair.

I smooth the cream over the thin, fragile skin under her eyes to hide the shadows that pool there after many nightmares. Then I brush on the powder that hides the dark veins that have begun to cross her cheeks. She begins to relax, though I can see her pulse beating rapidly at her throat. I tilt her head back and drop the nightshade into her eyes so that they will be dewy and wondering rather than hard and suspicious. Her full red lips are swollen from the nettles that I use to make her lip rouge.

Eventually the nightshade will blind her and the venom on her lips will make it impossible to form words. Surely not even she can withstand the poison forever.

"There." I back away as Solena touches her fingertips to her face and examines herself in the mirror. She sighs as the tension in her shoulders ebbs away.

"I'll go then," I say.

Her eyes snap to me. "Don't be hard to find. Be ready to attend to me." Damn, I'd hoped that the more potent mixture would make her mind foggy.

"As you wish, My Queen." I keep my head lowered so she can't read my expression.

I have chopped only a few more swayleaves when there is a knock on my door. "Queen Solena requests your presence," Darien calls through the door. I toss the knife down with a clatter and curse as a few blossoms flutter to the floor. "Immediately," he adds, and I curse again.

I am wearing Mother's tunic and pants, which are stained and smell sour and bitter. *Fine*, I think. *She needs me immediately? I will come immediately.*

Just as I reach the door, I turn back for my favorite scarf, the one that is the exact shade of the Turquoise Sea, and drape it around my neck. There is another knock. "All right!" I shout as I tuck my knife into my belt and conceal it with my tunic before going to the door.

A half dozen men stand waiting in the courtyard, one of them standing slightly in front of the rest. He swallows as he watches our approach, then shifts so that he is standing a bit straighter. His dark skin gleams with perspiration and sweat slides down his temple. His white shirt is covered with a fine dusting of sand and dirt streaks his light pants. A blue medallion on a heavy gold chain is draped across his chest. This must be the Prince.

At his shoulder stands another man, slight as a shadow. His dark hair is pulled back from his gaunt face. Unlike the Prince, this man's face is unreadable as he watches Solena.

White roses are twined through her tresses, which glow like mahogany in the sunlight. The golden gown cascading from her shoulders brings out a gleam of amber in her dark eyes. She lifts a languid hand to brush her hair over her shoulder.

"Welcome, Prince Arlo," she says, her voice warm and thick as honey though there is still a razor edge to her smile. She offers her hand.

Bowing, Arlo takes it and kisses it. He is certain to have nightmares from the lotion on her skin. "This is my adviser, Khalen." The man at the Prince's shoulder bows deeply.

"My sister, Najma," Solena says, and Najma offers a solemn curtsy. "These are my Ladies, Petra and Yadira." They curtsy, though Yadira is a bit unsteady. "And Diya."

I mutter, "That's not my name," as I curtsy. I rise in time to see a smile flicker over Solena's face. The advisor raises his eyebrows.

"Your Ladies rival the Queen in beauty," says the Prince.

Solena stiffens, her smile turning to ice. Petra's eyes flicker from Arlo to Solena. Yadira stares vacantly before her as if she has not heard.

"Your Grace is so kind and chivalrous," Petra says smoothly. "But everyone knows that none of the Queen's Ladies could rival her beauty." She elbows Yadira, who belatedly dips her head in agreement. I see a smile flicker across the adviser's face as I roll my eyes.

The Prince looks over his shoulder at his adviser, whose smile disappears. He gives a slight nod and Arlo turns back to Solena.

"Stories of the Queen's loveliness have traveled across the Lost to all corners of the realm," Arlo says, "and to my amazement, I find them to be true."

Solena's smile widens and she takes the Prince's arm. "Come. You must be famished and thirsty after your long journey." She leads him toward the Dining Hall where servants are darting to and from the kitchens. I imagine the frenzy as they try to prepare a feast for our unexpected guests.

I fall behind, hoping to slip back to my potions unnoticed. I've hardly gone a few steps when Solena turns and calls, "Diya, where are you going?"

I curtsy, something I hardly ever do. "I wasn't sure you'd need me, My Queen."

Her eyes flash. "Oh, I do need you, Diya. Please join us."

I feel the eyes of Arlo and his adviser on us as I bow my head, muttering curses that I hope are too low to hear as I follow the entourage into the Dining Hall. As we enter, the men look around, Khalen with interest, the Prince gaping in awe. The Kings' effigies watch as we seat ourselves around the table. "She'll eat him alive," Petra mutters from beside me. On her other side Yadira smiles vaguely.

Khalen sits across from us. I hope he hasn't heard her. "I notice you've brought no Witch. That is quite unusual." *And foolish.*

"Oh?" he says.

"Witches are deft at intervening with the demons and other Witches." Other warnings come to mind, though I don't speak them. *The Wind Demons might have whispered things that would drive you to despair, things from your past that you thought you'd buried but they unearthed. The Witches who might have found you at your most desperate hour and tricked you into trading something you couldn't live without. The ghosts that haunt you until you become one of them.* I say instead, "Many do not dare make the journey here. They find the risks to be too great."

"It is not an easy journey," he concedes, taking a slice of bread and drizzling it with honey. "But we moved quickly and our horses are swift. I am not unfamiliar with the dangers of the Lost."

"Even the wind?" I press.

For an instant his eyes darken. "It is persistent." His hand moves absently to a chain around his neck, a gesture I think must be habit. Whatever hangs from it is hidden beneath his shirt. Despite his smooth demeanor, he is not as confident as he would have others believe.

The servants enter carrying trays of oranges, dates, and meat. Our visitors eat the food eagerly. Arlo takes a huge bite of meat, the grease smearing his chin. Khalen mimes wiping his chin until Arlo catches his meaning and swipes at his chin with his napkin. Petra takes a drink to hide her laughter.

"Do tell us of Tanera," Solena says.

Arlo begins to speak, despite the fact that he has a mouthful of food. Catching Khalen's frown, he tries to swallow. His face reddens and he begins coughing. A piece of chewed meat flies from his mouth and lands on Petra's plate. She grimaces and hands her plate off to a servant who appears at her shoulder. Khalen pounds on Arlo's back as Solena taps her fingernails on the table. I stiffen. She can't possibly be thinking of eliminating him, not already. What about the riches and security?

"Tanera is on the eastern edge of the Lost," Khalen continues, as though the Prince were not hacking beside him. "It is built on hills." Arlo's coughs have begun to subside and he drinks from his water glass. "It's very green and there are a lot of trees. The Calla River empties into the Eastern Sea there."

"There are waterfalls," Arlo breaks in, his voice hoarse from coughing. "And pools to swim in. It is green and cool." He looks at his plate, his ears reddening.

"It sounds so lovely. Whyever would you be interested in our dry little city?" Solena asks.

"A trading route," Arlo says. Solena arches an eyebrow and smiles as if a child has just surprised her with its knowledge. "Our caravans could rest here during journeys across the Lost rather than keeping to the coastline."

"Our hope is to trade our lumber for the ore that is found in the west," Khalen breaks in. "Traversing the mountains in the north would take too long and it would be difficult to manage the heavy trees. We try to avoid the mountains to the north and the swamps to the south."

And the terrors in the Lost, I add silently.

"Legend has it that Aran was once the Pearl of the Lost," Arlo says.

Solena's nails drum harder.

"We'd like to find the most direct path to Mera as well," Khalen says as he picks up an orange and peels it.

"Diya knows Mera," Najma says. She smiles at me and I try to return it, though I hardly wish to speak of Mera to these strangers.

Arlo looks up, gaping, his eyes still watering. "You've been to Mera?"

I nod. "I lived there."

"Why would you come here?"

I try not to flinch as the drumming of Solena's nails increases. "I came with my mother."

"Diya's mother was a Witch," Solena says, as if she were commenting on the music. "She's dead now."

"She wasn't a Witch." The table falls silent and the Prince and Khalen look from me to Solena. The smile has vanished from her face. I drink deeply from my water to cool the heat in my face.

"Ugh, let's not bore them with this," Petra groans. "It's so dull. Tell us, Prince Arlo, about your true intentions in coming here." She rests her chin on her hand and leans forward flirtatiously. I notice one of the Prince's men, tall and thin, swallow as he watches her.

Arlo clears his throat. "I have come to court Queen Solena."

"Oh! Isn't that wonderful!" Petra cries. Yadira, momentarily alert, echoes her. Najma spreads more honey on her bread.

"The Duke of Dorros certainly tried to talk us out of coming," Arlo says. The table once again falls silent.

"The Duke of Dorros?" Solena repeats.

"Dorros isn't far from Tanera," Arlo says.

Once again Khalen breaks in. "We passed the Duke's caravan last night; they were in quite a hurry to return home. Apparently he suffered some sort of accident during his visit here. His court thought he died, but then he awoke."

"Cursing and demanding wine," Arlo adds.

I widen my eyes in shock. I did not expect the Duke's entourage to encounter anyone until they reached Dorros.

Solena taps her nails. "We certainly thought he was dead when he left here," she says, her eyes flicking toward me. "His heart gave out, wasn't that it?"

"Evidently he'd caroused too much the previous night," I agree, holding her gaze.

"Well, thank the stars he is all right," Khalen says, raising his glass. We all follow suit and I drink deeply from my water.

"Aran is known for being incredibly hospitable to those who are lucky enough to reach it," Khalen continues, setting down his glass. "Your father was famous for welcoming travelers."

"There haven't been many," Solena says with a small smile.

Until now, I think.

"He passed recently, didn't he?" Khalen asks.

My hand freezes on my glass. His voice is sympathetic, but I wonder how much he suspects of the King's death.

"It's been three years. But yes, he did." She lifts a hand toward her father's effigy. Even in stone his smile makes me shiver.

Khalen dips his head. "I'm sorry to hear that." Perhaps only I see him nudge Arlo, who mumbles his condolences a beat later.

"He ruled for a long time," Solena says with a catch in her voice as if her eyes were capable of forming tears. "And I plan to as well. Though it has been so difficult, so lonely—I'm sure you can understand," she says to Arlo. He nods.

"It's fortunate that you have your sister to support you," Khalen says.

"Najma is too young to understand." Najma frowns. "You must be tired," Solena says to the Prince. "Petra, Yadira, show them to the baths and the guest rooms. Diya," she adds as everyone rises, "I would like to speak with you."

I curse the bad fortune that led the two caravans to meet. "Actually, I must work in my garden," I tell her. "I am running out of powder for your eyes and cream for your lips. It would be awful to have to start watering it down." She glares, furious that I've revealed that her beauty isn't completely natural. She says nothing as I rise and hurry from the Hall.

✳

I keep to my garden the rest of the day, trimming feverishly and harvesting coldberries for a tincture to ease headaches caused by too much wine. After a while my fingers are stained with dirt and a sour taste lingers in my mouth. I tense with each sound, waiting for Solena to find me with accusations and threats. But she doesn't come; perhaps she's too busy trying to convince Arlo how wonderful our city is or sleeping off the effects of her cosmetics.

When my hands grow clumsy, I eat some of the courageberries but they are slightly green and make my stomach ache with the vague feeling of disappointment. I brace myself to take some bitterthorn, the acidic pulp stinging my throat.

The wind intensifies as night falls, driving the guard from the top of the Wall. I hear him curse as he passes, wiping sand from his eyes. Or perhaps they are tears, for the wind is particularly vindictive tonight.

Mother's lullaby fills the air and my throat catches with the sorrow in it. I climb the stairs and stare out into the sand as she sings to the stars with her head tilted back and the King at her shoulder.

"Careful," the Bones sigh. "It never ends well in this city when one becomes mired in their memories."

But it is too late. The wind glides slyly along the Wall, winding through my hair, lifting it so that it can whisper into my ear. The Fish fades and the Snake's eye glows brighter.

THEN

Mother and I left Mera five years ago on a night when a Blood Moon hung over the cliffs.

The air felt heavy and ominous, a late summer storm brewing over the ocean. We'd come to the beach to gather kelp. There was an edge to the wind that I should have heeded, but my thoughts were focused on a boy with a mischievous smile who caught my eye whenever we met.

"I'll be back, Badriya," Mother said suddenly.

I looked up, surprised, but her eyes were on a man dressed in white who was beckoning to her from the water's edge: Cayo.

He stripped off his shirt and beckoned again, laughing. Mother's hand was cool on my cheek, her eyes alight. She raced down the beach to meet him, running past him into the water. The waves churned around her knees and her dress clung to her legs. She scooped water into her hands and splashed him. With a shout, he lunged for her and caught her around the waist, carrying her into the water.

I held my hand over my eyes to shield them from the sunlight dappling the waves. The gulls wheeled and shrieked as Mother curved her arms over her head and dove into the water. Cayo followed and together they disappeared.

Don't leave me, I thought. The kelp in my hand dripped onto the sand and the wind bit through my shirt. A minute passed, then another. I began to shiver as the sand grew cold beneath me. The sun sank closer to the sea and the moon rose from the water, edged in red.

They have been gone too long. I rose and ran to the water's edge, my legs stiff. I pushed into the water, ankle-deep, knee-deep, then waist-deep, my eyes darting over the waves. But I could not see them. I cried out for my mother, but the waves swallowed my voice. The seagulls wheeling overhead seemed to mock me. The sun disappeared and the water darkened.

Finally I heard my name over the rush of the ocean. I searched the water but saw nothing. Suddenly I saw a shape struggling toward me. I recoiled, wondering if it was one of the merfolk coming to terrorize me as they were said to do during a Blood Moon. "Badriya." The voice was my mother's. I nearly sobbed with relief, though I could hear the exhaustion and grief in her voice. She dragged something heavy with her.

I fought toward her to help. When I got closer, I saw what she dragged: Cayo. His eyes were closed and his face was blue. I grabbed one of his arms, trying to help, but the surf kept breaking over us.

One final wave pushed the three of us onto the sand. I collapsed to my knees, gasping with the effort of hauling him onto the beach, but Mother began thrusting her hands against his chest, oblivious to the surf breaking over her. She pushed down so hard that I thought she might break his ribs. She'd stop and press her mouth over his, blowing air into him, then begin pressing again, her breath becoming more ragged. I stared at him, willing him to draw a breath, to sit up and laugh at the trick he'd played. *Please breathe, please breathe, please…*

A shriek echoed from behind us. Frantic footsteps scrabbled toward us in the sand. Polina pushed my mother aside and collapsed beside her husband, sobbing as she fell across his chest. Mother wrapped her arms around herself, rocking back and forth on her knees. Kohl ran down her face and the remnants of last night's Moondust glittered in her eyelashes. I put my arm around her cold, wet shoulders trying to warm her, but she did not seem to know I was there. Cayo lay on the beach staring up at the Blood Moon that was rising over the ocean. On his right shoulder, just visible, was a pale birthmark in the shape of a starfish.

Others gathered around as Polina sat up and glared at my mother. "He couldn't swim." Her voice was as rough as the barnacles on the rocks. "You tricked him. You enchanted him. You made him think that he could keep up with you. You can't stop wanting, Narisa. You're a poison that can't stop destroying everything around it. If you couldn't have him, no one could. Isn't that right?" Her voice rose to a shriek that tore at the air. "Isn't that right? Was it not enough that you cursed our marriage and kept us childless? Now I'm alone, completely alone." Her words dissolved into sobs.

One of the women whispered to another, and both crossed their arms and glared at us. Another woman tugged her child away from the beach. I recognized her as someone who'd come to my mother for a tincture to help ease the child's stomachache.

Mother's face didn't change, as if she didn't hear Polina. She just kept rocking.

"Mother?" I tried. "Mother, can you hear me?" She didn't react.

I felt sick for Polina, helpless. But as quick as the wind, her voice rose again. "Arrest her! She is a Witch! Arrest her! It will be your husbands and your sons next!"

The woman who whispered gave her husband a shove. He stepped forward but stopped uncertainly.

Anger overpowered my sympathy. "Don't talk to her that way! She did nothing!"

Polina's eyes flicked to me. "You're just like her—I can see it in your face. Poison." The hatred in her voice chilled me.

"Take your daughter and leave, Narisa," Polina said. "There is no future for either of you here. Nothing that will end well." She lay her forehead against Cayo's chest and continued to sob.

I rose, my fists clenched. "This is our home. We are not leaving."

I looked at the crowd. Many people glared, some whispered, and a few refused to meet my gaze. They wouldn't confront Mother, not if they wanted their serums and potions.

"We'll go." Mother's voice was so quiet I could barely hear it over the roar of the waves. I opened my mouth to protest, but Mother spoke over me. "We'll go, Badriya." I closed my mouth, the grief in her eyes silencing me. With one last long look at Cayo, she rose and walked toward the path that led away from the beach, leaving me to follow.

The Lost begins a few miles east of Mera. The meadow fades and the grass becomes more and more sparse until there is no green at all, only sand. The rush of the ocean and the cry of the gulls are lost—the only color is the silver sand that is painted by the moon.

Mother looked over her shoulder constantly, as if someone were following us. But who would venture into this void? We carried packs that held our clothes and the herbs and leaves that we'd wrapped in cloth. Mother's pack jingled with the sound of her bracelets. At her waist hung a purse containing the silver that she'd traded for Moondust.

The shell Cayo had given me was wrapped in my clothes.

"Why the Lost?" I asked Mother on the first morning. "Why not another town by the sea?"

"I belong in the Lost."

"I don't," I muttered, but she didn't bother to answer. Where would I go if I didn't stay with her?

"So we're blindly wandering into nothing?" I couldn't keep the resentment from my voice.

"No. We're going to Aran."

"Aran? What is that?"

"A city."

"In the Lost?"

"At its heart."

I stopped in my tracks. "Why?"

"Because, Badriya. There is nothing left for me here. In Aran I can be healed."

"Healed from what?" I demanded. I think of the blankness on her face and the way she hadn't seemed to hear me back on the beach.

Turning, she strode on. I looked back over my shoulder to see the tip of the lighthouse. I could still hear the rush of the waves just past the long, sharp grass.

It wasn't too late for me to run back to our old house. I could live on the beach, sleep in a cave, catch fish in the shallows.

I thought of the eyes of the villagers over Cayo's body and Polina's wails. I couldn't return.

Besides, if going to this city in the Lost meant that Mother would smile and dance again, I wanted her to go there. So I followed her, although I left a few yards between us.

The rush of the sea quickly died away and the wind became hot. The grass was brittle and cracked beneath my feet, sand seeped into my sandals, and my feet were sore and blistered.

One night I stopped in my tracks as a long, high cry of despair echoed across the sky. "What was that?"

Even Mother's footsteps faltered. "There are a lot of strange sounds in the Lost," she said. "You can't jump at them all or you'll never get anywhere."

My throat was dry and hoarse as I asked, "What is Aran like?"

"It was built on a magical spring. It is green there, and there are orange trees and apples."

"In the middle of the Lost?" My voice was sharp. Was she addled from the poisons? Perhaps she wasn't as wise as I'd always thought.

"That is how the magic works. A reckless man tried crossing from Mera to Tanera, and many men in his party slowly died from the heat and exhaustion. When they were too weak to resist, the demons pulled them under the sand one by one.

"Some of the survivors abandoned him and returned to their home. But just as the man began to despair, he found a trickle of water in the Lost. He drank from it eagerly, though it was more sand than water. Suddenly a Witch appeared, and she cast a spell over the water. It became clear and fresh. The survivors felt their strength return as they drank.

"The Witch offered the man a bargain, which he agreed to. He and the other survivors then built the city of Aran, and the man became the First King. Now, those who are willing to brave the Lost to travel to Aran are rewarded with the youth and beauty that the spring provides."

"What was the bargain?" I asked.

"The King traded his daughter."

"What?" I choked. "He traded his daughter?"

"Magic has its price, Badriya."

I rolled my eyes despite the goosebumps sprouting on my arms. "What a horrible place."

"Your future there will be better than in Mera." Mother's voice sharpened. "It is a beautiful place, a magical place. Those who live there enjoy beauty, health, and happiness." She took a deep breath. When she spoke again her voice was calmer. "It will be worth it, Badriya. Trust me."

Overhead, the Horse constellation urged us onward, but the Fish was beginning to appear, its points faint for now. In a few weeks it would cavort among the other stars; it would not be a good time to make decisions.

I wanted to trust my mother, to believe in the power of this enchanted place to bring happiness and peace. The only alternative was a despair as yawning and empty as the Lost.

"How can we reach this city when this group of men almost didn't?" My voice was shrill with panic.

"I have something to trade."

"What?" As far as I knew, we only had a few coins left from Mother's dancing and two gold bracelets. The shell I carried was hardly worth trading.

"My blood. They love the blood of merfolk."

"But you're not…" I think of her flitting among the waves, impossibly fast, easily outdistancing the boats. I think of the suspicious, angry looks people cast us in Mera.

"I'm not full-blooded, but my grandmother was," Mother says. "It will be enough."

"Mother, wait. You can't give them your blood. What will I do without you? You can't leave me…" My voice rose until my words tumbled over each other.

She touched her hand to my cheek. It was cool despite the heat pressing in on us. "They only require a few drops."

She turned away, her eyes skimming the Lost. I wrapped my arms around myself as I shuddered. "Who are you looking for?"

Under her breath she hummed a song that she'd danced to with Cayo on a starlit night in Mera, both of them too lost in laughter to notice the hurt and anger on Polina's face.

"He's not here! He's dead! You're being ridiculous!" I was furious with her for going mad, for dragging me out here and staring out at the sand with her sad eyes.

"It's my only chance to see him again."

"What are you talking about?" I sputtered. I remembered the cry I'd heard and knew better than to tell her that there were no such things as ghosts.

"What would he be doing here in the Lost?" I demanded. "If anything he'd haunt the ocean!" I scooped up a handful of sand and threw it, even angrier with myself for entertaining her madness.

She turned back and reached for me, but I jerked away. "There are things you don't understand. And I hope you never have to, my little Toad."

"Stop calling me that! Stop treating me like a baby." I folded my arms as tears filled my eyes.

Mother studied me for a moment. "Save your tears," she said. "You may need to trade them." Then she strode away, leaving me to follow.

CHAPTER FIVE

My eyes burn and my head aches. I haven't cried since the night the King died. My tears have built up, threatening to poison me—if only I could let them fall.

"Maybe you will cry sooner than you think," the Bones muse as I hear footsteps on the stairs. "Behind you."

I touch my fingertips to the knife that is hidden beneath my tunic. No one dares to climb here, not since the night my mother died, and definitely not on a night like this when the wind circles stealthily.

I step back into the shadows. A few seconds later a figure appears at the top of the stairs: Khalen. Gripping the Wall, he stares out into the Lost so intently that he doesn't see me. His eyes lock on something. I try to follow his gaze, but I see only shifting sand. He takes a small vial from his shirt and pours its contents into the sand below, just as my mother had done years before as an offering to the ghosts.

"Who do you see?" The question bursts from me. He whirls toward me, and for a moment we stare at each other. Traces of grief are written on his face.

"I do not like to be spied on," he says finally, his voice thick. He turns his back and strides toward the stairs.

My temper flares. Who is he to speak to me this way, on my Wall? "I do not like trespassers in my garden!" I shout after him. He does not answer as he clatters down the stairs.

He saw something, or someone, but what?

I rush back to the Wall and search the Lost, but I see only sand and darkness.

So, the Prince's stoic adviser sees his own ghosts. I stare out over the Lost, wondering. What regrets lie in his past? Who has he lost? Who, or what, haunts him?

The Bones are silent, though scorpions hiss in the garden. I can feel the Snake watching me with its red eye. The wind bites through my cloak, but there is nowhere to go except back to my chamber.

Under the Snake, one must be careful of hidden danger. I know that well, yet I am not as wary as I should be as I enter my chamber.

"Diya." The voice cuts through the dimness as I enter. I gasp and clutch at my chest as Solena's pale face looms from the shadows.

I must get a lock for my door. "My Queen. I was not expecting you. I would have left my chamber in a better state." Forcing myself to recover, I cross to the table and light a candle.

"As the Queen I may enter wherever and whenever I wish. Perhaps you should be in the habit of keeping your chamber neater."

"To what do I owe the pleasure of this visit?" I ask, turning to face her. "My Queen," I add, as she frowns.

"I only wanted to ask how a man I ordered you to assassinate has suddenly been seen alive."

"The poisons are not exact. I've told you this before." I force my voice to remain steady.

"Then why would you not use more than enough to ensure his death?"

"I did not wish to risk wasting my supplies. They're not easy to replace, you know. Why were you so determined that he die, might I ask?"

Her mouth tightens. "You saw him. He groped me as we danced— he treated me like a common servant." Her mouth twitches. "But I suppose that seemed acceptable to you given who your mother was."

I resolve to add an extra pinch of achevine to her powder so that her head pounds all day. "He won't be returning anytime soon. As far as you're concerned, he might as well be dead. Now others who have considered taking liberties with you have been warned as well."

She tilts her head and taps her long nails on the table. One, two, three. "I am warning you as well, Diya. Disobey me again and you will find yourself hanging from the Wall." She sweeps from the room, leaving the scent of lilies laced with something bitter in her wake.

I decide not to light the candle in the window. What would be the point? Solena would have frightened off any potential visitors.

Breakfast the next morning is late. Lightning had once again streaked across the sky last night, illuminating all the secrets that are usually hidden in the Lost. I imagine no one slept well. I certainly didn't.

Solena looks slightly ill, rubbing her temples—a sure sign that she has a headache. Good. The extra pinch of achevine that I added to her powder this morning is working.

Solena is seated on one side of Najma, while Khalen sits on Najma's other side. As I enter, he half rises and nods with a rueful smile. Feeling Solena's sharp gaze, I return his nod and seat myself across from Najma.

"Where is the Prince?" I ask.

"I have no doubt that he is in the library, My Lady," Khalen says with a bow of his head. *My Lady? He really is trying to get in my good graces.* "It is quite an impressive place."

"And a good place to hide," I observe, my voice cool. I am not ready to forgive his trespass.

"My father was a lover of books. He had them brought from all corners of the country. I've never had time to enjoy them, though." Solena sighs prettily. "The task of managing the kingdom keeps me so busy, of course."

Khalen raises his eyebrows. "I imagine it does, My Lady. Reading can be such a distraction for rulers. I imagine it's led to the downfall of many." He helps himself to some olives and pops them into his mouth.

Is he mocking her? I can't tell; his expression does not change.

Solena's smile freezes. Beside her, Najma looks from Khalen to Solena. "Which books does he read?" she asks.

We all turn to her. She hardly ever speaks at meals.

"Many," Khalen replies, swallowing an olive. "He enjoys history, as well as old legends. And you?"

Najma's eyes flicker to Solena before she answers. "I enjoy those that combine history and myth."

"Najma is very bookish," Solena says.

"A good quality," I say, smiling at Najma as I take more bread. Solena takes a deep drink from her goblet.

Khalen leans forward with one elbow on the table, "What are your favorite stories?" he asks Najma.

She hesitates before the words pour from her. "There is the legend of the First King, Medacus, who bargained with a Witch to make a tiny stream in the Lost abundant enough for a kingdom. As part of the agreement, she enchanted the stream so that Aran and its citizens would be healthy and beautiful."

"How did he do this?" Khalen asks. I flinch as she answers.

"He traded his daughter."

"How would that have saved Aran?" Khalen asks.

"If the Witch refused to enchant the spring any longer, it would become a muddy trickle again and Aran and all of its citizens would die."

"Hmm. Do you believe in this enchantment?" Khalen asks.

"You tell me, Sir Khalen." Solena turns her most radiant smile on the table. The servant filling Khalen's glass with water loses track of what he's doing, mesmerized by her. It's only when Khalen gently tilts the pitcher upright that he comes to his senses.

"And is this enchantment supposed to last forever?" Khalen asks.

"No," Najma replies. "Only three hundred years. You can already see it's wearing off…"

"Najma," Solena says. Najma continues, undeterred.

"If the Witch could be found, Aran might be saved again." *Only if she is given something with enough value*, I think. "Then Solena wouldn't have to marry—none of our Queens would."

I look at her, surprised. For years I've only seen her as a child who needs to be protected from the adults around her. I never suspected the maze of thoughts and opinions hovering just beneath the surface of her solemn dark eyes. I've underestimated her—we all have.

"Oh, Najma," Solena says with a silvery laugh. Perhaps only Najma and I can tell it is forced. "She fears losing me. Nothing will change, darling."

Najma looks at her plate. "A good ruler learns from the mistakes of the past," she says so quietly that perhaps only I hear her.

"You will make a good ruler yourself, someday," Khalen says to her.

"She is only thirteen," Solena says.

"That is young," Khalen agrees. "But some of the greatest monarchs have also been the youngest. Hector the Third was only twelve when he took the throne, yet he was one of the finest rulers the world has ever seen. And Andromilla the Second…"

"I plan to rule for a very long time," Solena says, her voice now etched in stone. "You'll understand if I do not want my sister's head filled with nonsense that will only cloud her judgment."

Khalen speaks again. "I would love to be shown Aran by someone who knows all of its secrets." His eyes rest on me.

I shake my head ruefully. "I'm sorry to disappoint. Despite what you've heard, there aren't any interesting secrets here."

"Oh, I am not so sure about that." Something in Khalen's voice makes me uneasy.

"Why don't you go now?" Solena says.

I suppress a groan; I need to return to my potions. "I am still hungry."

"You hardly need more to eat," she says with a laugh. "Your tunics are fitting a bit tightly these days, wouldn't you say?"

I smile brightly and remind myself to add a bit more stinging nettle to her lip rouge later. "Shall we?" I ask Khalen. He sets down his cup and rises.

I lead him from the Hall and out into the sunlight.

"Well, what would you like to see?" I ask. Behind us the water bubbles cheerfully in the fountain and tuberoses float on the surface, their scent sweet. Those who look closely might notice that the petals are edged in brown and the water carries the faintest odor of sulfur.

"First I must apologize," he says, offering a wry smile. "You were correct last night. I should not have trespassed onto your Wall. I had no right."

His words throw me off. I am still irritated, but I want to know what he saw, so I match his conciliatory tone. "It's hardly my Wall. I should not have been watching you without your knowledge."

His voice is smooth as he replies. "I was just surprised by how beautiful the Lost looks from the top. I wasn't expecting it. Our journey here was rugged, so seeing it from that vantage helped me appreciate it more. Having a full meal helped as well."

"I noticed you poured something into the sand," I say. "May I ask why?"

He smiles ruefully. "A habit from my childhood that I should have outgrown by now. My aunt was very superstitious. She always recommended that we leave an offering for luck or safe passage."

He is lying, I am sure of it. The way he gripped the Wall and stared into the Lost, he must have seen something. But his smile is unyielding and I can see that he will not say more.

"Where shall we start?" he persists.

"How about the Gambling Hall?" I ask, trying—and failing—to keep the frustration from my voice.

"Is that all there is to do here? Besides dining and dancing, of course," he says.

"Aran does love its games of chance," I reply.

"Very well." He gestures for me to lead the way.

We walk toward the pool that stretches in a long, clear rectangle in front of the Gambling Hall. Children splash about, their laughter echoing from the stone buildings. They stop and bow their heads as we pass. I smile at them, but they don't meet my eye.

"A pool, when your spring is drying up?" Khalen asks.

"Not very logical, is it?" I agree. *Then again, not much about Aran is logical.*

"I have a question. I hope it's not too personal," he says.

I knew this wasn't going to be a simple tour of the city. "What is it?" I ask lightly.

"Your name. Forgive me, but it seems strange that a mother would name her child after a beetle."

"No. That is a nickname Solena gave me when I first came here."

"Hmm. So you didn't get along?"

Actually, she hates me. "When I first arrived Solena was envious." *That's an understatement.* "We were young. The nickname stuck, unfortunately. My real name is Badriya."

"Badriya," he says slowly. "That's lovely."

He opens his mouth to ask another question, but I cut him off. "Here is the Gambling Hall."

We step past the pillars into the cool dimness of the arched doorway, and I lead him inside. The cloths that normally cover the round tables are being laundered. At this hour it is quiet—there are no shouts of triumph or dismay echoing from inside, and the lamps are extinguished. The air is laced with the metallic smell of coins and sour wine. I've come to associate this combination of scents with gambles lost and debts unpaid. It makes me uneasy.

"I've heard that the Queen enjoys gambling," Khalen says.

"She does," says a voice from nearby. We turn to see Safiya sitting alone in one of the high-backed chairs at a table, a glass of wine at her elbow and a stack of silvers in front of her. Only three nights before, she had dared to win a hand of Fortune against Solena. There had been silence, then nervous laughter after Solena made a jest. Safiya had been wise enough to lose the rest of the game to Solena and make self-deprecating jokes about her luck, but Solena's eyes had gleamed as she smiled.

Perhaps Solena has noticed, as others surely have, that her legendary luck has begun to sour. Has she wondered, as I have, if her fortune is tied to the slow decline of Aran and to the fading of the spell that was forged centuries ago?

"What are you doing here at this hour?" I ask.

"Practicing. I am sure our Queen will be out for revenge. I must be at my best when she challenges me."

Unfortunately the revenge won't come in the Gambling Hall. I groan inwardly, wondering how I will be expected to punish her. "Be sure to wager only what you are willing to lose," I say. She rolls the dice and curses.

"That is sensible," Khalen says to me. "I take it you are a gambler yourself?"

"No."

"Perhaps not in dice or cards," Safiya says, rolling again. "But Diya doesn't mind taking a chance. Eh, Diya?" she says with a wink. "I'd say your interest in her is risky," she says to Khalen. "For both of you."

"It's a bit early to be drinking, isn't it Safiya?" I ask. She laughs good-naturedly and raises her glass, taking a long swallow.

"Your main currency is pentos, is that right?" he asks.

"Yes," I reply.

"Tell me about those, then," he says, nodding at the pile in front of Safiya.

"Those are silvers. They are rare and more valuable."

"Diya has stacks of them. She finds all kinds of ways to obtain them," Safiya notes.

I force a smile onto my face. "Good luck, Safiya," I tell her. She'll need it when I refuse to sell her the charm for luck, but we both know I need her silver.

I turn to leave, relieved when Khalen follows.

"So it is risky to show an interest in you? What exactly might happen? Forgive me, but I have to ask in light of the fate of the Duke of Dorros."

Steady, I order myself as I take a deep breath. By the time I turn to him I know my smile is calm and open.

"Solena is an envious Queen, as I'm sure you've noticed. She does not like it when she's not the center of attention."

"Yes, I can see that, but I feel like there is a story you haven't told."

"I could say the same to you." For a long moment we hold each other's gaze.

"What would you like to see next?" I ask at last, my voice sweet.

"I am eager to see the garden that blooms in the middle of the Lost. The White Garden, is it?" His voice is pleasant and bland.

"We saw it on our way to the Gambling Hall."

"Only the outside."

"There is nothing else very interesting about it."

"I must disagree. How is such a lush garden possible in the middle of the desert?"

I glance at his expression, but it is as polite as his tone. Obviously he suspects that there is something strange about the White Garden, and I have only heightened his speculation with my deflection.

"The legend of King Medacus explains that, remember?"

"Ah, yes. The King who offered his daughter for his kingdom."

"Yes."

"That seems rather heartless," he says.

"The Kings and Queens of this city are known to be quite ruthless."

"Hmm. So what was the fate of the poor daughter?"

"She was traded to the Witch and then married to a Wind Demon. Some say you can hear her cries on still nights, and if you are unlucky enough to be caught alone in the middle of the Lost, you can be driven mad with despair from the sound of it."

"Really?"

"That is the story." The cry I'd heard on our journey across the Lost echoes through my mind, and I can't suppress a shiver. His eyes sharpen and I silently curse; he noticed.

"How long has it been since this bargain was struck?"

"Nearly three hundred years."

"Then your doom is nigh. Perhaps it's time to make another trade?"

"If one believes the legend to be true. I suppose we'll see whether or not the enchantment actually ends."

"It seems risky to base your entire city's welfare on a spring. It would only take a few drops of poison in the fountain…"

"No one here is that evil—unless you are planning something?" *I've thought of doing it myself.*

He holds up his hands placatingly. "Of course not. I am merely here to guard my liege. So, what about this Witch? Najma seems to believe that another bargain could be struck. Could she still be alive?"

I think of the Witch who holds my mother's soul hostage and the Duke's Witch. It is impossible to tell how old they are. "Shall we visit the garden?" I ask, hoping to distract him.

"As you wish," he says. I begin walking and he follows.

"It's interesting that Aran has never been attacked," he says.

"Why would we be attacked? It would hardly be worth the effort. We are far from everywhere. Half the army would die of thirst before they could reach us, and we have nothing to offer."

"Didn't you just claim that your city is built on a magical spring? Whoever controlled it could also control the Lost, whether it was magic or not. Not to mention that you are a welcome respite for caravans traveling from one coast to another."

"The spring's enchantment is due to end any day now, remember? Besides, King Medacus struck the bargain. It has to be someone from his bloodline who rules Aran."

Unless someone else can strike another bargain with the Witch—if she could even be found. I cast him a sideways glance. "Aren't there other ways to win a city?"

"Of course. Forgive me, I was raised with a military background."

"I imagine that you hope to win Aran through a marriage between your Prince and our Queen."

"It's no secret that it is not just the city itself that intrigues many other rulers. Until recently, Queen Solena was only a myth—a young Queen known for her beauty and mystery."

Oh, how she would love to hear this.

"Do you think she would agree to a marriage with Arlo?"

I have only just met Arlo, but I know with certainty that he will be dead within a year of being married to Solena. "Is our city really worth so much?" I ask. "After all, you can see its decline."

"From what I have seen so far, yes." He holds my gaze a beat too long. "And Najma is next in line for the throne after Queen Solena, I presume?"

"Yes. Why do you ask?"

"As I noted earlier, she would make a good ruler—a shrewd one." Something in his voice makes me glance at him. Perhaps I have underestimated him as well. As usual his face is unreadable.

"As our Queen said, she plans to rule for a long time." At least until the madness takes over, but he won't learn that from me. "And her will is very strong."

Turning my back, I walk across the walkway. He follows me along the gravel path leading into rows of white lilies and roses. The smell, sweet and cloying, is nearly stifling. Just beneath their scent is the sharper smell of licorice. I stop at the edge of the garden, the hairs on my arms already standing up.

"The King planted this garden for his wife—her favorite color was white." Khalen moves around me, walking into the tunnel of flowers. The air shimmers beside him. "The gardeners prefer that we stay on the path," I call, but he ignores me.

"He must have loved her immensely," he says, inspecting a blossom.

"Immensely," I echo.

He looks back at me. "You seem reluctant to enter."

"Not at all." I allow my fingers to brush against the knife hidden beneath my tunic before I follow him into the garden.

"How did she die?" he asks.

"A terrible accident." An image flashes in my mind of the Queen's body half-fallen from the bed, her dark hair lying in a pool of Fairy Green, her eyes wide with terror at whatever nightmares had come to haunt her.

The scent of licorice overwhelms the air as if she is standing at my shoulder. I know that if I turn, I will see no one. "Some say she still haunts the garden." No Lost for her, even as a ghost.

"Do you believe that?" he asks, running a finger over a leaf.

"Of course not." Petals rain from a nearby bush as if they were brushed by the wind or an invisible hand. I force myself to breathe out and unclench my fists.

Khalen catches some of the falling petals. "The way it drifts down like that makes it look like snow."

"Snow?" I had read about it in a volume in the library one afternoon when I was hiding from Solena and her friends.

"But real snow melts the moment it touches you. Every flake is unique and has its own tiny pattern."

"Where did you see snow?"

"When we crossed the Ash Mountains on a journey to Mera."

"I can't imagine the cold."

Death is cold, breathes the Queen at my shoulder.

"You truly don't remember anything except the Lost?"

"No," I lie. I remember cool and salty air, the rush of water on the rocks, the lighthouse with its stone walls that were warmed by the sun. But I can't afford to become mired in those memories.

"Perhaps when we are brother- and sister-in-law I might escort you to the mountains." For an instant I imagine standing atop a mountain, cold flakes dancing around me, cooling my skin and covering the ground like sand. There wouldn't be any demons lurking beneath the surface.

His next words jar me from my reverie. "Many say that the King loved your mother even more than he loved the Queen. Some even believe that she bewitched him."

"Where did you hear that?" My voice is far too sharp.

"Stories travel, even across the Lost."

Of course she bewitched him, hisses a voice at my ear. I take a step backward toward the path.

"Your questions are very personal. We are just strangers."

"Forgive me," he says, bowing from the waist. "I am not usually so impolite, perhaps it is the wind."

"Maybe the scent of the flowers is going to your head. I believe we've seen everything. Shall we return? It grows hot."

"We could seek shade in the garden."

"We are in the garden."

"No, the other one, at the foot of the Wall."

"You've seen that one as well." I hear my voice growing tense.

"I would like to know more about it. It seems important to you."

The heat pulses around us. "The only things in there are bones and sand, as you know."

"Nothing more?"

I cock an eyebrow. "You seem interested in something that you saw there. Perhaps you would like to discuss it?"

The air has gone very still. We can hear children's voices raised in argument and the splashing of water in the pool. He shakes his head. "You're right. I saw nothing of interest."

I nod. "We should go inside. Prince Arlo will no doubt need your help with negotiations. I believe Solena planned to meet in the Council Room."

"But what about the Crypts?"

My footsteps falter, but I straighten my back and continue walking. "What about them?" I call over my shoulder, as nonchalantly as I can.

"I have heard they are wondrous—definitely worth seeing."

"Someone has exaggerated. The Crypts are dark and dusty, and it's impossible to see anything."

"Crypts usually are, but the effigies are supposedly works of art— true testaments to the Kings, Queens, and founders of Aran."

"Who have you been talking to?"

"Queen Solena recommended that I see them. She also suggested that you could be the one to show them to me."

Damn her. I feel a flush of anger and fear creeping up my neck toward my face, threatening to betray me. I turn to face him, forcing my face to remain expressionless. *Don't even blink,* I remind myself. The flush slowly recedes.

"The Queen loves a good jest." *At the expense of others. The more cruel, the better.*

"So you do not want to show me."

"As I said, there is nothing to see."

I don't like the expression on his face: the raised eyebrow and the sideways lilt of his mouth. I turn my back on him and begin walking back to the palace.

He catches up in a few steps. "Thank you for the tour," he says. "It was quite informative."

"I am glad to be of help." To my relief, my voice is as bland as his.

"Will I see you at dinner?"

"Of course," I reply.

"Perhaps you will dance with me." There is a hopefulness in his smile that I do not like. "I do like a little bit of risk, and according to Lady Safiya, it is risky for me to show interest in you."

The memory of a laughing face flashes through my mind. "That is foolish." My voice is sharper than I intend, and he raises an eyebrow. I force myself to take a deep breath and then another.

I will ask Petra to make sure his cup stays full and slip the dancer a few extra coins to keep his attention for the rest of the night. Perhaps I will even slip a powder into his drink so that his curiosity is dulled by a pounding headache.

He bows, his expression hidden. "I did not mean to make you feel uncomfortable, but you should know that it is necessary for us to get acquainted. After all, my liege and yours are to be married."

"She has promised nothing yet. Good luck with your negotiations." I turn and walk away.

THEN

Mother and I traveled early each morning when the skies were still dark and the stars were like sharp jewels. The Horse constellation galloped overhead, brave and relentless, leading us onward.

We walked until the sun hung high in the sky, its heat pressing on us relentlessly. It was too hot even for the demons. We might hear their grumblings under our feet, but they didn't emerge.

We buried ourselves like the demons, covering our faces with Mother's long, light scarf. I held Cayo's shell to my ear so that the sound of the ocean would lull me to sleep. In my dreams the hush of the waves turned into the whisper of the shifting sand. I heard the stirrings and groans of the demons as they woke, and dreamed that Cayo was trapped beneath the ocean of sand, calling for help.

"Get up," my mother said grimly, pulling me from sleep. After a few bites of bread we began to walk again, but not before she poured a few drops of wine into the sand. "For the ghosts," she said, "to stave off their thirst." In the moment before the wine disappeared into the sand, it looked like a drop of blood, and I wondered what the ghosts actually thirsted for.

Each night I searched behind us for a glimmer of the lighthouse in Mera. I imagined that I saw it, just at the horizon, though perhaps I only wished that I did. For a few moments I would hold the shell to my ear and listen for the ocean.

Sometimes I would hear the despairing cry, usually just before dawn. It always sent an arrow of fear through me, and even Mother's mouth tightened, though she said nothing.

In the mornings when the air was clear, before the heat warped it, I could sometimes see the peaks of mountains to the north, capped in white. I stared at them, imagining how cold it must be there.

They inspired me to ask questions before my throat became dry and parched.

"Is it true what Polina said? Are you poison?" My voice was parched and coated with sand.

Mother sighed, the sound as despairing as the rumblings beneath the sand. "Some think so," she replied. "Some will always think so."

I ran my dry tongue over my lips, tasting the toxins that lingered there. *I don't want to be poison.*

"Did you really curse their marriage?" I swallowed, the question thick in my throat. It had been building since we left Mera, and now I finally had the courage to ask.

She stayed silent for so long that I thought she might not answer. "No. Her doubts cursed their marriage." But she did not sound convinced. She sighed. "I know tricks, that's all. I know how to use plants to my advantage. For people like Polina it's so much easier to blame others, to blame magic, for their own problems."

The sand shifted before us and she took my arm to steer me away. "I see things others don't," she added, "but that's only because I'm willing to face what others can't, or won't."

The second time I saw her pour wine into the sand, I asked, "What would the ghosts want with that?"

"It fools them into thinking they're getting blood," Mother replied. "It used to be the Creator's task to feed them, but then he threw his goblet and it shattered. Look, you can see the pieces." She pointed up at the sky where thousands of stars winked and glimmered. "The shards of the Creator's goblet took the shape of twelve animals, one for each month of the year. Right now the Horse is guiding us. But look, the Fish is ready to appear."

"Why would the Creator be so clumsy?" I asked doubtfully.

"Strange, isn't it? But think about it: he created Mera and the sea to the west; the mountains to the north; forests and waterfalls in the east. But then he left the south to the swamps, and the middle to…this."

The Lost stretched out in every direction, deceptively calm, heat rising from the sand in waves, concealing the danger that lay just beneath it.

"Was he drunk?" I asked. "Is that why he threw his goblet?" I waited to be chastised for speaking against the Creator, for lightning to flash from the sky and strike me down. But neither happened.

"Some say so, yes," Mother answered to my surprise. "Others thought that he started to create this land but grew bored with it. His wife took pity on us and created the oceans, the mountains, and the forests to make it nicer for us here. But when he found out, he was so furious that he threw his goblet and it broke. She didn't get a chance to improve the Lost before she was discovered."

I was too old for such stories. If we were in Mera, I would have scoffed and rolled my eyes, but here in the Lost, as a line of scarlet on the horizon warned of the sun's imminent rise, I asked, "What happened to his wife?"

A sad smile flickered across my mother's face as she answered, "They say she came to Mera to join the merfolk and infuse us with her magic."

I shook my head in disgust. "I didn't get any of that magic."

Mother stopped and took my chin in her hand. When I pulled away she took my shoulders. "Your magic is different. It's not Mer, but maybe Earth." She sighed. "You're lucky if that's true. Mer magic is known to take a toll on the mind."

"Has it hurt yours, Mother?" I asked softly. She didn't answer, but she didn't need to. I remembered the blankness of her face in Mera, and the way she had hummed and danced the night before as though Cayo were still with us.

"There is magic in you, without a doubt," she said, as though I hadn't spoken. "In your blood, or in your tears where no one can see it. Remember that, but don't tell anyone. It would be dangerous for anyone else to know."

She turned away and began to walk, leaving me to follow and wonder what kind of magic ran in my blood.

As the sun rose, Mother laid a sheet out across the sand. Once we were settled, she pulled another sheet over us to protect us from the light. She pointed up at the fading Horse. "When the Fish appears we'll be in Aran," she told me.

As I listened to the demons muttering to one another deep under the sand, I didn't know which made me shiver more: the thought of a drunken creator or a cruel one.

One night when the moon rose full and pink, my mother danced beneath it. She spun in the sand with her eyes closed and her arms weaving a graceful pattern. Her face softened and her mouth curved into a near smile. It reminded me of our happiest nights in Mera, when the ocean was just a few yards away and the air was soft and green. When she danced, the shifting of the sand stilled and the grumbling beneath it silenced. I watched, forgetting all that had happened in Mera, if only for a moment. I was filled with the joy of the night, the music, and the moon.

But then she spoke so quietly that I almost didn't hear her. "You shouldn't have followed me here."

The spell of the night chilled. "Where else would I go?" I demanded, confused and angry. Would she have left me behind? She continued as if I hadn't spoken.

"You belong with Polina. She grieves for you. You should have stayed with her."

I caught my breath, shivering; she was talking to Cayo. I peered into the air around her but saw nothing.

Finally her movements slowed, and her eyes opened as if she'd awakened from a trance. She began walking again without a word, and I followed just as silently.

A few nights into the journey we came to the ruins of a palace, its stones bleached white from the sun. A girl in a ragged dress, her hair knotted about her face, skittered over the top. She held my gaze for a moment. Her black eyes were raw and greedy, and I fell away, sensing that she would devour me if I got too close. In a moment she vanished into the sand.

"Did you see that?" I cried. Mother turned and her forehead creased. "Mother! We have to help her!" I raced back to where I'd seen her disappear, but I hesitated as I remembered her hungry eyes. What if she dragged me down with her?

"You can't help her now," said a voice from beside me. "Not unless you have a lot of silver, which seems doubtful."

I looked up to see a woman dressed in a green silk dress that was far too fine for the Lost. Her hair was piled on her head and coins winked from the tresses. "Where did you come from?" I blurted.

She tilted her head. "Have you any tears?" She smiled, her silver teeth glinting in the moonlight.

Before I could answer, Mother returned to my side, grabbing my wrist and dragging me away. We didn't stop running until we'd crested a dune, then descended it, and the woman was out of sight.

"Who was that?" I demanded, bending over, pulling in breaths.

"That was a Witch. The girl must have bargained with her, and now the Witch owns her soul until her debt is paid."

"How is she supposed to pay when she's buried in the sand?"

"The Lost is a haven for the desperate, until it swallows them and they become ghosts. There's nothing you can do for her, for any of them."

"She asked me if I had any tears."

Mother looked sharply at me. "Did you promise her any?"

"No!"

She blew out a breath of relief. "Good. She'd expect you to make good on your bargain. We need to keep moving." Mother started off, but I hesitated, looking back at the dune. "Badriya," she said, and her voice did not allow for argument.

Over the next few nights we passed other ghosts. Once we saw a boy whose eyes were blank as he sat cross-legged on a dune and stared up at the stars. Another night a man shoveled at the sand, his hole never growing deeper. He paid no attention to us as we passed, muttering in a low voice.

I later wondered if I was able to see them because I was also destined to bargain with Witches.

Just before dawn on a night when the wind bit at our necks and faces, I heard the long, forlorn cry of the forsaken daughter.

"Only the coasts are free of them," Mother told me. "There are more ghosts in the Lost than there are people."

"Why are we here then? We aren't ghosts."

"Some people prefer ghosts to the living."

"Do you?"

She didn't answer.

"Can other people see ghosts? Like the people in Mera?"

"If they did, they'd never admit it." Mother's voice was grim.

I thought of what she had said—that she belonged here. Perhaps this was where she could still see Cayo. Maybe she was haunted by other ghosts that I didn't know about.

Occasionally bony hands pushed up from the sand, grasping. Sometimes we barely side-stepped them, their fingers brushing our legs and grabbing onto our tunics before we managed to pull away. The ghosts and demons circled through all hours of the night as we walked, sighing, singing, and murmuring until I could no longer tell when I was awake or asleep.

The Horse faded from the sky and the Fish took its place, splashing among the stars. "You said we'd be there when the Fish appeared," I told my mother grumpily; she sighed in response.

That night I woke to fingers tracing my cheek. I bolted upright, a cry in my throat. Beside me crouched a boy with half his face missing. His lips stretched into a grimace of hunger and greed, his teeth showing through the tears in his cheek. My scream trapped in my chest, choking me. I could not draw a breath. His fingers went to my throat, tightening.

There was a roar and the ghost vanished in a cloud of sand. Mother knelt beside me as I gasped for breath. "You are susceptible," she muttered. "They are drawn to you."

I shivered, trying not to think about how close I'd come to being pulled beneath the sand to join the invisible groaning masses. Maybe they could sense what I would be willing to do in the future—the acts I would commit out of desperation.

Light still hung at the edges of the sky but Mother pulled me to my feet. "We need to go."

I followed her even though I was still tangled in feverish dreams. In one dream I thought I was dancing alongside Mother at a feast in Mera, only to discover that the flesh of the guests had fallen away, leaving only bones that clacked as they gamboled with us.

"Badriya." My mother's voice pulled me from the nightmare. I opened my crusted eyes to see grand white walls rising from the sand, moonlight pouring down on them to illuminate its stones as if it were a mythical city from one of Mother's stories.

"Where did it come from?" I croaked, swaying on my feet.

"Hush." She pulled her scarf over her head. "Now come, we are safe."

Two great dark horses pranced before the gate, their riders eyeing us curiously. Atop the gate another guard stared down at us. He gave a shout and the huge gate opened with clanking and creaking.

Beyond the gate was a courtyard where more guards stood with their hands on their swords. They were dressed in blue shirts and pants that were the same color as the sand. Another gate stood open behind them, revealing tiled walkways and buildings made of stone. Above everything stood a dome that was plated in blue and gleaming in the moonlight. I could hear the bleating of goats and smell their ripe odor, but I also smelled citrus, the sweet scent of flowers, and water—clear, fresh water.

One of the guards finally stepped forward. "Where did you come from?" he asked. Even in my tired state I could hear the wonder in his voice.

"Mera." Mother answered. The guards muttered among themselves, and the man who'd spoken to us tilted his head.

"Are you Witches?" he asked.

"No," Mother replied. "Witches can't have children."

He looked at her in silence.

"Please," Mother said. "The demons nearly took her." I shivered, realizing she was talking about me. "She's so hungry." My stomach gurgled in response.

The guard's face softened. "Come," he said, leading us further inside the city.

Though it was night, a few people still strolled along the path. Women in floating gowns strolled on the arms of men in shirts the color of the sky, their laughter floating on the night air. Among them people in rougher, but still beautiful, clothing darted around. They stared at us as we were led to a building made of white stone that was inlaid with colored glass. Nearby, water splashed merrily in a fountain, and I realized that this is where the scent of the fresh water came from.

I caught glimpses of a garden filled with white flowers and a building from which light poured and shouts echoed. In front of it stretched a long pool full of water and blossoms.

We were led inside a building that was draped in tapestries and cloth. The room was filled with empty tables made of a light wood. The most ornate tables stood on a dais. Nearby was a second dais that had musical instruments laid out on it. A row of sculptures lined one wall; judging by the crowns at their brows they must have been rulers. Their eyes watched as we were led to a small table.

A servant poured water into a cup for me and I drank it so fast that water ran down my chin. She laughed as she refilled my glass. Other servants brought food: bread with honey, orange slices, and a few bites of meat. The meat was cold and the bread was hard, but I could not get it into my mouth fast enough.

"Badriya." My mother nudged me. I looked up mid-bite to see a man standing before us, tall and golden-skinned with a close-clipped beard and light brown hair that flowed to his shoulders. His dark eyes shone like stones and his smile was kind.

Mother stood and curtsied, and I followed her lead, my mouth still full of food.

"Welcome to my city," he said, spreading his hands. "Who are you?"

"My daughter and I traveled from Mera, on the coast, My Lord King."

He raised an eyebrow. "And what was your trade in Mera?"

"I was a dancer, My Lord, and I created potions and tinctures. Perhaps some of your subjects could benefit from them."

"A dancer?" His eyes lit as his gaze swept over her body. "We have need of a dancer here." I noticed he did not mention a need for tinctures. The food in my stomach suddenly felt heavy.

Mother, perhaps sensing my unease, squeezed my hand, but the smile she gave the King was radiant. "I would be honored to fill the position, My Lord."

"It is impressive that you survived the trek from the coast, just a woman and a child. Entire caravans have been lost on that journey. You must tell me how you did it someday."

"Yes," came another voice from behind him, her voice as smooth as water. A woman with sharp cheekbones and eyes like a cat stepped forward holding a goblet full of a bright green liquid. "Someday you must." She took a long drink.

From the moment we arrived in Aran, the King could not keep his eyes off Mother, despite his beautiful wife and their two daughters.

We were given a chamber near his, on the side of the city where trees shaded the rooms from the sun and the breeze was softened by the whisper of leaves. The floors were made of cool tile, and the mattresses were thick and draped in brightly colored silk and sweet-smelling pillows. Here it smelled of oranges rather than goats. I later learned that this was where all the King's favorites resided.

The King offered me my own room, but I shook my head as Mother drew me closer. "We are happy to share, My Lord," she said, and his face darkened for a moment.

Though we didn't sit with him at meals, the King would send us dishes of tender lamb and plates of rich cheese. For Mother there was always a glass of spiced wine. The Queen watched as she sipped the bright green liquid in her goblet—it was called Fairy Green.

The King's oldest daughter, Solena, always sat close by. She was close to my age and had the same sharp face as the Queen. A flurry of girls attended her, dressed in light gowns the color of the sky: the blue of midday, the pink of dawn, and the maroon of dusk. Each time

I saw them I tugged at my tunic from Mera and glanced at my mother, but she hardly seemed to notice, her eyes closed in delight as she tasted the food and wine.

On the other side of the Queen sat a small girl with the same dark eyes as her father—the King's younger daughter, Najma. The Queen stroked her hair lovingly as she sipped her drink. Najma watched her father longingly, waiting to be noticed, but his gaze never left my mother.

When the music began, the King would stand and offer his hand to the Queen. She smiled radiantly and allowed him to lead her to the floor where they floated into an elegant dance. She leaned into the King, who smiled politely in return.

Soon the drums began to beat a wild rhythm while the pipes lifted into a daring melody and the lute hinted at longing and desire. When the rhythm changed, the King stepped away from his wife with a bow. She always smiled demurely and curtsied, but the King had already turned in search of my mother.

As the two of them leaped and twirled to the wild music, Mother's eyes would light up. The music in Mera had been softer and more wistful, but she had no trouble adjusting; her steps quickened, and for a moment the King struggled to keep up. Other courtiers soon joined, awkward and stumbling compared to Mother. She laughed breathlessly as the King's arm encircled her. I knew from the dreamy expression on her face that she was imagining herself in Cayo's arms back in Mera. She'd lost herself in the embrace of another man who could never be hers.

The Queen watched from her table, sipping her Fairy Green and laughing a bit too loudly at something a courtier murmured in her ear. She watched her husband and my mother, her blood-red nails tapping the table. I wanted to shout a warning to them—could they not see the danger?

As the music died down, the two of them slipped from the Hall. The Queen stared straight ahead, her face set like stone until a courtier, bowing gallantly, asked her to dance.

I left the Hall soon after and returned to our chamber where I paced and fretted. Why had Mother given herself to him so quickly? *Because he is the King, of course,* I answered myself. *Our life here is safe, luxurious even.* He was also handsome, there was no doubt about that.

Perhaps she was trying to recapture what she had felt for Cayo as a way to ease her grief. When she danced with the King her eyes shone but not with the same elation that I'd seen in Mera.

All night long I lay awake in our chamber with these thoughts spinning through my mind. Mother would return in the morning. She was always flushed and happy, often wearing a gift from the King: sometimes a sapphire ring or maybe a gold bracelet. Sometimes there would be a finely woven scarf or a cake made of rich chocolate for me. My protests and concerns would soon subside, the bright daylight chasing away the fears that lurked in the night.

Gowns made of materials that were as light as a cloud and dyed to match the shades of the sky were delivered to us. Mother spun in one that flared from her hips; it was perfect for dancing. There were some for me as well, but I stubbornly wore my tunic and pants even though they were stained with sand and sweat. Sometimes, when Mother wasn't watching, I would finger the delicate fabric of the gowns.

But Mother hadn't completely forgotten our life in Mera. She found the remains of a garden that was growing in a forgotten corner of the city behind the kitchen by the Wall, and together we coaxed it back to life. The earth was cool and damp against my fingers; it reminded me of Mera. The potions and tinctures that we created weren't quite the same as those we'd crafted before, but they had their own unique effects.

Sometimes when we were in our chamber, Mother would call for the musicians. She would insist that I wear one of the new gowns while she taught me new dance steps or ordered sweets. She even let me try on the jewelry that she received from the King.

When a servant would deliver the message that the King had sent for her, she would hastily dab perfume behind her ears—the one with the scent that could make men promise anything—and then she would brush a hasty kiss onto my temple and rush from the room in a flurry of silk and flowers. She wouldn't return until the next day, her breath tinged with sweet wine.

My loneliness became as oppressive as the heat that bore down on the city. When I could no longer stand the silence of the chamber, I would venture out in search of someone to talk to. Laundresses, gardeners, men sweeping the walkway—everyone bustled about and called good-naturedly to each other, but they ignored me completely.

One day I found a group of Solena's friends sitting in a circle whispering together in the empty Dining Hall. Solena was not among them which gave me the courage to approach.

I still had some leftover chocolate that I hadn't eaten yet, so I held it out to the friendliest-looking one. "Do you want some?" I asked. She had freckles and light reddish hair. Petra, I'd heard her called.

She shrugged and scooted over, but a girl with golden hair glared, first at me and then at Petra. "Ugh. No. It's probably poisoned."

"Come on, Yadira," Petra said it low enough that Yadira could pretend she hadn't heard.

"We don't talk to Witches," the boy said. He had a face like a ferret and cold blue eyes.

I lowered my hand. "I'm not a Witch." The old hurt throbbed like an open wound.

He looked me up and down. "Then why do you have hair like a Witch?" he asked.

"Fallon!" Yadira shrieked, then burst into laughter. Even Petra's mouth quirked as my hand rose instinctively to touch the ends of my hair; it was wavy and coarse like my mother's.

"You should go," Petra said, though not unkindly. "It's only going to get worse."

"Careful, she'll bite you with her Witch teeth," Fallon added, sending Yadira into hysterics.

A retort formed on my tongue, but tears were already building in my eyes so I turned and fled rather than let them see me cry. From then on I kept to my chamber, only venturing out to the garden to take refuge among the herbs and flowers. I returned to the Dining Hall only when Mother forced me to. There I had to endure Solena and her friends eyeing me, whispering, and then bursting into laughter. Sometimes I felt Mother's eyes on me, but she never asked why I didn't have friends in Aran, so I never told her.

I loved the nights when no one came for Mother and she would order apples to be brought to our chamber. We would lie in bed as she told me stories from her childhood in Mera or stories of merfolk who tricked humans into doing stupid acts in order to repay them for their duplicity or greed. Sometimes she would recount romances in which heroes or heroines committed acts of bravery in order to prove their love.

One day she found a strange, prickly bush in the garden. To my dismay, she ordered me to chew the leaves and swallow the pulp even though it left the inside of my throat raw and my head spinning. Whenever I ate these leaves my dreams were laced with dread, so I named them bitterthorn.

One morning Mother and I were summoned to serve the Queen. "You must use the same cosmetics on my face that you use to enchant my husband," she told Mother.

Mother knelt, pressing her forehead to the floor. "My Queen, I have done no such thing," she murmured.

"Oh? You suggest that it is your thick waist, your rough skin, and your nest of hair that enchants him?" The Queen took a long drink from her Fairy Green as her ladies tittered. "You will come to serve me every day," she said, her voice like iron.

Mother's face went blank and the light in her eyes dimmed, but she nodded. "Yes, My Queen."

During our subsequent appointments, the Queen would smile indulgently on her husband's lover. She gave Mother a place among her ladies, and I served as one of her maids. In front of the King, she smiled at my mother and treated her as a Lady of Honor, but when she stroked my hair she left scratches on my scalp and her breath smelled of licorice from the Fairy Green.

Out of the King's hearing, however, she forbade the other ladies of her court from speaking to us. Every morning as Mother assisted the Queen with her toilette, the Queen and her ladies whispered that Mother's husband, if she ever had one, must have been so sickened by her that he cast her out into the middle of the Lost where she would have surely died if not for the kindness of the King. They whispered about how she must surely be a Witch—what else could explain his attraction to her? Despite the cosmetics that Mother used on the Queen, the King could not keep his eyes off Mother.

Mother stayed silent, so I did too, even though I wanted to upend the bowls of powders and creams over the Queen's head. I painted her eyelids the way Mother showed me, using the smoky powder that she had ground from the pods we'd found in the garden. Mother added a silvery mineral to the pods that made the Queen's eyes dance and shine like starlight.

The first time I watched her make this powder, she had pressed the point of her knife into her skin until a drop of blood appeared and then let it fall into the powder.

"You have to give her your blood?" I asked incredulously.

"Magic has its price, Badriya," she reminded me as she pressed a small cloth to her wrist.

"But why give it to her when she's been so horrible to us?"

"We've taken something from her as well," she said sadly. "Remember to only dust a little of this across her eyelids. Too much will make her mad. She'll crave more and more until she's willing to do anything for it."

"Like the Moondust," I said.

"Yes."

"She's already mad," I muttered.

"She's envious, and the Fairy Green doesn't help."

"Then why do you flirt with her husband?" I could not stop the question from coming out.

She turned on me, her eyes dark, and gripped my shoulders. "Would you rather be in the Lost?"

She held my gaze, refusing to look away until I stammered, "No." She released me and my shoulders throbbed as I sullenly retreated to the opposite side of the room.

There were times when she simply sat at her vanity staring at her reflection, a brush forgotten in her hand. I remembered what she had said in Mera, that she did not intend to live long enough for the cosmetics to have an effect, and a chill passed through me. I began to wonder if the cosmetics she used on herself were driving her further into madness. I would put my arms around her, hug her, and shake her, but she didn't seem to notice. I would curl up next to her, weeping, until I felt her gently shaking my shoulder and coaxing me to bed. The next morning she would wake up brisk and cheerful, as if the previous night had never happened.

"I wish we could leave," I told her in these moments.

"And go where?" Mother asked lightly as she dropped belladonna into her eyes.

"Back to Mera."

Her voice hardened. "We can't go back. You know that."

"Someplace else, then."

She shook her head. "You wouldn't survive another trek across the Lost, Badriya. The demons nearly took you."

"We could take horses," I told her. I had watched the Favorites ride the powerful animals out into the Lost, racing each other across the sand. Though the horses terrified me, I was sure they could outrun any danger in the Lost.

"Badriya, no." Mother's voice was like steel. "This is our home now. I want to hear nothing more about it."

"This will never be my home," I muttered.

She sighed. "I know it is hard for you here, Badriya," she said, her voice softer. "But you must find a way to be happy."

"How?" My voice cracked.

"Please try. For me."

What choice did I have?

The Fish soon faded, and the Snake took its place. This was the most dangerous time of the year, when despair could take hold of you without warning.

Mother disappeared with the King one night when the wind was particularly vicious. Sitting alone in the window seat of our chamber, I held Cayo's shell to my ear and listened to the sound of the ocean. I tried imagining that we had never left Mera; I pictured us in the town plaza, music that was lighter and faster than the music here filling the air, the Lights of Mera streaking overhead, and my mother laughing and happy.

I was so lost in my daydream that I leaned back a little too far, forgetting that the window was open to the cool night air. My heart stopped for a moment as I caught myself in the window frame. The shell fell from my hands and landed on the cushioned seat. My hands, still clumsy with fear, knocked the shell from the window seat.

I scrambled to my knees and leaned out the window. I could barely see it in the moonlight.

I raced down the stairs and behind the building to the strip of land behind our chambers. Long blades of sharp grass grew wildly from the sandy earth; it was clear that no one ventured here often.

Light flowed from the nearby windows and voices floated out into the night, amplified by the wind. Nearby, a man murmured something, followed by a woman's throaty laugh. A voice from another room, this one low and furious, ranted that he'd been cheated. A woman cried from a nearby window.

The voices were as ominous as the wails of the ghosts in the Lost. I spotted the shell and darted toward it. The soft ground beneath the window had broken its fall and it had suffered only one long crack.

I had only a moment of relief before a scream rang through an open window.

"What have you done!" The voice was the Queen's.

My heart stopped and I ducked, sure that she had spotted me. I held my breath as I waited for the guards to drag me from my hiding place.

There was the sound of a loud slap, and I flinched as a girl cried.

"Stop your crying you hateful, ugly creature," the Queen snarled. "It's your fault he won't look at me anymore."

"Mama, no!"

I caught my breath. The voice was high-pitched and full of fear, but it was unmistakably Solena.

My eyes darted to the other windows. The nearby conversations hadn't faltered; everyone was too absorbed in their own drama to hear the Queen's words to her daughter.

"Oh, he called you ugly—make no mistake. And you are. Ugly on the inside as well as the outside."

"It's the Fairy Green talking, not you. That's why I poured it out." Solena's voice was thick as if she were holding back tears. I couldn't help but feel slightly impressed that she had defied her mother.

"He called you ugly and me as well. And it is the truth," the Queen said, her voice slurred with tears. "Being your mother has aged me. It's made me as ugly as you are."

My stomach turned. I had wished horrible things on Solena since we arrived, but this was too much. "If it weren't for you, he'd still be in love with me. Only with me!" The Queen's voice rose to a shriek.

I heard sobbing and knew it must be Solena.

"Get out of my sight," the Queen said.

"Where will I go?" I could hardly understand Solena through her tears.

"I don't care."

"Mama, please. I'm sorry. Let me stay." Her words were lost in sobs. I heard a door open and then slam closed, and then there were only sighs and sniffling.

I stood in the dark for a long time, holding my cracked shell. My stomach twisted on itself as I thought of the fury in the Queen's voice. My mother was mad, but she would never send me away. *After all, she had dragged me all the way across the Lost,* I thought wryly.

I could only imagine what Solena would do if she knew that I had overheard what her mother said. I cowered in the long grass, afraid that she'd see me.

But I couldn't stand there in the dark forever, so I finally gathered the courage to make my way around the building to the stairs. The wind gusted around me as I slipped up the stairs to my chamber.

The gallery was empty and silent—no sign of the Queen or Solena. I breathed a sigh of relief. Just as I reached the door to my chamber, I heard a sound that was no louder than a breath. I knew before I turned that it was Solena, crouched in the shadows against the wall with her face pressed into her knees and her shoulders shaking.

I took a step toward her. "Are you alright?" I asked.

She moved her face so that only her eyes showed. "You heard, didn't you?" she asked.

"No," I told her, my heart thumping.

"Yes, you did. I saw you scuttling around like a rat from the window." There wasn't any venom in her voice, just sadness.

I clutched the doorknob, ready to duck inside, when Solena spoke again. "It *is* my fault. He would love her more if it weren't for me." She heaved a shuddering sigh. "At least they love Najma."

I looked down at the shell and back at Solena. She'd buried her face in her knees again. "That's not true," I heard myself say. "Come inside. I'll make you something to help you sleep."

I regretted the words right away. Why had I invited her into my only safe haven? She looked up at me for a long moment and I held my breath. At last she rose. "Alright."

I had no choice but to open the door and lead her inside. Lighting a candle, I quickly got to work. I wanted to make her salve as quickly as I could so that I could send her away.

She looked around the chamber as I found the jars of dreamsigh, clearvine, and slumberweed. I watched out of the corner of my eye as she fingered the cloak that Mother had left lying across the bed and picked up a bracelet that the King had given to my mother. She set it down without comment.

She came and stood next to me, examining the bowls and vials as I measured the ingredients. "Don't touch those," I said before I could stop myself.

She held a jar closer to the candlelight. "What's this?" she asked.

It was the new powder that Mother had made, similar to the Moondust she'd made in Mera—the powder for which women would pay too much. "It's nothing," I told her. I could tell that I'd spoken too quickly by the way she watched me. She set the jar down slowly.

"What's in that?" she asked as I tipped the sleeping mixture into a tiny bag.

"Add hot water to this, like a tea. Then you won't hear or dream anything all night."

She frowned, staring at the bag. "It's not poison, is it?"

"Of course not."

I waited for her to leave but she stayed where she was. Even in the dim light I could see the traces of her tears and the redness in her eyes. For a moment I thought she might thank me, but then she turned abruptly and left the chamber without a word.

The next morning in the Dining Hall she was flanked by Fallon, who whispered in her ear with a sly smile on his lips; Yadira and Petra leaned in, smiling with delight. When I saw her look my way, I allowed myself to hope that she might invite me to sit with her and her friends. That hope was dashed in an instant.

"There's the spy," Solena's voice rang out. "Standing outside my window like a disgusting, ugly insect. I mean, look at her!" Her friends all swiveled to stare at me.

"No, I wasn't," I said, feeling my face get hot.

"Repulsive," she continued, her eyes narrowing. "Hair like hay for the goats and skin like a lizard. Just look at her stare!" She broke into peals of laughter along with Fallon and Yadira.

Fury built up inside me, so suddenly and swiftly that it threatened to erupt. I opened my mouth, ready to tell everyone what I'd heard, but Petra gave a shake of her head so slight that I thought I imagined it.

I hesitated long enough to realize exactly what would happen if I revealed what Solena's mother had said to her. Solena's revenge would be terrible, for certain, but no tincture could help me sleep through the guilt I would feel.

I turned on my heel and rushed from the Hall, my face burning at the mocking laughter that followed.

Chapter Six

Prince Arlo finished yet another goblet of wine, and the servant had barely refilled his glass before he drained it again.

Catching Petra's eye I raise my eyebrows, but she just shrugs in return. She has tried all evening to persuade Khalen to drink, even challenging him to a game, but he has somehow remained clear-eyed and sober while she must catch Fallon's arm when she stands, hiccupping and giggling helplessly.

I hear a voice at my shoulder, lovely and sad, singing softly to the plaintive tune that Theron strums on the lute. I know without looking that it's Mina, holding a carafe of wine, lost in the music, and forgetting her bitterness for a moment while she waits for someone to need their glass refilled.

"What wonderful hospitality, My Lady Solena," Arlo says. His words are an ominous echo of the Duke's. I shudder and turn to see Khalen watching me. He raises his glass with a small smile but returns it to the table without drinking. Is he mocking me?

Solena smiles. "Tomorrow we shall celebrate the Festival of the Full Moon. It will truly show the beauty of Aran."

Arlo mutters something in return as grease from the meat dribbles down his chin. "Perhaps some dancing?" Solena says, turning away. She signals to the musicians, and I see Theron's mouth tighten as they end their plaintive song and strike up a livelier one, the drums beating a lively rhythm and the tambor ringing.

"Will you dance with me?"

I look up to see Khalen holding out his hand.

"Please?" His dark eyes are pleading. I can feel Solena's eyes on me. "If you were to say no, I would have to think that you are avoiding me."

"Of course I'm not avoiding you." His mouth quirks up at one corner: he has baited me. I cover my agitation with a smooth smile. "Let us dance, Sir Khalen."

He rests his hand on my waist, drawing me into the dance. Nearby, Petra is singing loudly and making up her own bawdy lyrics to the music as she dances with Fallon. Khalen raises an eyebrow and smiles crookedly, and I can't help but laugh in return. Without warning he grasps my waist, and we spin as the music and lights swirl around us. He tips my body back and then pulls it upright again, laughing as I catch my breath. For a moment I am lost in the dance and the feel of his arms.

Over his shoulder I see the fabric against the wall blow outward, and just before they settle back against the stone I catch a glimpse of sharp eyes. Najma. When will I remember that I am always being watched?

"Thank you for the dance," I tell him, stepping out of his reach, "but it is late and I must see to Najma."

Before he can answer I've slipped away to pull the curtain aside. Najma rolls her eyes.

"Come on," I tell her. "I'll give you a little of the tuberose rinse." Her eyes light up. She begs for the hair wash often but I have never offered it. It is said to compel those around you to give you whatever you ask for, but at thirteen she doesn't yet know how dangerous that can be. Besides, my clients are willing to pay a lot of silver for it.

"Khalen thinks you're beautiful," Najma says, a smile curling her mouth.

"Oh really? And what makes you say that?"

"I can just tell," she says, her eyes gleaming. I nudge her, but I can't help smiling like a silly courtier.

As I glance over my shoulder, I see that Khalen is now dancing with Petra. "Well, he seems to think Petra is beautiful as well."

"He's not looking at her the same way he looked at you."

Khalen laughs as Petra murmurs something to him, and I feel a little deflated. Most likely the only interest he has in me is to try to determine what the risks of an alliance with Aran are and whether they are worthwhile. Safiya's warning was needless. I should feel relief, but instead I feel hollow.

We step out into the warm night. "You think he is handsome," Najma says.

"Do I?" My attempt at nonchalance sounds strained, even to my own ears. Najma smiles. "What do you plan to ask for once you've used the rinse?" I ask.

"Perhaps a new scarf," she replies.

"A new scarf," I echo.

"What else would I ask for?" she asks, her eyes wide and innocent as we pass through the archway.

I fill a basin with water from the pitcher and add some tuberose blossoms. While we wait for them to steep, Najma unwinds the intricate braids from her hair and wraps a towel around her shoulders. She lies across my bed with her hair dangling over the edge, and I position the bowl under her hair, which is so long that it nearly sweeps the floor. I dip a cup into the water and wash it over her hair a few times. She shivers. "It's so cold!"

"It's lukewarm like it's supposed to be. You're more likely to get what you want this way."

"You're making that up." She shudders and then laughs as I pour yet another cupful over her hair.

"I am not." The sweet smell of the tuberose fills the room, threatening to give me a headache.

"So what do you really want? You can't really be going to all this trouble for a new scarf."

"Mine are all threadbare."

"Remember what I told you..."

"I know—beauty isn't the most important thing," she recites in a sing-song way.

"It's true."

"It's the most important thing in this city, though, isn't it?"

"It doesn't have to be."

"But it is."

"Maybe you'll change that someday," I tell her as I massage my fingers through her scalp.

She is silent for a while. I've nearly finished when she says, "Well, there aren't any new books to be found—no one ever brings those, maybe they're too heavy."

I smile. "Perhaps Prince Arlo will bring books from Tanera."

"And perhaps you could speak to Sir Khalen about this." She raises her eyebrows and I roll my eyes at her.

I rub the tuberose in as thoroughly as I can while wishing something else for her and for me.

Later that night four women come, one right after the other. The first wants a tincture to ward off headaches; she presses her lips together when I ask for three silvers rather than two, but she pays them. The second wants the lotion that erases wrinkles from beneath tired eyes. She only has a thin gold chain for payment, but I accept it, thinking of her newborn child. The third wants the same cream, but balks when I ask four silvers for it. She leaves without the cream and without paying. The fourth woman pays one silver for a wash that brings sweet dreams for herself and whoever shares her bed.

At midnight I extinguish the lamp and stare at the four silvers I've earned.

It is a good hour for gathering herbs because they will be at their most potent. I take up the basket that I use for gathering and slide my knife into my sleeve. Before I leave, I tie the little pouch filled with silvery powder to the belt at my waist, then I slip from the room and walk toward the garden.

I cut and gather until my basket is full and my fingers are stained. Finally, I rise and stretch, rubbing my aching back. The moon is nearly full, its light pushing through the branches that hang over the garden. Before I know it, I am walking up the stairs to the Wall, drawn to it like a moth to a candle flame.

The Lost is busy tonight. Just at the edge of the shadows a pale, bony hand thrusts up from the sand: a demon hopeful for unwary victims. Somewhere nearby a cricket sings and a scorpion hisses. The air is laced with the scent of jasmine. In the sky, the Snake eyes the Fish hungrily.

Mother is merely a shadow flickering in the sand. If she sings, I can't hear her. After three years I have just over eighty silvers. It's not enough.

The wind rises and the Bones rattle gently against the Wall. "Footsteps," they sigh. I grit my teeth, knowing who approaches. *Can't he just enjoy wine and dancing like everyone else?* I brush my hand against my knife as Khalen reaches the top of the Wall.

"Your friend Petra seemed very anxious to keep my wine glass filled," Khalen says as he joins me.

"She's not my friend."

"Really?"

"Really."

He is not deterred. "Luckily I have a high tolerance from my years as a soldier."

"Luckily," I echo, feeling exasperated.

"I hope you don't mind that I've joined you."

I offer a noncommittal shrug.

"I enjoyed our dance, and I thought you did too." I curse under my breath as he leans against the Wall. "Who were you thinking of just now?" he asks.

"What do you mean?" I reply, keeping my eyes on the Lost.

"You looked sad, quite unlike yourself. Usually you look so...serene."

Good. That is what I strive for.

"I wasn't thinking of anyone at all," I tell him. "I thought we agreed not to spy on one another."

"Forgive me. I didn't realize I was spying."

Now he'll leave, I think, but he looks up at the sky. "My aunt told me that the moon itself has a voice," he says. "That some nights it sings and offers secrets to those who can hear it."

Or those who are haunted by regret. In the darkness the shadows around his eyes betray sadness. His fingers idly brush his chest, as if reaching for something beneath his shirt.

"Hmm. Your aunt sounds as if she had quite the imagination."

"She believed in the ghosts and spirits of the Lost. She had reason to."

I look at him sharply but can't read his expression.

"Do you miss Mera?"

I keep my eyes on the horizon. For a moment it is as if Rumin is standing beside me, but it will benefit neither Khalen nor myself to become close. "Why would I want to do that? I have everything that I need here."

He snorts. "I've only known you for a few days and I can tell that this place has hardly given you everything you need."

I turn on him. "Know me, did you say? We met only two days ago, Sir Khalen."

"Has it only been two days?"

The wind carries the scent of something that has died in the Lost as the Bones scrape against the Wall.

"I think you would like the mountains," he says. "There are trees and plants that you've never seen before. Shadows. Many places to hide."

I think of the white peaks I'd seen in the distance during our journey to Aran and how quiet and calm they seemed.

His voice softens. "What keeps you here? You don't belong."

"I think you overestimate your tolerance for wine," I tell him sharply.

In the moonlight Mother twirls, suddenly visible, and the King stands at her shoulder. Khalen's body tenses as he grips the Wall and leans forward, staring out at the Lost, his jaw set. I catch my breath. "You can see them." *Is it possible?*

He looks sharply at me. "Them?"

I close my mouth, feeling foolish. Of course he can't see my ghosts. But then, who or what does he see?

After a long moment he closes his eyes and takes a deep breath. He pulls on the chain around his neck until a flat, brown stone emerges. It looks like a rock anyone could find lying in the Lost, yet he rubs it with his fingers over and over as if it were a talisman.

Catching my gaze, he says, "It's from my aunt, to help cross the Lost. She bought it from a Witch. It's supposed to keep the demons and other Witches away, but it doesn't work on the ghosts, or help quiet the wind."

For a moment, the only sound to be heard is the sound of the Bones scraping against the Wall.

"Ever since we entered the Lost, I can hear my father's voice calling to me," he says, his eyes fixed on the Lost. "And now I see him."

Khalen seems calm and clear-headed, but even he is haunted. Questions swirl through my mind, but before I can choose which one to ask, a willow branch cracks in the garden below.

Khalen's head snaps around. I groan inwardly, knowing who has entered with such desperation.

"Diya?" The voice is ragged.

"Wait here," I tell Khalen, and I hurry down the stairs, trying to think of how to appease her and send her away.

Yadira stands in the garden, her gaze darting around and her body twitching. Her fingers dance over her cheek, her nails bitten to the quick.

Her tongue flicks out over her lips. "Do you have it?"

I do. The silver powder that makes her eyes look like they are filled with starlight rests in the pouch at my waist. Now she craves it so much that she has nightmares until she gets more.

"The payment," I murmur.

She steps close enough that I catch the scent of roses laced with bitterness; it's the scent she always carries with her. She thrusts a little purse at me and I peer inside. Opals wink up at me.

"Where is the silver?" I ask.

"You took it all—I don't have any more. These were my mother's. They are all I have left of her." Her voice shakes. "Give me the Stardust."

Her eyes fall on the pouch at my waist, and her hands whip out to tear it away, fast as lightning. She unwraps it hastily. "Careful!" I warn as some of the sparkling dust spills.

Dropping to the ground, she scrabbles at the dirt, salvaging what she can. She brings her fingers to her lips, her tongue darting out as dirt mixes with the glimmer on her tongue. "It's meant for your eyes!" I whisper, but she pays me no attention. Tilting her head back, she closes her eyes and sighs. My stomach turns.

"Have you been swallowing it?" I grip her shoulders and give her a shake. "Have you?"

She shakes her head. "Please," she mumbles. "Please."

Groaning, I stare up at the sky. The wind is sharp and cold.

Taking her wrist, I push the bag of opals back into her hand. She stares up at me and blinks hard, trying to focus. "But it's your payment." Her words slur.

"Opals are of no use to me."

Her eyes widen fearfully. "I don't have any silver right now. But I will get it. I will."

I shake my head. "Don't ask me for any more Stardust."

Her mouth opens, her lips trembling. "But I have to…" her words die away.

I pinch her arm hard. "Listen to me." She blinks. "I am out of Stardust. It's gone. There's no more." There is actually an entire jarful that I just prepared last week, but in that moment I vow to pour it out the window.

It takes a moment for my words to penetrate. "No!" she cries. "I'm sorry. I'll find you the silver, I will…"

"There's no more, you silly fool!" I tell her fiercely.

Her face hardens. "Then I'll tell," she snarls. "I'll tell everyone what you made me do the night the Duke died."

My heart rises into my throat, but my voice stays cold. "You're speaking nonsense. You have no idea what is truth and what isn't. No one would believe you—you're so addled."

She falls to her knees, her mouth slack.

"Now listen to me. You will have nightmares, the worst of your life, for three nights. Then you'll feel better than you did before the Stardust. And you'll be more beautiful. Do you hear me? More beautiful."

"More beautiful," she echoes.

I rush to a tangle of branches that grow against the Wall. Among them are berries with hard, green shells and a pungent odor: coldberries, for hangovers. I snatch a handful and rush back to her. "Here." I thrust them at her, but she merely sways. I snatch her hand and push the berries into it. "Chew these," I tell her. "Say it."

"Chew these," she echoes.

"Chew them when the nightmares wake you. It will ease the fear." I close her fingers over her fist, then I pull her to her feet and push her toward the entrance.

"Go home," I tell her. "Go to bed, chew the berries, and have sweet dreams."

"Sweet dreams," she sighs. Her hair catches in the branches as they fall closed behind her.

"So."

I whirl to see Khalen leaning against the willow tree, his arms crossed. "Spying again?" I ask coldly.

"I wasn't spying. I was standing right there at the top of the Wall, if you recall. Anyone could have heard you two—you were hardly subtle."

I am grateful that he can't see my expression in the dark. "Well, now you know one of our dark secrets." My voice is brittle. "Some women are willing to do anything for their beauty."

"And some are willing to take advantage of this."

I feel the blood rush to my face and my fists tighten. "I warned her not to misuse it."

"But you perpetuate it and profit from her misery."

I glare at him as my stomach turns, but then I am gripped with anger. *Who is he to judge me? Why must I explain myself? What do I care of his opinion?*

"Don't presume to understand me or anything about this place." My voice is nearly as ragged as Yadira's had been. "You'd better return to your Prince."

I stalk toward the entrance, but he reaches out an arm, blocking my path. This is really too much. I turn on him, but he forestalls my words.

"Tell me, what will you do with the payment?"

"I do not need to answer to you." I look at his arm. "Are you going to forcibly keep me in my own garden?"

He keeps his arm in place for another long moment, his eyes searching my face. The warmth that had been there is now gone, replaced with suspicion and disappointment. I feel a heaviness that might be regret. What he doesn't realize, and what I've nearly forgotten, is that anyone who gets close to me meets a terrible fate.

At last, he drops his arm and I pass by. After a few steps I turn to face him. "It is risky to be close to me, as you've been warned, and as I'm sure you've noticed. You'd best keep your distance." I push through the willow door and he does not follow.

THEN

Mother and I might have had more time—months, perhaps years— had I been able to control my temper.

I returned to my chamber one afternoon to find Solena there with Fallon and Yadira. She held the shell that Cayo had given me.

My chest tightened. "Give that to me."

Fallon hooted at the tremble in my voice. "Give that to me," he repeated mockingly.

Solena held it out to me. As I reached for it, she let go. It shattered against the tile.

Fallon stopped laughing and drew in his breath and Yadira covered her mouth with her hands. Solena, however, held my gaze. Lifting her chin, she smiled.

I dropped to the floor and gathered the pieces. *I can fix these*, I thought feverishly. *I can glue them together*. Dimly I heard them leave the room, snickering and whispering.

I tried the stickiest of Mother's creams and the thickest of her ointments. Even when the pieces stuck together, they fell apart again as soon as I tried to hold them to my ear.

Mother found me sitting among the shards, tears rolling down my cheeks and dripping into my lap. She managed to fit the pieces together, though cracks spiderwebbed across it. But when I held it to my ear, I heard nothing. I had lost the ocean.

She tapped my chest. "You don't need a shell to remind you of the ocean. It's here with you, always."

My sudden fury took me by surprise. Leaping up, I brought my heel down on the shell that we'd worked so hard to piece together. The sound of it breaking could have been my own heart. "I hate it here! I hate you!" Then I rushed from the room and into the night.

There was nowhere to go. I circled the city, past the Rooms of the Favorites, the Lesser's Quarters, the stables, the White Garden, Mother's garden, and even the Dome. In the end, the only place left was our chamber.

Mother was gone, but she had cleaned up the pieces of shell. For a moment I felt sick. Had I driven her away when I told her I hated her?

My anger soon returned. Why hadn't she stayed this one night, knowing how upset I was?

I knew by now that Solena hated me because I'd heard what her mother said and seen into the darkest corners of her life. It wouldn't be enough for her that she and her friends had broken my shell.

I didn't think they would follow me to the garden, so I went there when the emptiness and the silence of the chamber grew too much to bear. The air was thick and hot by midmorning, and everyone was in a foul mood. As I walked past the White Garden, Solena emerged without warning, flanked as always by Fallon and Yadira.

"Where's your mother?" she asked in a voice that was sickeningly sweet. Her eyes were as sharp as a viper's as she tapped her cheek in mock thoughtfulness. "I didn't see her at breakfast."

My heart began to beat faster. I tried to push past them, but Yadira stepped into my path. She'd eaten so much chocolate at breakfast that I could smell it on her breath. She never could stop herself from indulging too much, thin as she was.

"Wasn't she with your father?" Fallon asked in a tone of false interest. The shine in his eyes told me he knew exactly where my mother was, and it wasn't with the King.

"She displeased him," Yadira said with relish.

Solena turned on her, swift as a scorpion. "Did anyone ask you to speak?"

A flush rose in Yadira's pale cheeks and she pressed her lips together.

"Your mother overstepped her place, as she always does," Solena said, turning back to me. "But her spell is wearing off. My father finally saw her for who she is: an ugly Witch who will do anything to make him love her."

"Where is she?" I demanded. Fallon's smile widened, and I knew he could hear the tremor in my voice.

"He sent her to the Crypts," Solena said, her mouth curling.

The bodies of the Lesser—the servants and those not included in the shining warmth of the King's inner circle—were burned in the Lost when they died. Their families gathered around a pyre, but not for long because the ceremonies tended to attract demons. You could hear them scrabbling just under the sand, grinding their teeth hungrily as the smoke rose into the air. The bodies of the Favorites—the royals and those who were the most beautiful—were interred in the Crypts below the Great Hall.

I had never been inside the Crypts, and I hoped to never have a reason to, but now I raced there as fast as I could.

The doors leading to the Crypts were built into the side of the Great Hall. One door stood slightly open, and I shivered despite the heat as I stepped into the cool darkness. Oil lamps set into the walls provided dim light, revealing stone steps leading down. They were covered in dust and I grimaced, wondering if it was the remains of the dead. I slowly made my way down.

At the foot of the stairs, I swallowed. "Mother?" My voice was engulfed in the darkness.

In the flickering light I could see rows of effigies: Kings and Queens of the past lying on their backs and staring up at the ceiling. Many of the Kings held stone swords, while the Queens held painted flowers. The faces of the effigies flickered in shadow. I shrieked as one appeared to open its eyes, but with the next flare of the flame I saw that its stone eyes stared up at the ceiling.

There was a movement in the shadows. In the next instant a child stood before me. I screamed and backed away so quickly that I collided with the stone behind me.

"Careful," someone said. I imagined that the voice came from the effigy of the young woman holding a rose.

The voice spoke again. "If you can sit here in the dark with the dead, then you never have to be afraid of anything. That's what my mother told me." It was Najma, looking solemn and pale. "But my mother never comes here. I think she is always afraid."

"What are you doing here?" My voice was a rasp. I tried to slow my breathing.

"Visiting my grandmother." She nodded over her shoulder. "That's her. My mother's mother." Slowly I stood and risked taking a look at Najma's grandmother. Even in stone, the woman's face looked more benevolent than the others, her cheekbones softer, her smile more kind. "My grandmother is the only one with a crown." Dimly I registered the gleam of silver on the brows of the effigy. "My mother said not to tell Solena because she will pester Father to let her have it, or just take it herself." Najma shrugged. "But she never comes in here. If she knew about it, she'd make me bring it to her." She turned back to me. "What are you doing here? No one you know is buried here."

"My mother is here. Have you seen her?" I shouldn't have trusted her—she was Solena's sister after all—but I was desperate.

"She's not here. I'm the only living person here. Well, and you."

From the top of the stairs the door groaned, then shut with a great shuddering echo. At that moment I knew Mother wasn't here, and she never had been. The lamps flickered for a moment and fear clutched at me. "How will we get out?" I demanded. "Najma?"

"A heartbeat," creaked a voice that didn't belong to Najma.

"Listen to how fast it drums," someone else wheezed.

"And now it's stopped," observed the first. The voice was right—my heart had stopped mid-beat.

My breaths came quick and shallow. Sparks of light began flashing before me and my fear exploded into terror. I turned and raced for the stairs, racing up them so fast that I fell, cracking my chin against the step. I ignored the pain, scrambling the rest of the way up the stairs to the door. I began pounding on it. "Let me out!" I screamed over and over again.

Without warning, the door slid open. The light blinded me as I took great breaths of hot air. Over my gasps I could hear laughter, loud and cruel.

"Let me out! Let me out!" Solena, Fallon, and Yadira mocked, falling over each other in their mirth.

Petra held the handle of the door; she was the only one not laughing. "The door was never locked. Are you alright?"

My rage overtook me like poison. I strode up to Solena, drew back my arm, and used all my strength to hit her right in her lovely face. She cried out, pressing her hand to her eye. The laughter died abruptly as she fell to the ground. Fallon shouted something wordless.

Solena lowered her hand as her smile widened, and I raised my fist to hit her again. To my savage satisfaction, her smile disappeared and she flinched away.

Fallon grabbed my arm. "What did you do?"

"You really are mad!" Yadira added her voice to his as Petra kneeled beside Solena.

Dimly, I noticed that Najma had come to the door of the Crypts, watching the scene in silence.

I yanked away from Fallon and raced back to my chamber, the dust of the dead drifting from my clothes. "You'll hang from the Wall for this!" Fallon shouted after me, but I never slowed.

I fled to our chamber to wait for Mother. She would defend me. She would speak to the King, and then he would speak to Solena. She would have to apologize, and Fallon too. I paced the room as hours passed.

Mother returned when the light outside the window started to dim. Her face was as still as stone.

"Mother, where have you been?" My voice trembled. All my fury had ebbed, replaced by cold fear.

"It's time for your medicine, darling." Her voice was vague, as if she spoke from a dream. Her eyes were large and dewy, and she blinked slowly as she removed the lid from the familiar jar and held out a spiny leaf. She'd dropped a lot of belladonna into her eyes, perhaps too much, and now she was sleepy.

"They locked me in the Crypts!" She didn't respond. "Did you hear me? They did it on purpose!"

"Take it." Her voice was hard. I took the leaf and chewed it bitterly.

"You are overheated. Here, drink this." Mother held out a goblet of clear liquid with blossoms floating in it." I hesitated; no more poison today. "It's only water, darling."

I took the goblet and sniffed it. I could only smell the blossoms, sweet and fragrant. There was no trace of bitterness. I took a drink, and then another, the cool water soothing my raw throat and slowing my pounding heart.

A moment or so later there was a knock at the door. Mother made no move to answer, so neither did I. Would they give up and go away? I should have known better. The door opened and a guard stepped inside. "The Queen requests your presence," he said. "Both of you."

Mother's expression didn't change as she rose and drifted after the guard. I followed, my legs feeling wooden.

The Queen sat on her padded chair with Solena at her side, holding a hand over her face. Nearby stood Fallon and Yadira. "Look what your whelp has done," the Queen said. She pulled Solena's hand away, revealing a black eye.

"She locked me in the Crypts," I burst out. "They all did!" Fallon merely smirked and Yadira looked away.

"Do you honestly think the King will tolerate this behavior? He will cast out your daughter. You may have enchanted him, but he will not allow his own, true daughter to be threatened this way."

"Badriya will apologize," Mother replied, her voice still vague and her head bowed.

"He will tire of you. He will see you for who you are: an aging enchantress. You will be cast back out into the Lost, and you will be doomed there. You and your daughter."

I thought of the sensation of the ghost's fingers on my cheek, the grumblings beneath the sand, and the way the ghosts and demons surrounded me hungrily. *You are susceptible*, my mother had said. Fear slithered through my belly like a snake. What had I done?

"My Queen," Mother said as she knelt, pressing her forehead to the floor. "I will give you what you want." The Queen leaned forward eagerly, the goblet shaking in her fingers. "But no harm must come to my daughter."

"What does that mean, Mother? What will you give her?" The words tumbled from my mouth. My tongue felt thick with poison and the edges of my fear dulled. My voice sounded far away, even to my own ears. The water, I realized. She had tricked me and given me some kind of draught.

"Quiet, child." Mother turned and laid a cool hand on my cheek, just as she had in Mera before swimming with Cayo. "It will be all right. I'll never leave you."

I wanted to protest, but the words swam just out of my reach.

Mother turned back to the Queen. "No harm must come to my daughter," she repeated. "Her safety must be guaranteed by you, My Queen. You must treat her as your own."

The light in the Queen's face dimmed.

"You must vow."

The Queen pressed her lips together, but she nodded.

Mother untied a cloth the color of blood from her waist and held out her arm.

"Tonight," the Queen said, her voice low and trembling.

Mother stared at the cloth in her hand and nodded. "Your arm."

The Queen thrust out her arm and took another drink. Mother wound the cloth around their arms, fastening them together. She began to sing, her voice shaking with tears. I could see a vein throbbing in the Queen's temple.

Mother stopped singing. "That's it?" the Queen asked. "Is it done?" Mother's hand moved and the Queen gave a startled cry. Mother held up her tiny dagger, its edge lined with red, a small scrap of cloth hanging from its point. "How dare you!" the Queen cried, yanking her arm away. Mother calmly unraveled the cloth and rose as the Queen stared at her with eyes full of poison.

Mother gave a low, slow curtsy to the Queen. She nodded for me to follow, then turned and left without another word. By now my eyelids were heavy, my legs tingled, and my breath was slow. I was already on the edge of a dream, the cries of seagulls carrying me off to the sea.

"Get in bed, darling." I felt a rush of relief that Mother was speaking at last. I realized we'd returned to our chamber. She tucked me in and sang me a soft lullaby that was mournful and full of longing. I allowed myself to drift off to sleep. For that I would never forgive myself, but it was so much easier to believe everything would be all right.

When I woke in the night she was gone. My head pounded, full of cotton. My throat was thick and my tongue dry. I felt my mother's absence before I saw that I was alone in the room.

Her jewelry lay in a pile on her vanity, even the tiny band that she'd worn since Mera. I caught my breath when I saw her knife, its blade stained with her blood and the silvery mineral she had been cutting only hours before. Beneath it was a note:

My darling,
  I was wrong. The magical qualities of Aran were not enough to heal me, so I must try somewhere new. Another realm, altogether.
  I am sorry to leave you, but the Queen has promised no harm will come to you. You will be safe here, safer than in Mera. The King will watch over you too, until you can make your own way.
  Remember, you have magic even though it may not look the way you expect.
  And never forget—

To have good luck: goldenray, a spoonful stirred into tea.
A fingernail of sugar will make the luck sweeter.
To persuade others: swayleaf, dried and crumbled, then added to
butter. It makes a delicious spread.
To forget: greenbell, gathered when the moon rises.
I will always be with you. Be strong and remember what I've taught
you. You need only look over the Wall to find me, and you need only
listen to hear me.
   I love you.
      Mother.

No. No. No. No.

Even though I felt as though my legs had sunk in sand, I stumbled through the door and outside in search of Mother. Instead, I found Solena standing in the gallery in her nightgown with Fallon at her shoulder.

"Your mother jumped from the Wall," she told me as guards rushed past and orders were shouted. She smiled.

I shoved her as hard as I could, and she fell to the tiles with a cry.

"You should jump too!" Fallon shouted after me as I raced barefoot along the gallery to the stairs and down the path past the fountain. Late-night revelers and couples stood transfixed at the sight of the guards rushing toward the Wall.

Pushing through the willow door, I charged into the garden. "Mother?" I called, but the garden was hung with silence as though the plants mourned. It couldn't be true—my mother would never have left me. "Mother?"

Atop the Wall I heard cries and the sounds of a struggle. "There was nothing I could have done! She was over before I could stop her! How could I have known what she would do?"

"King's orders," another voice said. "Sorry, friend." Then there was the sound of chains, a strangled cry, and the sound of something heavy crashing against the Wall.

I stood frozen in the garden, my thoughts a whirling storm. If I climbed the stairs, she would be there, waiting. The sound of desperate grunts and wheezes, the scrape of chains, and the sound of scrabbling kept me from moving.

Without warning I heard her voice, as clear as if she sat beside me, singing into my ear. I sighed with relief and turned to look for her, but the garden was empty. Her voice continued to fill the air with the lullaby that she'd sung to me on the darkest nights in the Lost, when the starlight felt like the pricking of icicles and the weight of the sky felt like it would crush us. Then, it had filled me with hope, as if the moon were filling my chest and its light protected us from any danger. Now the night went still and the scent of jasmine hung in the air as thick as sorrow.

At last I could make my legs move, and they carried me up the stairs.

The amber moon was like a lamp in the night sky that somehow illuminated the Lost and threw it in shadow at the same time. The Snake lurked nearby in the sky.

Two guards stood at the top of the stairs. One paced back and forth, rubbing his face; the other was turned away from the Lost, and even in the darkness I could see how pale he was. A chain was looped through an iron ring at the top of the Wall. It creaked and rattled as though something heavy were attached to it.

As Mother's song grew louder, I drew a great breath and looked over the Wall. A man hung by his neck from the chains, his legs twitching. Beyond him, standing in the Lost, was my mother. Her face was tilted back to the sky as she sang, and her hair was shorn.

I screamed to her. One of the guards cursed and reached for me, but I ducked beneath his arms and raced for the stairs. If she would not come to me, I would go to her.

I kept to the shadows that pooled at the base of the walls, out of the moon's searching light, until I reached the main gates. The guard stared off into the Lost as if entranced—perhaps he heard the echoes of Mother's voice.

I slipped into the stables where the horses stamped restlessly in their stalls. Their riders were nowhere in sight—not even they would brave a race tonight.

It was nothing to slip through the stables to the gate where the horses raced into the Lost. Outside the Wall, the wind blew ferociously as fine sand stung my face and blinded me for a few seconds. Both Mother and her song had disappeared.

Sticking close to the Wall, I fought my way around to the eastern side. Above me there were urgent voices, fearful and angry. I struggled out into the sand, my eyes sharp, searching for bony hands reaching from its depths.

"Poor child."

I whirled to see a woman standing a few feet behind me. She wore a gown made of fine green silk, and coins were woven into her hair, jingling softly in the breeze. This was the Witch I'd seen before in the Lost. Now she wore a plait of hair around her neck with reddish-gold strands gleaming among the ebony. From it rose the scent of jasmine and the sea. Mother's scent.

"You're an orphan now, aren't you?" she said. "She's left you all alone."

"Help her!" I cried, turning in a circle. Was she beneath the surface? Had a demon pulled her into its depths? Dropping to my knees, I began to scrabble at the sand.

"You won't find her there."

"Then where is she?"

"Someplace she can't hear you."

"Can you bring her back?" She folded her arms. "You can! Bring her back!"

"She jumped into the Lost willingly. She forfeited her soul—it is mine." She touched the hair around her neck. "To seal our bargain. It's only a symbol, but I do have a flair for the dramatic."

Her words were like a blow to my chest. "You're lying. That's impossible."

The Witch laughed, a soft sound like the wind over the sand. "Don't pretend to know the rules of my desert."

"Let her go," I persisted, my voice shaking.

The Witch cocked her head and tapped her chin. "What could a little mortal girl give me that I don't already have?" She made a show of looking all around herself. "I know!" She brightened as she looked up into the sky. "I do love stars."

My stomach clenched. "You know I can't give you stars."

She laughed again. "Didn't I just say you are only a little mortal? Silver. It's the silver in the stars that I love. Yes. You must bring me one hundred pounds of silver. Surely her sacrifice is worth at least one hundred pounds. Then I'll set your mother free."

"She sacrificed me too," I said softly. "She left me here alone."

"And yet, alone as you are, you're still alive, while she is not," the Witch replied slyly.

The Lost stretched out in all directions. The walls of the city were at my back and demons hissed beneath my feet.

Fingers poked out from beneath the sand and wrapped around my ankle. With a shriek, I yanked away and brought my heel down on the hand. It slid back beneath the surface.

"Ah. Not ready to give up after all," the Witch noted.

"Where am I supposed to find one hundred pounds of silver?" I choked.

"Think of the gifts that the King gave your mother; all of those jewels he showered on her," the Witch said. "That will be a start."

"None of them are silver." I wondered if this was deliberate.

"Oh, come now. Aren't you the daughter of the King's tragic lover? He'll give you whatever you want now."

She sank into the sand and disappeared. I stood shaking and alone.

The bargain between my mother and the Queen came to nothing, because when my mother jumped from the Wall she became sainted in the King's memory. She was the woman who would stay eternally beautiful and never grow older or tiresome as his wife had. She would always be the mysterious woman who appeared like magic from the Lost. "She will forever hold my heart," the King repeated to whoever would listen.

The King commissioned a stone effigy of my mother. Her lips curved into a sweet smile, though I'd never seen her smile this way in life—her smiles were more mischievous than sweet. Her eyes were painted as no other Queen's were: blue and looking directly at the beholder, though my mother never looked at anyone directly and had brown eyes.

Was this how the King saw her?

Only a few nights later the Queen also died, leaving Solena without her mother as well. Any promises that had been made between the two were void.

All I had left of my mother was her knife and her ghost.

Chapter Seven

The next night I light the lamp in my window again, even though I find it hard to concentrate. I must do anything I can to earn more silver. My thoughts are muddied by Khalen and the disdain in his voice. His own past haunts him, he'd said so himself, so why would he judge me? Why do I care?

Five women visit, one after the other. Two ask for something to hide the shadows beneath their eyes, so I exchange some of the cream I use on Solena's face for three silver rings. A young woman who is married to a much older man asks for a sleeping draught, but she only has a thin gold chain to trade. I suspect she will give it to her husband so that he will not wake when she slips from her chamber to dance with the young tambor player. Another trades a brooch for a pot of the rouge that I paint on Solena's lips.

The last woman asks for Stardust. When I hesitate, she pleads. "I'll only wear it for the Festival of the Full Moon. That's all. Please?" When I still don't answer she presses five silvers into my hand. I give her a bag filled with just enough to brush over her eyelids for one night.

I have eighty-six silvers now. It's not nearly enough.

I should work more after she leaves, create more Stardust, but my exhaustion and fear will bleed into potions and bring heartache and bitterness. Instead I fall into bed.

My dreams won't let me rest. In them, Mother casts herself from the Wall, her voice filling the sky. The sand below turns to green and gray ocean waves that churn hungrily. She disappears beneath the surface, though I can still hear her singing. Silver coins, enough to pay the Witch, hover in midair, just out of reach. I clamber onto the Wall and reach for them when the Wall suddenly vanishes, and I fall toward the water. Just before I reach the surface, the water turns into sand and the King rises from the waves, reaching for me, ready to devour me…the laughter of the Witch rings in my ears, turning into screams that shatter the air.

I sit upright, the cries echoing from the room adjacent to mine. Najma. I fly out of bed and rush to the door, not bothering with a wrap. Her guard stands beside the open door, his eyes wide with fear. "I did nothing," he stammers. "She woke this way…"

She is quivering and pale in her bed. I shoulder past him to her side. "Wait outside," I tell him.

Kneeling beside her, I smooth her hair from her face. "What was it, Little Crocodile?" I ask.

"Mama," she says, her face crumpling. I know that in her dreams she's relived the moment she found her mother, three years before, on a warm and humid night like this one.

It had been soon after my own mother had jumped from the Wall—perhaps the Queen was haunted by her song as well. She drank even more Fairy Green and slept through the day more and more often, until one morning Najma found her lying half out of bed, her eyes open and unblinking, and her hair floating in a green puddle of vomit on the floor. An empty goblet rolled nearby, her fingertips grazing it as if she'd reached for it even in her last moment.

"I'll get you something to help you sleep," I tell Najma.

"Don't leave," she begs, catching at my hand.

"I'll only be a minute," I soothe her, and then leave her shivering beneath her covers.

From the table in my chamber I grab the vial of clearvine, dreamsigh, and slumberweed that I always have mixed and ready in anticipation of nights like these. I pour the mixture into water and return to her in less than a minute, stirring as I go. "Here," I tell her, "drink this." I hum the songs Mother sang to me in the Lost as she drinks. In only a few moments her face relaxes and she sighs, lying back.

"Now your dreams will be sweet," I murmur. "Sleep now, because the Festival of the Full Moon is tomorrow and you will be up all night."

I rise as her eyes droop, but she catches my hand. "Stay," she begs.

With a sigh, I drink what's left in the glass and settle myself beside her. Her breathing deepens as she slips back into sleep.

I am not so lucky. Despite the sleeping tincture, I lie awake thinking of the rawness in Khalen's eyes as he rubbed the talisman over and over. I listen to Najma's breathing, trying to match mine to hers, and at last my muscles begin to relax and my heartbeat slows. I fall into a dreamless sleep.

It seems only a few minutes have passed when the door slams open. I bolt upright as Solena enters in her nightgown, her hair standing out about her white face, her dark eyes small and hard. I put my finger to my lips and glance down at Najma, who turns over but doesn't open her eyes.

"What is it?" I whisper. "My Queen," I add.

"Assist me." Though her voice is low, the cords in her neck stand out.

"With what?"

"I must prepare for my betrothal."

"Betrothal?"

"Yes, you imbecile!" Her voice rises.

"When?"

"This evening!"

"It's only been two days!" Najma stirs in her sleep.

"He is truly enchanted by me," Solena says.

Or his adviser convinced him that he needs to act to quickly in order to gain an alliance with Aran before he is poisoned.

"The cosmetics are taking their toll," I warn Solena in a whisper, watching Najma. "Perhaps you should use them less."

"And perhaps I should announce the truth behind the King's death at the ceremony, as a gift to my groom. Tell him that you tried to seduce my father, just like your mother did, then murdered him when he wouldn't succumb to your wishes." Her chest heaves as she watches me with wild eyes.

My heart stops, then begins to beat slowly as we stare at one another. One, two, three beats.

Her madness is even worse than I thought. I look at Najma again; she lies still but I can't tell if she is just pretending to sleep. I slide from the bed and exit the room, crossing to my own chamber. Solena follows.

Once inside I turn to face her. "That is not what happened." I don't have to keep my voice down anymore.

"Who would believe you?" She crosses her arms. "I'll hang your body from the Wall as a gift to my groom."

"And he'll vomit all over your lovely wedding gown, My Queen."

She slaps me across the cheek. I gasp, despite myself. She is even more disturbed than usual today. Her veins pulse beneath the fragile skin of her cheekbones.

I want to tell her to paint her own face, but instead I take a breath and force my voice to stay even. "You need to use less of the powder. It is leeching into your blood, making it too thin. You'd better stop using the belladonna too. It can blind you."

"You will come to my chamber, now," she says. With that she turns on her heel and strides from the chamber.

Rage fills me. Snatching up a jar of rouge, I throw it to the floor. It shatters against the stones. Powder as red as blood rises in a cloud.

I will not follow. I will leave now, right now. I would rather face the demons in the Lost.

The truth is, I can't take the chance that Solena will hang me from the Wall or cast me out into the Lost. Then my mother will never be free. As brave as I try to be, I don't want to face the demons, not on my own. The only thing that I can think to do is follow Solena, leaving the floor littered with glass and poison.

As the sun sinks lower in the sky, we gather in the Great Hall for the ceremony. Arlo shifts from foot to foot and glances over his shoulder at Khalen, who smiles reassuringly. Our eyes meet and his gaze slides away. Dark shadows pool beneath his eyes. *All for the best,* I tell myself. I have no time for the judgment that I read in his expression just before he looks away.

I am still wearing the same earth-colored tunic and shapeless pants that I'd slept in. A stain blooms on the knee of the pants from when I'd collected the pods and crystals that I needed for Stardust, and the sleeve of the tunic is raveling.

A smirk crosses Mina's face as I enter. She leans over to whisper to Fallon and both of them snicker. With a serene smile on my face, I take my place next to Petra, who looks lovely, but not too lovely, in a flowing green tunic. She eyes me head to toe pointedly, but I avoid her gaze. Yadira is on her other side, pale and red-eyed. Najma stands at the foot of the dais, her eyes darting about; she has not yet learned to hide her thoughts.

The court falls silent as Solena arrives. Her face is smooth and calm, thanks to several layers of powder that hide the enraged blotches, and her eyes are large and limpid. Despite my warnings, she'd insisted on her usual regimen. She smiles at Arlo as she comes to a stop before him.

Khalen gently prods Arlo forward. "Queen Solena, I would be honored if you would accept my offer of marriage."

There is a long, heavy silence. Then Solena's smile lights the courtyard. "I accept your offer with great pleasure." A spattering of polite applause fills the Hall.

Arlo moves forward to kiss Solena, his face damp and mottled. At the last moment she turns her face so that his mouth lands on her cheek rather than her lips. He pulls away with a grimace as if he just tasted something bitter. The taste of poison on her cheek is what he can expect every day of his marriage to her.

Musicians wander among the tables, playing quiet ballads. The curtains are drawn across the windows, blocking the sunlight, but the room is lit with lanterns that fill the Hall with soft light while providing plenty of shadows for secrets. The conversation is threaded with flirtatious laughter.

Prince Arlo gazes around the Hall silently, his mouth turned down. He picks up the bottle before him and frowns, then signals to a servant, who quickly arrives with another. He lifts the glass to his mouth as soon as she finishes pouring and drains it, then claps it back on the table. He wipes his arm across his mouth as the servant fills it once more.

Petra sits beside one of Arlo's courtiers. One of her hands alights on his forearm, graceful and light as a moth. He watches, his mouth open slightly, as she reaches for his glass and drinks from it, her lips stained with red wine. His eyes never leave her face.

Arlo sways to his feet holding a goblet. Several empty bottles lay on the table in front of him, winking in the lamplight.

"To my beautiful future wife," he slurs, gazing down at Solena, struggling to focus. She smiles up at him, her eyes gleaming.

Khalen rises. Leaning over, he murmurs into Arlo's ear, but the Prince waves him away clumsily. Arlo thrusts his goblet upward with such enthusiasm that wine sloshes out and splashes Yadira. She hardly seems to notice.

"My beautiful wife, Sonela." His voice rings through the Hall. Petra sucks in her breath. The court looks at the lamps, the glasses, anywhere but at Arlo or each other.

"You might be cold, but I'll take care of that on our wedding night. Isn't that right, my love?" He begins to laugh but the sound ends in coughing.

Khalen takes a firm hold on the Prince's arm, and the mirth drains from his face. He slowly sinks into his chair and stares at his plate. Taking a slice of meat, he chews it slowly, swallowing hard. Solena's face is as hard as stone, her smile etched into her ivory face. The only sounds for a time are the clink of cutlery and the tap of her nails against the table.

Her eyes fall on Safiya. "Safiya, my dear, I must try to win back some of what you've taken from me. Perhaps some gambling after dinner?"

Safiya carefully swallows her bite before she turns to Solena with a brilliant smile. "I've been so lucky lately, My Queen, it's true."

"Perhaps your luck is about to run out, Lady Safiya," I break in.

"And you, My Lady Badriya? Will you play?" Khalen asks me.

Solena laughs. "She's hardly a Lady, Sir Khalen. And her name is Diya."

Ignoring her, I match Khalen's smile as I reply. "As I've told you, Lord Khalen, I do not gamble."

"She has nothing to gamble with," Solena says. "Nothing you're interested in, at least."

"I doubt that," he says over the rim of his glass. Next to Solena, Najma looks from him to me.

Popping an olive into my mouth, I stand and curtsy. "Forgive me, I have a pounding headache." I nearly collide with Mina as I turn, but I do not slow as I leave the Hall without waiting for Solena's leave.

I spend the day in the garden, cutting and digging until I am dizzy from the aroma of dreamroot and slumberweed. As the light dims, I rub the ache in my back and climb to the top of the Wall. Tonight the Lost is dark and still. No ghosts show themselves, not even my mother.

I look to the sky, remembering the way the Horse urged us forward on our journey. The moon is nearly full, but the Snake refuses to be eclipsed, its mouth open wide as if to swallow it.

The points of the Bat's wings are appearing just above the horizon. I am running out of time to earn the silvers for the Duke's Witch. I have to think of another plan.

"What a boring party." I whirl to see Najma at my elbow. How can she still sneak up beside me so easily?

"And yet I can never get you to leave when it's time."

She shrugs, holding out an orange. I take it and peel it, its tart scent sharpening the edge of my dulled consciousness. "I'd rather look at the stars," she says, tilting her head back, following my gaze. "The Snake. Trouble ahead, then." She glances at me, then looks away. Again I wonder how much she sees and hears from her hiding places. "I hate that my sign is the Crocodile."

"Why? You are the perfect Crocodile. She sees everything from the water, but no one sees her."

"I'd rather be a Fish," Najma replies, popping a slice of orange into her mouth.

"Crocodiles are graceful; they can swim in the water and walk on land."

"They have giant heads and short legs."

"But in the water they glide along gracefully. No one threatens them."

"I'd rather be a Bat, or even a Toad, like you."

I smile. "That's why I'm so comfortable in the dark."

"Not in the Crypts."

The memory of being trapped in the dark clamps around me like a fist. "That was different. We were locked in the Crypts with the dead." I take a deep breath of the warm night air that is laced with the scent of lilies. "You weren't afraid, though."

"Crocodiles are fearless." She smiles.

I poke her in the side, forcing away the old panic, and she giggles. "That's true."

A despairing cry rises from the Lost. We stop laughing and stare out into the darkness. Najma can hear it, too, I realize.

As it fades away, Najma's mouth tightens. "The magic is almost finished."

"Do you really believe that story?" I ask her.

"All the enchantments are growing thin. We're foolish to ignore the signs and pretend it's all a fairytale."

Her chin is set. She drums her nails on the Wall like Solena.

"So what should we do?" I ask.

"Dig for more water. The Witch enchanted a source of water that was already there, so there must be more below. Solena should suggest it to Arlo as a term for their marriage."

She speaks with a determination I haven't heard before. "A good idea," I agree.

"And," she adds, "perhaps another bargain with a Witch wouldn't hurt."

"And who would you trade?"

Her eyes sparkle. "I have some ideas."

I break into laughter and her mouth quirks. She turns back to the stars. "Does Arlo know that Solena is a Scorpion?"

"I doubt it," I sigh. "They're not all bad, you know. They are ambitious and protective."

"And horribly vengeful if you cross them," Najma says. "Poor Arlo, I would be a better ruler than he is."

"I believe you would," I reply.

"Poor Arlo," the Bones echo.

We stay atop the Wall for a while, the Bones rattling companionably, until Najma turns to look back at the Rooms of the Favorites. "You have customers," she observes. I follow her gaze and see a hooded figure pacing the gallery outside my chamber. Another waits at the foot of the steps. "You really should be a Bat," I tell her with a sigh. Loathe as I am to return, I need the silver.

From my chamber I hear snippets of the revelry from the Dining Hall. The tambor tinkles merrily as voices call out enthusiastic toasts, one after the other.

I listen as I chop and slice. As the sky begins to lighten, I draw the knife across my arm. The blood that flows into the powder is sluggish, reluctant, but it will make the person who drinks the goldenray tea so lucky that they will be nearly invincible, and whoever takes the swayleaf will be able to convince anyone, even Solena, of their point.

Only a little longer, I tell myself.

The door opens and Solena enters. I curse under my breath at the shine of sweat on her brow. I feign nonchalance as I inspect the cream I've created.

"Why aren't you celebrating?" I ask.

"Ugh. He is repulsive."

"Security and riches," I remind her. "This is a great sacrifice that our Queen makes for Aran."

"Don't mock me, Diya."

"I would never, My Queen." I can't help smiling to myself. "I thought you were gaming tonight. What happened?"

"You know what happened. That little worm thinks she can cheat me."

My heart sinks. "Safiya won again, I take it?"

She taps her nails on the table, the blood-red polish gleaming in the lamplight. One, two, three. "She must pay the consequences."

"Why don't you just order her to give it back?"

"Then she will have won."

I study her. Scarlet veins show just below the surface of the skin at her temples, her dark pupils fill her eyes, and her cheeks are sunken like a cadaver's. "Perhaps you should get some more rest."

Rage flickers across her face. She takes a deep breath and closes her eyes. When she opens them, she smiles prettily.

"Very well, Diya," she murmurs. "I see I cannot convince you." She turns and leaves the room.

My eyes rest blearily on the door. *Why has she conceded so easily?* I wonder as I return to slicing stems. My fingers are sluggish and my thoughts slow. I haven't slept well in days. The knife slips and a bloom of pain wells from my finger. Blood runs onto the table, staining bits of the stem. Unwilling to waste it, I fumble for a vial and catch as much of the blood that spills from my finger as I can.

I wrap my finger in a cloth and lie down on the bed. *I'll only close my eyes for a minute*, I promise myself, *then I'll get up at dark when it's time to light the lamp.*

My head grows heavy. In my mind I feel the past approaching like a specter, but I can do nothing to keep it at bay. Though I hear the tentative scratching at the door that means a desperate woman has come, I cannot answer as memories crash over me in waves.

THEN

For days after my mother jumped into the Lost I felt as though I had sunk to the bottom of the sea. I barely heard the taunts of Solena and her friends; I stayed in my chamber, refusing to eat or bathe. I didn't know whether it was morning or night.

One morning I opened my eyes and stifled a scream. Najma stood beside the bed. Had she come to deliver a taunt? To break something on her sister's orders, or perhaps on her own?

But tears hung in her lashes as she held out an orange. "I'm sorry about your mother," she said softly.

I was too surprised to do anything but take the orange. She left the room as silently as she'd entered.

I sat up and peeled the orange. The sharp scent penetrated my despondency, and the sweet juice softened the edge of my sadness. Before I knew it, I'd devoured the entire thing.

Later she returned with bread that was drizzled with honey. Another time she brought an apple.

I began to look forward to her visits. She told me some of the legends she'd read in the library about the Kings and Queens of the past. I told her some of the stories my mother had told me while we were in the Lost. I got out of bed, dressed, washed, and combed my hair again. I even ate in the Dining Hall, but only occasionally. I couldn't bear to watch the King sob into his meal as if he were as entitled to grieve as I was. Meanwhile the Queen stared straight ahead, stony-faced, her glass of Fairy Green in her hand. Solena and Najma watched their parents, Solena's eyes sharp and Najma's sad.

Then the Queen died, and I began to think of escape.

One evening I returned to the stables that Mother and I had passed through on our first night here. Groomsmen and riders in blue livery swaggered about, calling out taunts and wagers to one another.

I was terrified of the horses. They were huge and muscular, tossing their heads and racing along the sand as their riders shouted exuberantly.

I approached the Master of Horses, who was watching from the gate. Swallowing, I squared my shoulders. "I would like to learn to ride."

He bowed politely but did not look at me.

I cleared my throat. "Did you hear me? I said I would like to learn to ride."

"You shouldn't be here," he said, casting me a glance. He shook his head slowly. "I must refuse your request."

"Why?" I demanded. "I am a favorite of the King."

He turned to face me. "It is the King himself who has given the order that you are not to ride, and no one is allowed to teach you. In fact, you should not even be near the stables. It's for your safety." He turned away.

To keep me imprisoned is what he meant. I could tell by the way the Master of Horses' gaze slid away that he knew it to be true as well.

I watched two horses thunder toward the gate, sand flying up around their hooves. Clearly they could outrun any danger in the Lost. Their riders shouted, cursed, and laughed.

A plan took shape in my mind: I would sneak down to the stables under the cover of night, like the heroine of a story, and win one of the horses over. It would allow me to mount it and then it would carry me out of the city. Together we would fly over the sand and across the Lost to Mera.

My reverie was interrupted by a man's shout as he was thrown through the air. The horse raced away as its rider rolled about in pain. Cursing, the Master of Horses ran to the gate that led outside. "Get away from here before you get me hung from the Wall!" he shouted over his shoulder.

Despair washed through me, wave after wave, as relentless as the sea in Mera. Without watching where I was going, I wandered back through the inner gate, toward the city. I stuck close to the Wall, passing the Dome, the Gambling Hall, and the Lesser until I'd reached my mother's garden.

Pushing through the willow door, I stalked past the achevine that had wound itself around the serenity blossoms and threatened to choke them. Meanwhile the swayleaf nearly drooped to the ground, in dire need of a trim. Since Mother had died I hadn't cared for them as I should. Still, I went up the stairs to the Wall.

The wind had been relentless lately, and my heart ached with longing for my mother. I had been plagued with nightmares of silver gleaming just ahead, then sinking into the sand before I could reach it. Mother called to me from beneath the sand. "You'll never free her at this rate," the Witch's voice admonished me, though she remained out of sight.

I longed for rest.

I lay on the edge of the Wall, hoping I could sleep at last. Maybe I would fall painlessly into the sand below, already dead before the sand could swallow me. Mother seemed happy enough, didn't she? Oblivious to me and the King, she danced, free of all the sorrows that plagued her from Mera. The wind whipped my hair around my face. The stars appeared one by one in the sky, as thick as the sand below.

It was only then that I realized the Snake had disappeared and the Bat had taken its place. The urge to fall faded.

Perhaps I can see the Lights of Mera tonight? I thought.

If Mother appears, it's a sign that she wants me to join her.

The night grew darker, the stars brighter. Mother never appeared. But I still didn't jump.

I turned quickly at the sound of footsteps, and the world reeled. A hand took my arm, steadying me.

"Careful. Others have become so dizzy with starlight that they've lost their balance and fallen."

I blinked and looked into the face of a young man in a guard's uniform. His light windblown hair was coated in sand, and his eyes were a shade of green that reminded me of the ocean on a bright day in Mera.

"Maybe that wouldn't be the worst thing in the world," I said. *Falling surrounded by stars.* "What are you doing here?"

He shook his head. "Oh, no. Don't even think of jumping—I don't want to join him." He nodded toward the Bones below as they swayed in the wind, creaking like laughter.

"I wouldn't want to endanger you," I said bitterly, and turned to go. I couldn't even find peace on top of the Wall.

"I imagine things are hard for you right now," he called after me. "It would be understandable if you wanted to jump."

"I wasn't going to." My voice was sharper than I intended.

He raised his hands placatingly. "Alright. You don't have to go, you know. You'll miss it."

Stopping in my tracks, I turned to look at him. "What are you talking about?"

He nodded at the horizon. "You can see the Lights of Mera from here."

"No you can't." Despite my words, I couldn't stop hope from blossoming in my chest.

"If you say so." He stared out into the darkness.

There is no chance that he can see the Lights of Mera. I've looked for them every night since I've been here. This is a trick; he was sent here by Solena. Once I get too close to the edge, he'll shove me over the side.

I suddenly realized how little I actually wanted to die.

I remembered the way the air went still in the moment right before the great green flash filled the sky, how the fireball streaked over the ocean and set the world alight, at least that's how it seemed. A breath later there would be a boom that echoed to the ends of the earth, sending the seagulls shrieking and wheeling.

He pointed out over the Wall. "Look over there."

"There's nothing." The sky near the horizon was black and empty, devoid of even the stars.

Suddenly a ball of bright green light flashed just above the horizon. Just as quickly as it appeared, it was gone, though the sky still held the dim glow.

"Did you see it?" he shouted. I couldn't speak, my throat thick and my vision blurred with tears. The heaviness that had plagued me fell away.

"I knew they would come tonight! The Lights of Mera!" He beamed.

"How?" I asked. "How could you have known?"

"The air. It's electric."

"But we're over a hundred miles away."

"I'm only telling you what I know."

I studied him as he stared out at the Lost, this young man dressed in the uniform of Solena's guard. He could be lying, tricking me, so that he could repeat all of this to Solena and the two could laugh at me together. But his eyes held none of the sharpness or suspicion of most of Solena's court. Instead they seemed to me to be alight with wonder as he searched the sky. He hardly seemed to notice that I was there.

"Make a wish," he said suddenly.

Because he sounded so much like a child and not at all like a guard, and because his hair was a little long and his uniform a little wrinkled, I did. I closed my eyes and wished for enough silver to free my mother and return to Mera so that I could see the Lights of Mera directly over the ocean, and not from the top of a wall in the middle of the ghost-filled desert.

"What did you wish for?" he asked.

It was bad luck to tell someone your wish, but it was good fortune to dance under the Lights of Mera. I took his hands and led him into the twirling dance that Mother had taught me. We moved faster and faster until we spun and the remnants of the Lights became a bright greenish blur overhead. The pain of losing my mother, of the King's unwanted advances, of the harsh whispers and sharp laughter of Solena and her Favorites receded to the edge of my mind, though I could sense it waiting to regain its grip.

I could have danced for hours, mirroring my mother who spun below, but the boy slowed, laughing even as his breath came in huffs. "I think it's over."

"Oh." He was right. The Bat still darted among the stars, but the Lights were gone. I felt hollow and depleted as my mother's song died away.

But I no longer wanted to sink into oblivion. I suddenly remembered how it felt to dance beneath the Lights of Mera with the ocean roaring nearby, the pipe and drums combatting the sound of the seagulls, and the smell of the cool, salty air.

The boy squeezed my hands. "You didn't say what you wished for."

Instead of answering, I turned to him and countered with a question of my own. "Where are you from?"

"Here. Aran," he replied lightly.

"You're not from here if you know of the Lights of Mera."

One side of his mouth turned up in a smile. "No, really. My father was a guard, too. He's the one who brought me up here and showed me the Lights. It was the first time I realized there is more to this land than the Lost. You can see them even more clearly outside of the city."

I looked sharply at him, suddenly recognizing his voice. He was one of the riders I'd just watched who'd urged his horse to the finish line.

Envy prickled inside me like a thorn. He had the freedom to ride out of Aran and face the dangers in the Lost because his horse was strong and fast enough to outrun them. But he always chose to return. If I had that choice, I would ride away.

He watched me as if I'd spoken aloud, and only then did I see the danger. I didn't know him at all, and I couldn't trust him. Despite his kind smile and the fact that he'd danced with me under the Lights of Mera, I couldn't risk staying. It wouldn't be long before Solena poisoned him against me.

"I should go," I said, though I didn't want to go back to my chamber to be alone again. Servants had come and taken away Mother's clothes and jewelry, so there was no trace of her except for the scent of jasmine, tuberose, and her potions.

"You can come anytime," he said. "It gets lonely here on the Wall."

"That it does," the Bones agreed.

"My name is Rumin," he added.

"Badriya," I replied, and slipped away, feeling hope for the first time since I'd arrived in Aran.

My wish came true eventually, but if I'd known what I would have to do before that happened, I might not have been so quick to wish it.

At first I visited Rumin only occasionally, on nights when I thought we might see the Lights. We never saw them again, but it didn't matter as we spoke, washed in moonlight, the demons only feet away.

He always called me by my true name, Badriya, even though he must have heard that I was known by another.

Though my heart beat faster around him and my cheeks flushed, he seemed at ease around me. He never tried to touch me or take my hand as he had when we met atop the Wall. He spoke to me as if we were brother and sister.

It's because I'm so ordinary, I decided. So I had to seem extraordinary.

In my chamber, I found some of the pods Mother had used to make the Stardust powder that she brushed across her eyelids so that the King couldn't take his eyes off of her. I decided to grind them and add more indigo to better bring out my eyes. When I finished, the powder was the shade of the twilight sky.

As I worked, Mother's warning echoed through my mind. "This is dangerous, Badriya," she had said as she brushed it over her eyelids. "You must wear it very, very carefully. Use too much and you become hungry for it all the time. You'll do anything for more. Then you'll begin to see things that aren't real, things you want, until you aren't a part of this world anymore."

I hesitated, looking down at the mixture. *Magic has its price, Badriya.* Before I could think too much about it, I drew Mother's knife across my hand. Sucking in my breath at the pain, I allowed a drop to fall into the powder. I bandaged my hand as it dried.

I studied the powder on my fingertips, the silver in it gleaming like the points of knives. There were so many beautiful women in Aran who might catch Rumin's attention. I was so plain compared to them.

I'll just try it. I can always wipe it off.

When I brushed the powder across my eyelids, they sparkled like the night sky. It looked as if my eyes were filled with starlight, just like the powder Mother used.

As I entered the Dining Hall, the world seemed hazy at the edges, like a dream that could easily turn into a nightmare. The figures moving past were like teeming shadows. The King sat atop the dais, and next to him sat Solena, seething and watchful. All around the other ladies and lords of the court whispered and laughed as they plotted.

Yadira and Petra, closest to Solena, glanced at me, looked away, then looked back at me again, their heads together. I felt serene as I glided over to sit on the other side of the King in my mother's old spot. I'd never glided before in my life.

The King hastily set down the cup from which he'd been drinking. "Badriya. You look lovely this evening, more lovely than usual."

Solena's head snapped around and Najma watched, as she always did. "Thank you, Sire," I replied as I sipped my water.

Fallon hesitated before me and I braced myself for a whispered taunt, but instead he bowed from the waist. "Lady Badriya." My head began to ache. Had I imagined this? Shadows were already forming at the edges of my vision, ghosts perhaps, whispering to each other about what I would do next.

The King signaled to the musicians, who struck up a lively tune that had been a favorite of my mother's. He rose and took my hand, then pulled me to my feet and onto the floor. He spun me around the dance floor, his white teeth flashing in a smile; it was the same way he'd danced with my mother while the Queen looked on and drank her Fairy Green. I tried to slide away, but his grip on my hand tightened.

As the music died, he beckoned to a servant, who rushed forward with a small parcel. "I've been meaning to give this to you." He took a golden bracelet from the parcel; I recognized it as one he'd given my mother. It reminded me of a shackle as he slid it onto my wrist it.

"Do you like it?" he asked eagerly, his eyes searching my face. I nodded and tried to smile, though I felt as though I'd swallowed a rock.

He pulled me close, his arms twining about me, and kissed my lips. Gasps and murmurs floated around us. "You are like your mother," he murmured.

"Father!" Solena called, and I had never been so glad to hear her voice. "You promised me a dance!" As he turned, I slipped from his grasp and out of the Hall, the whispers of the courtiers following me.

I rushed directly to the Wall to meet Rumin. He could erase the memory of the King's lips, at least I hoped he could. The stars seemed to cartwheel across the night and the dark purple of the sky pulsed. I smiled, feeling a rush of relief when I saw him waiting for me, and the knot in my stomach loosened.

As I approached, he frowned. "You look…different. Not yourself."

I blinked for longer than necessary to allow him the chance to catch a gleam of the powder. "What is that?" he asked.

"It's Stardust," I replied, deflated by his lack of enthusiasm. Around me the night went still, and the stars slowed their acrobatics.

"He's not one for illusions," sighed the Bones from the Wall.

I waited, holding my breath.

Finally, he offered me his lopsided smile. "You're beautiful with it and without it."

He had said, "You're beautiful." The stars began to sing, echoing my heart, or at least I thought they did. It could have been the Stardust, or simply my heart dancing for the first time since I left Mera.

I don't know how long we stayed atop the Wall, nor do I remember what we talked about, but I did forget the King's kiss, at least for a time.

I finally drifted back to my chamber, floating on the memory of Rumin's words, his smile, and his gaze. I'd nearly reached my room when someone spoke from my shoulder.

"Diya." I whirled to see Petra, the girl with the laughing eyes.

"That's not my name," I told her.

"It's what Solena calls you, so everyone else will too." She shrugged.

"What do you want?"

She took a step toward me. "How did you make your eyes look so..."

"As if I'd tell you."

"I'll pay you two silvers." Opening her purse, she showed me the coins.

The sharp words on my tongue vanished. I was certain she wanted to catch the attention of Fallon. His long lashes made many of the ladies in the city sigh, though I thought he resembled a ferret.

Petra had never joined in with Solena and Yadira's torments. She smiled and laughed more often than the others at court, and the sound was loud and happy rather than low and unkind. Because of this, I told her, "He's terrible."

She frowned. "You know nothing about it." When I still hesitated, she asked, "Do you want the silver or not?"

I did, which is why I mixed her a vial of Stardust with an extra spoonful of powder to compliment her light complexion. I gave it to her under the cover of the shadows in the Cursed Garden in exchange for the silvers.

"You didn't poison this, did you?" she asked, frowning at the vial. I rolled my eyes and reached to take it back. "I'm sorry!" she cried, retreating.

The next evening when I entered my garden to gather more dreamroot, I found her hunched at the foot of the willow. The kohl ran down her face in black tears and the Stardust was a clumped mess on her cheeks. "This is what your powder got me," she said, her voice thick.

"I warned you," I replied sharply. The defiance in her face dissolved; hiding her face in her hands, she broke into sobs.

Though I tried not to care, it saddened me to see her happiness overtaken by darkness. I mixed her a different potion, this one made with the extract from the lotus blossoms that floated in the pool. The potion would help her forget and make whatever memories haunted her seem like bad dreams, barely remembered in the light of day.

When I saw her again, she strolled arm in arm with Yadira past the reflection pool, her laughing face turned to the sun. Only a shadow beneath her eyes remained. She said nothing to me but sought me out in the garden the next afternoon as I chewed on the poison leaves, their acidic juice burning my throat.

"Can you make more Stardust?"

"What?" I nearly choked. "Have you not had enough?"

"Not for me, for others. Nearly everyone has commented on it. Even Solena."

"I doubt that." Tilting my head back, I let the cool, green sunlight bathe my face as it passed through the willow tree.

"I bet you could even get some of the ladies to pay you for it."

My vision snapped back into focus. "It's not for sale."

She cocked an eyebrow. "Oh? So your pride and spite are worth more than silver? Alright. I guess you're not interested." She turned away.

"Who wants to buy it?" I called after her.

"Yadira."

"Why doesn't she ask me herself?"

"She knows that you hate her, but she'll pay."

"What does she have?"

"Jewelry. A lot of jewelry."

"Silver. It has to be silver."

"I will ask her." She left me sitting in the garden, wondering at this turn of fortune.

Through Petra, Yadira paid me a handful of silver for the vial of Stardust. That night, many could not look away from her eyes, including Theron. Within a few nights, he was singing a song that he'd composed about the woman with eyes of starlight.

The next night Petra slipped me a pair of silver earrings in the shape of songbirds. "What am I to do with these?" I asked.

"They're silver, aren't they?" she returned, her lips barely moving. "For Safiya." She nodded toward a curly-haired woman at the end of the table.

So I mixed another vial of the Stardust powder, this time adding indigo to bring out the blue in Safiya's eyes.

A few nights later, Petra came to me again. "You have another request," she said, hesitating.

"For whom?"

She bit her lip. "Fallon."

"No," I said flatly.

"He'll pay double."

"How can you want to help him?" I demanded.

"He's fallen in love with one of the groomsmen."

Ah, so she never had a chance with him. "Triple."

She nodded. "But you can't poison it."

I'd thought of adding just enough blackdust to make his eyes bloodshot and his long lashes fall out, but I sighed. "Silver only," I reminded her.

I slowly began to accrue silvers: a handful at first, and then a dozen. I hid the thick coins in a plain earthen jar that was different than the ornate ones in which I kept the jewels and gold that I often received as payment.

The Bat faded and the Rabbit took its place, followed by the Crocodile. Then the Scorpion took its place in the sky. It was a good time to dance, but I forgot that it was also a time for vengeance.

Rumin and I met regularly in the soft darkness of the garden. We sat shoulder to shoulder and spoke about our dreams of leaving the Lost. We'd earn enough money to buy one of the horses and ride to Mera.

He would lie with his head in my lap as he toyed with my hair and teased me. Sometimes, I would lie in his arms and tell him the tales that my mother had told me about the people who lived by the ocean who were part Mer. He would try to kiss me, but I would pull away, letting his lips graze my jaw, my neck, and my temple but never my mouth. It became a game, one that I desperately wanted to lose. I feared what might happen to him if he kissed my lips after I'd ingested so much poison.

Our happiness made us careless. I must have looked too peaceful and content.

Solena was waiting for me in my chamber one night when I returned from the garden, the ghost of his lips on my skin.

"You should be more careful with whom you associate." Her voice came from the darkness. She told me how Rumin had cornered her, attacked her, and tried to ravage her in her own chamber just minutes ago. All the while her eyes shone the way they did when she was about to deliver a cruel taunt.

Gentle Rumin, with his sandy uniform and sideways smile—he would never attack anyone. But I knew better than to call out her lie. It would only spell his doom.

"Where was your bodyguard?" I asked through numb lips.

"I'd sent him for wine. Rumin must have been watching," Solena sobbed, though her eyes were dry. "He must be punished, Diya. You must poison him."

My heart stopped for three breaths.

"No," I said, and her eyes narrowed.

"What do you think will happen if I tell my father?" She tapped her chin. "I believe he'd have him hung from the Wall." She swept from the room, leaving me quaking.

After she left, I sat on my bed and counted the silver over and over again. Two dozen. Not yet enough.

I paced, knotting and unknotting my fists. We could take a horse and ride away together. Surely the Master of Horses would be willing to trade the silvers I had for a horse.

I'd come back for Mother as soon as I could.

The door opened and I swung around, prepared to see Solena. Instead, Najma stood in front of me. "What are you doing here!" I snapped. She flinched and I took a deep breath. "I'm sorry, Little Crocodile. You frightened me. I would love it if you could knock." I stepped in front of the silver on the bed, trying to block it from view.

"You can't leave," she said.

"Leave? What makes you say that?" My voice was too high, too bright.

She glared. "I heard Solena. I know you love Rumin."

My façade crumbled. "Please, Najma. Try to understand. I don't want anything to happen to him."

She crossed her arms.

I took a deep breath. "Najma, please don't tell your father. Or Solena."

"Father will let him go." Relief coursed through me, but only for a moment. "But if you go, too, Father will kill him."

I knew she was right. "He'll have to catch us," I tell her with more bravado than I felt. "It would help if you didn't tell him anything." Turning, I began to gather the silver.

"It won't matter," she said. "Do you really think the Master of Horses will sell you the fastest horse? Father will catch you."

Her words gave me pause, but only for a moment. "That's a chance we will have to take." I dumped handfuls of silver into the bag I usually used for gathering.

"There were other bones," she said.

"What?" I turned.

"Before you arrived there was another set of bones hanging on the Wall. They're gone now—they finally slipped out of their chains and fell. They're buried in the sand." I searched her face, but her expression was as unreadable as ever. She might have been making up the story just to stop me, but I couldn't tell.

"He had flirted with Mother, and Father got angry. When the man tried to ride away on a horse, Father caught him. The next morning he was hanging from the Wall in chains."

I stared at her. "How do you know about this?" She must have been a small child when this happened.

"Solena told me."

"Then it was most likely to scare you." At least I hoped so.

"I saw them." She looked over her shoulder as Solena called from the gallery. She slipped through the door in an instant. A moment later I heard Solena's voice raised in question, and Najma's quiet answer.

I sat on the bed and pressed the heels of my hands into my eyes.

Najma might have been trying to prevent me from leaving, but I couldn't take that chance. With two of us, even the fastest horse could be overtaken. I had to convince him to go without me. If he hesitated, even for a moment, Solena would follow through on her promise, and then I'd be visiting his bones at the Wall every night. I couldn't risk it.

So I added some swayleaf to dreamsigh and let my tears fall into the mixture as I stirred it into a cream that I spread over my lips. My mouth burned, but I welcomed the pain.

That night he met me in the garden, the scorpions hissing in the shadows. When he held out his arms, I fell into them, as I had so many times before. The tears in my eyes burned with the poison that filled my body. His forehead creased, but before he could ask what was wrong, I pressed my lips to his, kissing him deeply, tasting the sweat, the sandalwood, and the sweet drink he favored. His arms tightened around me as he returned my kiss. The leaves whispered around us, and for a moment I believed that everything might be all right.

But then his arms grew slack and he pulled away. He blinked, already drowsy from the poison on my lips. The tears spilled from my eyes, burning my cheeks in narrow trails.

"Let's lie down," I breathed, pulling him with me and resting his head in my lap as we settled into the moss.

His hair was wiry and gritty with sand in my fingertips. I swallowed a sob as his eyes drooped closed, and I leaned close to his ear. "Badriya is poison," I told him, forcing the words out. "She doesn't love you. She only wants you to believe that she does. All of the whispers you've heard are true. You must run from here and never come back. Or you'll die." I paused for a moment. "To Mera," I added. I slipped ten of my silvers into his pocket. "Use this to buy a horse, but save some for the Witches."

Brushing my lips against his forehead, blinded by my tears, I stood and slipped beneath the arms of the willow tree. I waited there until he woke, passing a hand over his eyes as if wiping away cobwebs. I watched his expression harden as he leaped to his feet, eyes darting about, and then rushed from the garden. Slowly I climbed the steps to the Wall. The night held its breath, waiting with me. I tipped my head back and counted the three stars in the tail of the Scorpion.

The silence was broken by the pounding of hooves as a great horse streaked across the sand, its rider's too-long hair flying about his face. They raced straight toward the point on the horizon where we'd seen the Lights of Mera.

I wiped the poison from my lips with the back of my hand. I watched them until they were lost in my tears. No amount of poison I'd swallowed had ever hurt as much as this. The forsaken princess began to wail from the Lost.

In the next instant the King was at my side. He stood so close that his breath was at my ear. I turned, startled, and he smiled gently. "It's only me, Badriya," he said, and laid a hand on my waist, sliding it to my hip. I could smell the wine, sour and spicy, lacing his breath. "But where is the gift I gave you?" he asked, inspecting my wrist. I'd left it upstairs, buried in a drawer; I couldn't bear to look at it. I began to stammer out an excuse, but he spoke over me. "You must wear it. Always."

He leaned close, his eyes dark. "You look so much like her," he said. His lips were close enough to graze mine. I tried to pull away, but his arms locked around me.

The cry rose from the Lost again, and the King pulled away, looking sharply out into the Lost. His hands loosened and I pulled away, fleeing down the stairs.

Najma was right, I realized. The King hadn't bothered to pursue him. Rumin was safe because I'd let him go. The thought filled me with both relief and despair.

CHAPTER EIGHT

I wake up shivering, despite the sunlight pouring in through the window, once again wearing the clothes from the day before. My finger throbs and burns, and I reach for the pitcher of water on the table, drinking directly from it. Then I lie back, staring at the ceiling and thinking of Solena's visit the night before. Why had she agreed so quickly to my refusal to poison Mina?

No. I had poisoned Mina. I refused to poison Safiya. I close my eyes and their faces swim behind my eyes, their features blending into one in my mind.

I didn't help Mina, but I could try to help Safiya.

Forcing myself to rise, I grip the bedpost for support until the room steadies. I splash water on my face and change into clean clothes. It takes several tries to braid my hair, but I finally wrap a scarf around it and go look for Safiya.

If she were wise, she would be hiding in her chamber, but Safiya is not wise. She is most likely in the Gambling Hall, cherishing her victory and preparing for another, so I go there first.

The heat is already thick and oppressive, and not even the shade from the olive trees lining the path provides respite. Sweat pools on the back of my neck and trickles down my back. I pass a servant cleaning the stones in front of the Dining Hall, his movements slow. He averts his eyes as I pass.

I enter the shadowy coolness of the Gambling Hall, but the tables are empty at this hour. There is no whisper of cards or the jingling of coins, just the scent of stale wine, anxious gamblers, and the metallic smell of coins. I've come to equate it with the smell of risk, debts unpaid, and despair.

At least Safiya has the sense to stay hidden. Turning to leave, I catch my breath as a lean, tall figure fills the doorway. "Lady Badriya."

Is he mocking me by calling me Lady?

"Sir Khalen," I reply, unable to keep the impatience from my voice. "What brings you here? I am beginning to think you are following me."

"Aran is quite small. I was truly hoping to play Fortune with you last night. I do hope you're feeling better?"

"I just needed to sleep. Thank you for asking." I take a step forward, but he does not move.

"Do you feel well enough to join me?"

"Doesn't Prince Arlo need you?"

"He is reading. He cherishes his time alone. I sense you are a formidable gambler." He pats the purse at his waist. "And I have a lot of silver." Reaching his long fingers into the purse, he pulls out a thick coin. "Moons, as we call them in Tanera. Fitting name, isn't it? I think they are worth even more than your silvers."

I look over his shoulder into the courtyard, which is quiet at this hour. I should find Safiya and warn her. But then again, I am very good at Fortune, and he is right: the coin looks heavy, far heavier than the silvers hidden beneath my bed. They are sure to satisfy the Witch.

"I can see that you won't relent," I tell him with a sigh. "One game, then." I settle myself at one of the tables that is just out of sight of the doorway and he joins me. Opening the ornate carved box that houses the thick, worn cards, I spread them on the table to be sure that all the cards are there and unmarked, but there is no sign of duplicity. "Would you like to inspect them?" I ask Khalen.

"I don't know what to look for. I shall have to trust you."

"That's dangerous," I reply with a wicked smile. "Would you at least like to deal?"

He shuffles the cards a bit clumsily. Good. This promises to be easy. He deals the cards and I pick up my hand, studying his face over the tops of my cards. He keeps his expression blank as he plays a Wheel and then draws. I lay down a Hammer and draw another card.

"Such wonderful news," he says, playing another card. His voice is bland and distracted as he concentrates on the game.

"Oh?"

"About my Prince and your Queen."

"Ah, yes. Wonderful."

"You don't seem pleased."

"I am not sure how happy Prince Arlo will be in a marriage with Queen Solena. Is our kingdom really worthwhile?" I lay down a card and he snatches it up eagerly.

"As Arlo mentioned, it is a good stop on a direct trading route. The Lost is treacherous, as you know, so it would provide a safe oasis for caravans. Not to mention that being able to directly cross the Lost would also cut the journey in half." He frowns and begins to pull a card from his hand, then decides on another. The corner of his mouth twitches as he lays it down. "It is also beautiful—enchanted, perhaps, as the stories say."

Feigning nonchalance, I pretend to consider the card he's laid down before I finally pick it up with a sigh. "Outsiders do not fare well here."

"Have some of them ended up in the Crypts?" His face doesn't change as he studies his cards.

"No." I match my tone to his, light and careless, and look at my own cards without blinking. "Only citizens of Aran are buried there. I only meant that it is hard to fit in here. I speak from experience." I nod at his hand. "Are you going to play a card?"

"Don't worry. The Prince's primary home will still be Tanera, and I imagine your Queen will stay here. They might see each other a few weeks out of the year." He lays down another card, this one much less valuable. He is catching on to the game. "As might you and I." Again, his voice is bland. He might be jesting, but I can't tell.

"Not very often, then," I comment.

He glances at me with a raised eyebrow. "Could it be that you are sorry?"

Am I sorry? I think of the way he gripped the Wall as he searched the Lost and the way he rubbed his talisman. A kinship, I decide; someone else who is as haunted as I am. That is all I feel.

That's not what's important, I remind myself. What matters is winning his Moons. The corner of his mouth twitches and I smile. *His tell.* "Of course I am sorry. I am sorry that you will not be here more often so that I might take more of your silver." I lay down my hand triumphantly. "Fortune."

His brow furrows as he looks over my cards. "How does your hand beat mine?" he asks, displaying his cards. "I have a pair of nines, while you merely have a pair of fours."

"Mine are Hammers and yours are only Wheels."

"I should have known those would be the rules," he sighs, throwing down his cards in disgust.

As I stand, I hold out my hand for the Moons.

"Tell me, what will you do with all the silver you're collecting?" he asks as I slip the coin into the purse at my waist.

"That is a secret. You'll have to best me at Fortune if I am to tell you."

"Ah. Another round, then? I have a lot more Moons."

I look over his shoulder at the courtyard beyond the arched doorway. There will be time to warn Safiya later, I am sure.

"This time," he says as I sit back down on the stool, "if I win, you must tell me three secrets."

"Three secrets?" I sputter. "Then you must pay me three times our first wager if I win."

"Fair enough," he agrees.

"Shuffle," I direct him, jutting my chin at the cards. As he does, some of them skitter from the pile and fly across the table.

"I am surprised you agreed to this, as private as you are," he says as he retrieves the cards.

"I don't plan to lose."

He deals and makes a show of holding his cards high to hide his face. I can't help but laugh a little.

"Should Lady Safiya be concerned? Your sister seemed quite annoyed with her last night."

"She's not my sister." I retrieve the Hammer that he's laid down. Has he learned nothing?

"How could I forget? Let me try again: Queen Solena seemed quite annoyed with Lady Safiya last night." He considers the Gem that I've discarded, studies his hand, and then draws a card from the deck.

"The Queen does not like to lose." He lays down another Hammer. I consider warning him, but then remember the Moons in his purse and take the card for myself.

"Is she in danger?"

"Probably," I reply. "It is not wise to risk the ire of the Queen, especially deliberately. Your Prince should be careful."

"I doubt anything nefarious will befall my Prince. Our army would hardly sit back and allow our Prince's untimely death to go unavenged." His voice is light and distracted, but there is an edge to his words.

He picks up a card and discards another. The corner of his mouth twitches again.

"Fortune." I lay down my cards. I don't have a strong hand, but I suspect it is better than his, and I am right. He curses as he lays down his cards.

"Moons, please." Reaching into his purse, he slaps three coins down in disgust.

"Have you lost enough?" I ask as I slip the coins into my purse.

"No. We'll play again," he says, scowling. "And this time, if you win you can have the rest of my Moons."

"Are you sure you want to risk it?" I ask, raising an eyebrow.

"Yes. Remember, if I win you owe me three secrets."

Giddy with how close I am to my goal, I agree. "Very well. I will deal this time." I deftly shuffle the cards and flick them back and forth until we each have a pile before us.

Again, my hand is not strong. I watch his mouth for the telltale twitch as his brow furrows in concentration.

"Who do you see when you look over the Wall?" he asks as he draws a card.

I force my expression to stay neutral, but I study my cards a beat too long. "No one. There is only sand." I take a card and discard another. "I might ask you the same."

"I wondered if you might be remembering a lost love," he says.

I force a laugh as he takes a card. Without looking at it, he discards another. Feeling his eyes on me, I force myself to meet his gaze. "You'd be a fool to fall in love in this city," I say, and return to my cards, suddenly indecisive. Which should I discard?

"I am saddened to hear that." Is that a thread of regret in his voice? Before I can stop myself, I look up, trying to read his expression.

"For the sake of my Prince and your Queen, of course."

"Of course." *Idiot*, I curse myself. *What are you, a child?* I snatch a card from my hand and discard it.

"Fortune!" I look up to see him grinning in triumph, his cards laid out before me. Slowly I lay down my own hand. His easily beats mine. He winks. "I'm not the only one with tells."

My mind whirls. *What are my tells? How did I let this stranger use my own weaknesses, my own arrogance, against me?* "Well played, Lord Khalen," I tell him as I rise.

"Where are you going?" he asks, catching my hand.

I try to pull away, but his grip is strong. "I have other things to do besides play cards. I'm sure you understand."

"You have not paid your debt, My Lady. Our wager was three secrets."

I am furious. Who does he think he is? I vow to sprinkle powdered rageroot into the honey he loves so much. His insides will feel as though they are on fire, and then he will regret ever wagering with me. Or flirting with me, for that matter.

"Very well." He releases my hand as I sit back on the stool and school my features into a smooth smile. "What would you like to know?"

He leans forward. "Why are you saving silver?"

Perhaps this will be easier than I thought. "For a new gown."

He rolls his eyes. "Please. Don't treat me like a fool."

Maybe a half-truth will satisfy him. "To repay a debt."

"Gambling?" he asks, tilting his head.

"Yes." That is true enough. My mother did gamble her soul for my safety. "I was once as obsessed with Fortune as Safiya."

"Hmm. And to whom do you owe this debt?"

"Is that your second question?"

"No." He holds up his hand, then taps his chin, thinking. "What befell the Duke of Dorros while he was here?" he asks, his voice hardening.

This I expected. I shake my head, spreading my hands. "He suffered an ailment of the heart that was so severe we all thought he was dead. Fortunately, he woke during the journey back to Dorros before they could burn his body."

His third question comes swiftly. "What did you force Yadira to do the night the Duke died?"

My heart beats faster, pumping the poison that runs in my blood through my body. For a moment I feel dizzy, but I try to keep my face composed as I answer. "The Duke didn't die."

"Then what did Yadira mean that night in the garden?"

Forcing a smile, I reply. "She hardly knows what she is saying. As you noted, she is addicted to Stardust."

"Stardust that you've sold to her."

I raise my chin. "She is a grown woman. I'm not responsible for her choices."

He leans forward, his eyes dark. "Here is what I believe." All the blandness is gone from his voice. "I think the Duke was poisoned, and his would-be assassin was so skilled that she knew how to give him just enough so that he would seem dead but would wake later when he was well away from here. And I think Yadira was tasked with distracting the Duke's bodyguard so that the poison could be administered. Am I correct?"

For a long moment the only sound is our breathing.

"Am I correct?" he asks again.

"That would be a fourth question, and you've already asked your three." I stand and exit the Gambling Hall without turning back, the Moons heavy at my waist.

THEN

Here is a secret Khalen might have found far more interesting: the King died on a night when the Wind Demons scratched at the walls of the city, hissing poisonous words and laughing at the despair they wreaked. The Snake appeared early, when the sky was still vermillion but not completely dark.

Before dark, the gentlest servant woman slapped her child across his face. The most skilled meat-cutter sliced his finger and ruined a roast with his blood. Theron played the wrong notes over and over again.

Rumin had been gone for weeks. Desperate to escape into sleep, I drank tea infused with amounts of slumberweed that would be poisonous to anyone else. I finally resorted to chewing it, though the bitterness burned my mouth and tongue and made my eyes weep. But nothing helped. Instead, I was trapped between wakefulness and slumber, the world a place of half-formed nightmares.

It didn't help that I'd eaten almost nothing, only bites of what Petra or Najma brought me. I didn't leave my chamber until a servant was sent to fetch me on orders of the King.

At breakfast the King's eyes followed me like a hungry ghost. I sat as far from him as I could, pretending not to hear when he called to me. When he finally rose and moved toward me, I stood and fled the Hall. I'd never been so grateful to hear Solena's voice calling for her father. He hesitated long enough for me to duck out of the Dining Hall and out of sight.

All day long the wind howled and the demons in the Lost scratched at the Wall. I took refuge in the garden, pulling out greedy weeds and trimming the vines that ran like long, thin arms through the grass.

The willow branches rustled as they were pushed aside. I'd been looking over my shoulder all day, but he had never followed me to the garden. I kept hearing my mother's singing, even from my chamber. Perhaps he did, too, and now he'd followed it here.

The King stood above me, swaying slightly, gripping yet another bottle. He blinked slowly, his eyes focused blearily on my face. It was only midday. "Narisa."

"I'm Badriya," I told him, my lips numb from the slumberweed, lack of sleep, and fear—maybe all three. I rose clumsily to my feet and took a step back, but he followed me.

"Narisa."

A vine caught my foot and I stumbled against a tree trunk. He lay his hand against my cheek, wound his fingers into my hair, and moved his face close to mine, his eyes half-closed. The smell of wine on his breath was overwhelming. I turned my face away, but he took hold of my chin and forced me to face him. "Why did you leave me?" His teeth were bared and his eyes blazed.

"I'm Badriya." My voice was a fearful squeak.

He leaned in so close that I could smell something else on his breath—a trace of licorice. Fairy Green? His fingers tightened in my hair. "Have you come back to mock me?" He asked, spraying my face with flecks of spittle. "Do you want me to beg? You chose to die in the desert over a life of comfort with me!"

I gasped as his fingers wrapped around my neck. I tried to tear away, but I stumbled and dropped to the ground. The King fell on top of me, pressing me into the roots of the tree.

His mouth closed over mine. I couldn't breathe. My chest burned as I struggled beneath his weight. Blackness formed at the edges of my vision. From somewhere in the distance, I heard my mother's voice raised in the sad song that she sang on the bleakest nights.

Suddenly the King's mouth went slack and his hands slid from me. His weight on me was motionless—dead weight.

I fought my way out from under him, drawing in great gulps of air, and sat up. The King was beside me, his eyes half-open, pupils dilated; there was no brown left in them, only black. His mouth was open, tongue half-hanging out. It was black too. He was dead.

I vomited into the leaves, tasting the poisons that had killed him: the bitterness of the slumberweed and bitterthorn on my breath.

I rose unsteadily to my feet, wiping my mouth with the back of my hand, and knelt beside the King's body. My heart pounded and rattled, my thoughts tumbling tumultuously over one another; I couldn't pick out one from the rest.

"What happened?" The King's favorite bodyguard stood before the willow branches. His eyes fell on the King. "What happened?" he repeated, this time his voice was a terrified whisper. "What did you do?" He rushed forward to grab me by the arm.

"It was an accident!" I stammered. "He drank too much! He wasn't himself!" The guard was already shouting, pinning my arms behind me.

"Take your hands off her." The guard fell silent, then bowed. Solena stood at the entrance to the garden. "Surely you are not implying that she murdered him."

The bodyguard dropped my arm as if it burned. "Go. Get a physician," she said.

The man hesitated a moment longer, his jaw tightening as he looked once more at the King, then he raced from the garden.

Slowly Solena moved to her father's lifeless body, pressing her lips together as she gazed down at him. The rims of her eyes reddened. "You fool," she breathed. Her hands balled into fists and she pounded them against her legs. One, two, three.

"I did nothing!" My voice slurred with poison and shock.

She looked up at me. "Make no mistake," she hissed, "you murdered my father. Look at you. You knew exactly what you were doing."

The world blurred, then sharpened, then blurred again. "I didn't!" I felt as though I were shouting, but my voice was no more than a squeak.

"You will do as I say, or you will hang on the Wall," Solena said. "Now go and hide." I closed my mouth; it didn't matter what I said. All that mattered now was what Solena pronounced. Even through my disorientation I could see that. It wouldn't matter that everyone saw how the King followed me, grasped me as though I belonged to him, kissed me as if I were his to possess. I would be the one who had lured the King to his death, just as my mother was the one who had bewitched him.

I retreated to my chamber and buried myself in my bed. Outside, footsteps thundered across the gallery and shouts echoed against the walls.

"Call the physician!"

"It is too late."

"Carry him to his bed!"

"It is too late, I tell you!"

"What happened?"

My stomach twisted. I curled up in bed and pulled the sheets over my head, shivering. My bones quaked and my teeth chattered. I wrapped myself in the covers and shivered there until dawn, pushing back the memories of what had happened in the garden.

The King was buried at dusk, on a night when the air was hot even after sunset. The sun had been an angry red all day, and tonight the shadows were tinged with crimson. His body was wrapped in a sweet-smelling cloth, but I still covered my nose against a sour, desperate odor. He was taken inside the Crypts to be interred with his wife.

Mina sang, her voice soft and sad in the night air. Theron's fingers were poised to play his lute, but instead he watched Mina. Najma sobbed and Solena put her arm around her shoulders, careful to keep her face away from her gown as tears dripped from her chin. Solena's face was pale and her eyes were rimmed in red, but no tears fell. They couldn't anymore, thanks to the Stardust.

I stood behind everyone else, my nails cutting into my palms. I'd wanted to stay huddled in my chamber, but one of Solena's guards had escorted me to the ceremony. He stood in the doorway until I accompanied him, even though my hair was not brushed and I still wore my worn tunic and pants.

Another voice rose, winding in harmony with Mina's. I knew it came from behind the Wall, yet it floated among us as if the singer stood beside Mina. My heart quickened. Najma looked up as if she heard the second voice, too, but everyone else kept their eyes fixed on Mina.

Afterward, I pulled my scarf tighter around my face and slipped away through the crowd, past the fountain and the garden where Theron held Mina in his arms. I slipped through the willow door to my mother's garden and up the stairs to the Wall.

The sand was washed in red. My mother danced just as she had with the King, her arms curved over her head, spinning and leaping as she sang. The scent of water hung in the air, and in my memory I saw the ocean spreading out from my toes, my skin sticky from the salt.

As the moon rose, scarlet and shaped like a blade, so did the King. There was a flicker in the air beside my mother, and then he stood beside her, his hands stretched toward her as if he were asking her to dance. She didn't see him, spinning and leaping on her own.

Her voice died away as the sky lightened. The stars faded until even the Snake was gone. The King and my mother vanished as well. The smell of the ocean faded and the air grew dry again. There was nowhere to go but back to my chamber.

With the first light there was a gentle knock at the door. I heard it open and light footsteps drew near. I caught the faint scent of tube-roses as I peered from beneath the covers to see Petra, her face as pale as marble. "Badriya?"

"Yes," I said, my mouth as dry as sand.

"Queen Solena bids you to come to her chamber."

I closed my eyes.

"Now," Petra said. "I'm sorry," she added before she turned and left.

Solena's chamber was hung with dark cloth. Lilies spilled from a vase on the table; their sweet scent hung heavy in the warm air. Solena stood in the center of the room, staring into space, her face pale.

I fell to my knees. "My Lady. I am so sorry…"

Solena swept toward me, nearly trampling me. "You murdered my father. I will never forgive you for that."

My heart hammered. "No, no, it was an accident. Listen…"

"My father enjoyed his wine, but not once did he ever drink enough to become ill. The whole court saw you dancing with him. You drove my mother to her death, and then you lured him into the garden and poisoned him."

I shook my head. "I would never…"

"You wanted what you couldn't have, just like your mother." Her eyes narrowed. "Perhaps you are a slattern like she was, trying to seduce him like she did, and when he refused…" She shook her head, biting her lip.

I felt as though I might be sick. "That's not what happened." My voice was only a rasp. "It was him," I said, swallowing hard. "He came to me and kissed me…" *Kissed* wasn't an adequate description, but I couldn't bear to describe the weight of his body or the feel of his tongue pushing into my mouth.

She took a step toward me. "Do you expect anyone to believe that?" she whispered. "Everyone knows your mother bewitched him. Everyone saw you dancing together and accepting his gifts. You will be hung from the Wall like the traitorous Witch that you are. The crows will tear at you and the sun will cook you until there is nothing left but bones. When your bones finally slip from the chains, you'll fall into the sand and be swallowed down into hell."

I began to sob so hard that I couldn't breathe. *Please*, I thought, *please, please, please…*

"But," she said. I looked up, blinded by tears that burned but refused to fall. "I can't do that to Najma. For some reason she is attached to you. I can't do this to her, not after everything else…" She tightened her lips and made a fist, turning her face away. Were I not already in such shock I would have been stunned that she felt grief. She drew a breath. "We will say that he drank too much and stumbled into your garden, then collapsed there. You were the one to find him. His death wasn't your fault."

"Thank you," I breathed. But I should have seen the trap.

She studied my face and gave a short laugh. "Look at you," she said, "pretending to grieve. You can't even cry for him, can you?"

I'm too full of poison to cry anymore, I realized.

Her fingertips pressed into my cheek and I cried out as she raked them down my face. "You owe me," she said, bringing her face close to mine. "At any time I can tell everyone how you seduced the King and then murdered him. Any moment, Diya." She clutched my chin in her fingers, her eyes burning into mine. "I could have you killed. I could kill you myself and no one would blame me."

I pressed my fists against my face. The wound on my cheek throbbed.

She released me abruptly. "I will be merciful, though, as my father was. I will allow you to atone for what you've done. For your first act of atonement, you will rid me of Mina."

Mina, with her voice that hung like honey in the air as it accompanied the musicians.

I lowered my hands. "What?"

She began to pace. "She's stolen him. He loves her now and not me."

I shook my head. "He's dead."

Solena whirled, balling her hands into fists, her dark pupils filling her eyes. "Not my father, you imbecile. Theron."

Theron, the young lute player with a thin face and hair that fell in his eyes. I shook my head, trying to clear it. "How could Mina steal Theron?"

"His heart was once mine, but now he looks only at her." She resumed her pacing. "She's not even beautiful. She has that awful scrawny face with those bulging eyes."

No one could tear their eyes away from her when she sang, her head tilted back, slender throat exposed, her voice pouring from her to fill the Hall. All of us were under the spell of her voice as surely as if it were Stardust, especially Theron.

"She's always singing to get his attention. On the pathways, at dinner." She made a face.

Theron would often forget to strum the chords of his lute as she sang. Solena watched him with a smile that showed her teeth, running her blood-red nails along the table.

She is going mad from grief, I thought. *Or the cosmetics.*

"You must poison her," Solena said.

I swallowed. "Poison her? How would I do that?"

"Do you take me for an idiot? I know your mother taught you!"

"No, she would never—"

Solena picked up a vase of lilies and threw it to the ground where it shattered against the stone. "You will."

"No." My whole body quivered. I'd never seen her like this.

She plucked a lily from the ground and thrust it at me. "You owe me. You took my father from me, so you will do this for me. And if you don't, I will tell everyone what you did. Then you will hang from the Wall and the crows will tear your skin from your bones." She pushed the lily into my hand. "You will poison her."

I trembled so hard that my teeth rattled. But I nodded and she smiled, her eyes black and her lips red.

The next morning I entered the Dining Hall carrying a basket of pears. Each one had been soaked in a sauce that would eventually eat holes in the stomach of anyone who consumed them. To everyone else they looked and smelled as though they'd been soaked in brandy.

My head ached with regret and fear. If only I could let my tears fall, some of the pain might ease, but instead my eyes burned.

Theron sat on the musician's dais strumming his lute; Mina sat at his feet, smiling as she gazed up at him.

I wondered what Mother would say. She had never meant for our magic to hurt anyone—to kill anyone.

And yet it had.

I waited until Theron left to speak with the piper before sitting beside Mina.

"You must stop flirting with Theron," I breathed.

She looked at me with disdain. "You don't frighten me."

"It's not me you should be frightened of," I told her.

"Theron!" she called, her eyes dancing. In a voice that was loud enough for everyone in the Dining Hall to hear, she said, "I think the little orphan is in love with you." Laughter rippled around the court. Yadira's shoulders shook and Petra rolled her eyes. Solena smiled behind her fingers. Theron turned back to the piper, his expression unchanged. My cheeks flamed furiously and I fled the Hall with the basket of pears.

For a time I thought about giving Mina a potion that would make her clutch at her throat and fall to her knees, beseeching me for mercy with her eyes because she would no longer be able to speak. I even began to mix it, but then I thought of the King lying in the garden gasping for breath and ended up pouring the potion out the window.

Instead, I mixed something that would only hurt Mina's vocal cords: she would have a sore throat and her voice would be raw and gravelly for a few days. I hoped she would take it as the warning it was meant to be. Then she would return to singing ballads, never again looking at Theron or taunting me again.

But the anger I felt must have made its way into the drink I created. The liquid was perhaps a bit more amber than it should have been, the smell more bitter.

The next evening, she sang to Theron's lute, her voice rich and seductive as the court sat transfixed.

The spell of her voice still hung in the air as I approached her. "I'm sorry for how I've acted," I told her, my voice as repentant as I could make it. "I know your throat gets sore after a performance, especially one as breathtaking as that. I've mixed you a tincture to help. Please take it." I offered her the glass.

Her eyes narrowed. "Did you spit in this, little orphan?"

I forced myself to smile, though it must have been more of a grimace. "Of course not." I lowered my eyes. "I really am sorry for how I've acted."

She studied me for a long moment, and I held my breath. "I accept your apology," she said at last, and began to drink.

She was truly arrogant if she couldn't sense the resentment, fear, and anger in the drink. If she only knew the truth about the King's death, she wouldn't be so amused.

For a moment I thought about knocking the glass from her hand and warning her, but I waited until she drained the liquid before I turned and rushed from the Hall, the poison dripping from my fingertips.

For days I waited in my room. I knew better than to try to sleep or take a potion to help, so I worked feverishly through the night creating sleeping draughts, scents for luck, and salves for burns. On the second evening, I was thinking of slipping out to my garden while everyone was at dinner when there was a knock at my door. I opened it expecting to find a servant with a tray of food but instead I saw Petra.

"The Queen bids you to come to dinner," she said. I opened my mouth to ask a question, but she shook her head slightly and turned away, leading me into the gallery and down the stairs.

Music floated from the Hall and the usual chatter filled the room, but there was no singing. On the musicians' dais Theron plucked at the lute as he stared at the ground, his eyes shining with tears.

Gossip rippled through the Hall, whispered into bejeweled ears and mouthed over ornate goblets. "Her face is ruined. Her voice…" Eyes flickered to me and then looked away. There was no laughter or insults cast my way.

Good, I thought savagely. *They should be afraid of me.* I took a long drink from my goblet. It burned slightly as it passed down my throat and I wondered if it was poisoned, which only made me laugh. I was already too full of venom for any of it to affect me now.

I looked over at Solena, who raised her glass to me, a smile playing on her lips. My mouth was too inflamed with poison to return her smile, so I took another drink and looked away.

Later that night there was a knock at my door so soft it might have been a scratch. I was not surprised to see Mina on the other side.

She pulled down her scarf, revealing the lower half of her face where the poison had burned away her flesh. Her chin and the skin around her mouth was blistered and wrinkled. "You should have killed me," she said through her ruined lips in a voice that was barely a whisper.

"You're lucky," I told her. "She wanted me to kill you."

She slipped away without answering.

The next morning Solena summoned me to her chamber.

"What are you wearing?" she demanded.

I looked down at the tunic and pants I'd worn in Mera, which were now far too short and stretched across my shoulders. Mother's cloak was so stretched that it nearly touched the floor.

I heard a hiss from a corner. "I think you have scorpions in here," I told her. My voice was slurred. I was still floating between waking and nightmares.

"There are no scorpions here," Solena snapped. "Now, explain to me why Mina is still alive."

I shook my head and forced myself to focus. "I don't understand. It should have killed her. But who will ever look at her again?" I pushed away the memory of Theron, sadly strumming on his lute. "And she'll never sing again; the poison likely ruined her vocal cords." Solena's eyes narrowed. "For her that is worse than death," I said quickly.

Solena studied me for a long moment, tapping her nails against the table. One, two, three. I held my breath.

A smile played about her mouth. "Mina probably wishes she were dead. You've punished her more effectively than I hoped." She leaned forward suddenly, her smile vanishing. "But do not think that I have forgotten your crime or what you've taken from me. Do not forget that I can have you executed for what you've done. Your debt has only grown. Do you understand me, Diya?"

"Of course, My Queen," I said, bowing my head. I scrambled from the room like a scorpion.

The next morning Mina returned to the Dining Hall as a server. Though Theron's eyes followed her, and he only played plaintive, mournful music, she wouldn't look at him, pulling her scarf around her face whenever she passed. Sometimes when she passed by I heard her singing so low that I might have imagined it. She tried to hover in the background and lose herself among the other servants, but Solena called for her often asking for wine, more olives, and for her to clear her plate. "You've become my favorite servant," she told Mina sweetly. "Besides Diya, of course."

CHAPTER NINE

Ninety-one silvers and four heavy Moons that I won from Khalen. Hopefully the Witch will think they are worth more than the silver. It is nearly enough to free my mother, but not enough to appease the Duke's Witch. I could offer my tears, but they won't fall anymore.

The Snake lies in wait in the sky, but the outline of the Bat's wings are brighter than they were the previous night.

Despite what I told Yadira, I must make more Stardust. It's my only chance to gather enough silver. I push away the vision of Yadira's gaunt face and the hunger in her eyes.

The preparations have begun in earnest for the Festival of the Full Moon. It is always celebrated when the Snake is in the sky, which is reckless, but it also perfectly describes Aran.

Servants drape chains of shining paper from the olive trees and hang stars from the branches. In the brightness of the day they look ordinary, but when the moonlight washes over them they will look magical.

As part of a tradition started years ago by the King, Petra and Yadira scatter jewels that belonged to the King's mother and grandmother into the grass for children to find. Only the pieces that that were deemed too ugly and old-fashioned are used, of course. Petra looks for hiding places between the roots of trees and beneath stones, while Yadira scatters them haphazardly.

Inside my chamber I begin preparations of my own.

I have just raised the knife's blade to my wrist when I hear Solena's voice behind me. "I came to see how Safiya will meet her end."

Lowering my knife, I catch a glimpse of her bodyguard standing just outside the door. "Do you no longer care who hears?"

She shrugs. "It will be your bones that hang from the Wall, not mine."

She is especially pale today; I can see fragile veins pulsing through her translucent skin.

How much longer can she withstand the poison, I wonder. She should have succumbed to the belladonna by now, if not the arsenic.

I resume chopping, my cuts clumsy and awkward. But it's too late, I've studied her too long. "Diya? Do you have a plan for Safiya?"

"Yes," I sigh.

"And it will be done tonight?"

"What is the rush? Neither she nor her silver are going anywhere."

"Because I command it." Her voice is as sharp as broken tile.

"As you wish," I reply, my eyes on the acheroot. The pieces are cut oddly and their edges are ragged—they will cause whoever consumes them to lose their memory.

Solena leaves as silently as she arrived. I grind the Stardust, dreamroot, and fortunescent until my fingers are sore. My customers will be sorely upset when they discover that I've doubled the cost.

The musky scent of white lilies fills the air. The paper stars gleam overhead in the lamplight. Musicians pound their drums, strum their lutes, and blow their pipes, creating a weave of melodies that is both familiar and strange. A band of children carrying swords made of shiny paper and wearing crowns of stars thread their way through the grass, peering intently downward, looking for hidden treasure. A little girl gives a triumphant cry as she snatches a pretty stone from the ground and holds it aloft.

My throat tightens as I watch them. My first year here I had joined the children, thrilled to find a milky stone, hard and cool. "My mother hated that ring," Solena said at my shoulder. "She tried to give it to me but I wouldn't take it. You can have it, though, if you like it." Seeing the curl to her lips and the gleam in her eye, I dropped it back into the grass when she wasn't looking.

Earlier I had gone to Safiya's chamber and knocked, but there was no answer. I looked for her in the Dining Hall, the Gambling Hall, and even the White Garden, but Safiya was nowhere to be found.

Maybe she didn't need a warning; perhaps she had already come to her senses and planned to stay hidden away. I hoped so.

The music is lively, Theron's lute merry and joyful for once rather than plaintive. This is a night of mystery, after all, a night when anything can happen. I spy Mina among the dancers. Though her scarf is wound about her face, she weaves and sways with her eyes closed and her head tilted to the moon. Theron's eyes follow her, lit with longing. *Don't let Solena see you*, I beg silently.

Yadira drifts across the grass, oblivious to the revelry around her, and collides with Mina. Mina hardly notices but Yadira tumbles to the ground. She merely lies there, staring up at the sky.

I take a step toward her but someone has already reached her— one of Arlo's entourage: a solemn boy with watery eyes. He helps her up and guides her to the fountain where they both sit. She turns her head and seems to see him for the first time as he speaks to her.

Petra appears at my side, lilies winding up her arms. She hands me a glass of wine. "Here, you look like you need this. Your hair looks terrible," she adds as I take the wine.

"Thank you," I tell her. "That gown is horrible."

She runs a hand over the fabric. She knows that the gown brings out the unusual color of her eyes, and I know that my hair glows because of the moonflower petals I rinsed it in earlier. But we have fallen into the habit of pretending to be enemies, and it has become as comfortable as friendship.

"So, what is between you and the Prince's adviser?" she asks.

"Absolutely nothing." I realize that I've answered too quickly when she raises an eyebrow. "No, really. He is abhorrent."

"Solena has asked," Petra says carefully. "I thought you should know."

I'll be gone before she can punish him, I promise myself. And then I wonder, *why should I care?*

"Have you seen Najma tonight?" Petra asks.

"What?" My gaze whips back to her.

"I think someone has given her some wine."

"Lady Petra, will you dance?" It is a tall courtier from Arlo's entourage who stands bowed with his hand extended. With a radiant smile she takes his hand and twirls around him. He sways uncertainly, his eyes wide.

My heart beats in tune with the drums as my eyes search the crowds. Where is Najma? What does Petra's warning mean?

Mina sits beside Theron as he drinks her in, his lute forgotten in his lap. Solena didn't take into account that it wasn't Mina's face that he fell in love with, but her voice and her laughter, just like the Queen believed that my mother had bewitched her husband. After all, how could such a plain woman win his heart? The Queen never thought that someone could fall in love with the joy of a dance or with laughter.

Solena will always equate beauty with appearance, just as her mother did.

All around, couples twirl and laugh, reaching for the paper stars in the trees and drinking wine.

My eyes fall on Safiya as she strolls across the grass, her head tipped toward the sky and her eyes filled with starlight. I can tell by her unsteady walk that she's had enough wine for her guard to be down.

Najma materializes at her side, blocking her path, and offers her a goblet. Safiya dips her head in gratitude and surprise, then reaches for the offering. It is the way Najma's eyes slide away and the abrupt jerk of her shoulders that alerts me that the wine is poisoned.

I've been a fool. Of course Najma has watched me closely enough all this time to learn how to mix the potions and cosmetics, and of course Solena would not have missed that.

I can't let her become poisonous and let the darkness eat away at her the way it has me.

I stride forward and Najma's eyes fall on me. Without a word, she flees, still holding the goblet. Safiya turns and her eyes widen when she sees me. She takes a step back.

"You should be mindful about what's offered to you on nights like these. It's hard to guess people's intentions."

Safiya bows her head. "Thank you," she says quietly, and slips away. I hope she has the sense to stay out of Solena's sight.

I scan the revelers for Najma. White wine glows in goblets as courtiers dance with abandon to the drums and pipes. Petra is still caught in the arms of the boyish courtier, her laughter carrying over the crowd. Solena watches from the dais, her face pale in the moonlight. Arlo stands beside her.

Najma is nowhere to be seen.

"Will you dance with me?"

Startled, I look behind me to see Khalen with his hand extended.

"No." Turning away, I continue to search the crowd. *I do not have time for this right now.*

"Are you still angry with me? Forgive me. I have overstepped my bounds yet again. I am truly more chivalrous than this, most of the time. Perhaps you make me more nervous than I am accustomed to feeling."

He is babbling. I eye him with suspicion; he is probably play-acting again, hoping to trick me into revealing more than I should.

"Are you looking for someone?" he asks.

"My sister. This Festival can get too raucous sometimes."

The musicians finish their song with a great burst of drumbeats. Prince Arlo stands nearby, watching with his lute slung over his shoulder until Theron waves him forward. A broad smile spreads across Arlo's face. Moving forward, he stands beside Theron and strums along enthusiastically.

"Your Prince enjoys music," I observe. Then, just beyond the stage I catch a glimpse of dark eyes watching. I stride across the grass.

I should have looked here first. She stands just behind a thicket of tuberoses with only her eyes showing; she is used to hiding, fading into the background, and listening. She holds the goblet of wine that glows in the moonlight as if it were enchanted.

"Why aren't you out searching for treasure?"

Her eyes narrow, as I knew they would. "I'm too old for that."

"Well, you're certainly too young for that." I nod at the wine.

"You always do that. You always say I'm too young." Her eyes blaze even more intensely than her sister's. I change tactics.

"Then come and dance with me. Why are you hiding? You look beautiful. You should be enjoying the Festival." She doesn't move. "Najma, what did she offer you?"

I lean over so that my face is so close to hers that I can smell the chocolate she had for dessert on her breath. Her eyes slide away. I pinch her arm and give her a shake. "Najma."

She scowls. "Nothing."

"Her sapphire necklace? Her silver scarf?"

Her eyes narrow and I instantly regret it. Of course she wouldn't do something so dark in exchange for a scarf.

The cook's son rushes past us, a streamer trailing behind him and a troupe of children racing after him. Something catches in my chest; she should be chasing these children, searching for trinkets, laughing.

I lift the glass to my nose and breathe in the fumes. White wine, dry and sweet, but with an undertone of metal, pain, and grief. There is only the faintest thread of bitterness that betrays the poison that would force whoever drank it to relive every moment of grief, sadness, and anger in their life. And if there weren't enough of those, it would twist any moment of happiness into one of darkness.

"This is poison," I tell her. "I've mixed this myself." She looks past me at the dancers, the cook's son, and the game of tag.

"Listen to me." I take her shoulders, so fragile they are like the wings of a bird. She jerks away. "Don't follow her orders, no matter what she promises. Find me and I'll do it."

She doesn't respond. "Najma. It changes you."

She sighs and shifts, rolling her eyes. Then her gaze focuses on something just over my shoulder and a small smile touches her lips. "Hello, Khalen," she says, and for a moment she looks just like Solena.

I feel a zip like lightning up and down my spine. Khalen stands just behind me. *Can he not leave me alone for a moment? What did he hear?* The drums beat a wild rhythm as the pipes trill.

"You are far too young for this," I scold loudly for Khalen's benefit. "Don't ever let me catch you drinking wine again. What would the Queen say? Now get yourself back to the Festival. And stay where I can see you."

She looks up at me, resentment sparking in her eyes. Then she stalks off, her shoulders stiff and her chin jutted.

"She was bound to try it sometime. She's coming to that age." He nods at the glass.

"Yes." I force a wry smile. The wine winks in the moonlight. But she is still too young to understand that you become the poisons you mix. This is all a game for her, and the prize is Solena's approval.

"There'd be no harm in letting her try. Would there?"

I shake my head, feigning regret. "Her father was known to be obsessed with it. There's no sense in exposing her too early."

"Perhaps you should drink it, then. To save your sister."

"I don't care for white wine."

"Especially if it's poisoned."

My heart beats in my throat, one, two, three times. Holding his gaze, I raise the glass to my lips.

"Wait." His hand jerks toward the glass, but I turn away and tilt the liquid into my mouth and swallow, the poison pulsing at the hollow of my throat.

I manage a smile even though the lights, moon, and music all blur together in a silver streamer that wraps itself around my temples, eyes, and throat. Courage pulses through me. *I'm not afraid of you*, I think, though I'm not sure who I mean. "Let's dance," I rasp, dropping the glass into the grass and taking his hands.

His mouth tightens, but he allows me to pull him out of the garden and into the plaza among the dancers. Raising my arms, I sway, circling and smiling over my shoulder at him. At first he stands with his hands in front of him as if he doesn't know what to do. It is comical enough that I laugh. He rests his hands on my hips, awkward and unsure. I put my hands over his, holding him close. Together the wine and the poison muddle my thoughts. *I hope I don't regret this.*

Maybe he is infected as well, because it is only a few seconds before his hands are firm on my hips. I laugh again. Now I have the upper hand.

A different song threads itself through the pipes, this one of love and desire. The song floats over the Wall from the Lost: a siren's song, if they could exist in the Lost.

"You smell of rain," he murmurs, pulling me closer. We spin and it is as if I'm on top of the Dome again, surrounded by stars and in danger of falling.

Wrapping my arms around his neck, I pull him closer until I can taste his breath, quick and warm, and then our lips brush. *I shouldn't let him kiss my mouth*, I think vaguely, but it is too late. His lips are gentle at first, and then insistent. My hands tangle in his hair and I return his kiss though I can hardly breathe.

You're going to poison him, a voice in my head warns. I pull away, smiling as he tries to pull me closer, his lips warm on my jaw, my ear, my throat, and the places I allow him to reach. He must have already taken in some of the venom from my lips, for he, too, becomes giddy and careless.

Somewhere in the back of my mind I think, *Solena cannot see this.* Rather than leave him and return to my chamber alone, I catch his hand and draw him through the crowd, slipping up the stairs and into my chamber.

We fall together onto my bed, wrapped in one another's arms, our bodies intertwined. He takes my wrist and traces his fingertips across my scars. I shiver and pull away.

"Come away with me," he murmurs at my throat. "You don't belong here. You're too good."

No, I'm not, I begin to answer, but my voice fades as he presses his lips to the pulse in my neck. "I'll take you to see the mountains and the snow. It's cool and clean there."

"How?" I return, but the word is lost in a gasp as his mouth glides to my shoulder and along my collarbone. I can no longer speak, only return his touch.

As the music plays outside, I pretend that his passion for me is real and not the result of the poison he drank from my lips, and that he intends to keep the promises he whispers in the darkness.

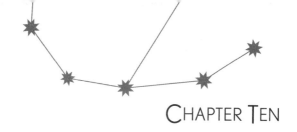

CHAPTER TEN

I wake to light pouring into my room and my head pounding. My mouth is dry and bitter. The edges of everything are blurry yet bright as I slowly pry my eyes open.

Slowly I turn my head to see that he is gone. Could I have dreamed the previous night—hallucinated it? I touch my fingertips to the rawness around my mouth and my throat. I didn't hallucinate him.

The poison, I think. *Damn the poison. I've acted like a complete fool. I should have left with the wine, poured it out. What was I trying to prove, drinking it in one swallow like that? Between that and the venom in my blood, it's a wonder I didn't die.*

I think of the warmth of his fingertips as they danced along my skin and the taste of his breath. I don't regret bringing him here to my chamber.

Does he regret coming here?

Of course he does. Why else would he have fled? I pull the pillow over my face with a groan.

Did he mean what he said? Does he truly believe that I'm too good for this place?

I need only glance at the empty space in my bed for the answer.

Don't be an idiot, I order, digging my nails into my palms until the burning in my eyes eases, though the ache in my throat persists.

And what will the after-effects of the poison do to him?

Well he isn't dead, otherwise his body would be lying on the bed next to me. But he might wish he was. He might feel as though his head is splitting open and see terrible monsters and threats from his past. He might lie senseless for a few hours and forget that he ever asked me to leave with him. Maybe he will finally realize how full of poison I truly am and how wrong he was to offer to take me with him.

Pressing the palm of my hand to my temple, I rise and shuffle to the table where I grab the pitcher of water. It sloshes all over the table as I try to pour it. I drink what I've managed to get into the glass. It is lukewarm and leaves a bitter tinge on my tongue, but I pour another glass and drink that as well. My throat is raw and rough, still coated with poison. I close my eyes to slow the spinning of the room.

I hear a knock at the door, but I don't bother to answer.

"Badriya." Petra's voice.

Before I can respond, the door opens and she sweeps inside with a basket on her arm. She closes the door and takes off her scarf, draping it across the chair. "How is it possible," she asks, wrinkling her nose, "that it smells worse in here than before?"

"Perhaps you shouldn't just walk in," I tell her.

She settles herself across from me, sweeping the jars and bits of leaves and blossoms out of her way as if they are merely clutter.

"I brought some cards, shall we play?"

I shake my head, then regret it as my temples throb. "I can't concentrate."

"Good." She has already brought out the cards and begins shuffling them. "Then it will be easier for me to win." She deals us each a hand, then studies hers with a frown.

I stare at my cards as the Hammers and Gems blur together. From the Dining Hall I hear the sound of voices and cutlery on plates. My stomach rumbles.

"When did you last eat?" she asks.

I try to think but my thoughts are too foggy. "I don't remember."

She reaches into her basket and takes out some bread wrapped in a cloth, a jar filled with olives, and an apple. I take an olive, but it tastes like acid on my tongue, so I spit it out.

"It's not poison," she says.

"I know, I'm just not hungry."

She takes a bite of the apple. "Well, you certainly created a stir last night." She draws a card, then lays down a Wheel.

"Really," I reply dryly, my eyes on my hand. "I couldn't possibly have been more interesting than you. That boy is not your usual type." I take the Wheel and lay it down with another. She makes a face.

"It's refreshing to be with someone more playful and less selfish," she says.

I grin at her. "Oh, I bet he is playful, alright, like a puppy."

She takes another bite of apple as she draws a card. "Stop deflecting. I want to know what is between you and Khalen."

"Nothing." The ache in my throat strains my voice. She raises an eyebrow as I lay down a card. "Nothing, Petra. I mean it. How can there be?"

"It was clear to everyone at the Festival last night that there could be something between you, including Solena."

A chill dances down my spine. "Did she say something?"

"She didn't have to. You could tell by her face. And she did that tapping thing with her nails."

"There's nothing between us." My voice is tight. "And after last night he'll never want to see me again."

"Really?" she says, her eyes on the chafe marks around my cheeks and neck. I pull up the neck of my tunic.

"Really. Do you see him anywhere?" I ask, laying down a Gem.

She snatches up the Gem and lays down her cards. "You used to be better at this game."

"I've been a little distracted lately," I tell her, making a face.

"I noticed," she smirked. "I wonder what Sir Khalen will do after the wedding?" She gathers the cards and begins shuffling again.

"What do you mean?"

"Well, he is so smitten with you. I wonder if he'll stay here as an ambassador of Tanera."

"He's not that smitten with me." I pick up the hand she's dealt and stare at it without seeing it.

"Or you could go with him."

I look up at her. "What?"

"They're due to leave right after the wedding. Ask him to take you with him." She leans forward. "What if you took a chance, just this once?"

I shake my head. "You must be mad."

"He would take you with him in a second. Anyone can see that."

I doubt that. "I don't need anyone to take me away. I'll leave on my own."

She crosses her arms, her cards forgotten. "Where will you go?"

"To Mera."

"Why Mera?"

"It's home." I begin straightening the bottles and vials that she swept aside.

Petra purses her lips. "Whose home?"

"Mine."

I don't have to look up to know that she's rolling her eyes. "Really? Weren't you exiled from there? Wasn't it more your mother's home?"

"It was my home too."

But was it?

She leans forward. "What if you tried somewhere new? Somewhere out of your mother's shadow?" She taps the cards thoughtfully. "I've heard Sir Khalen describing the mountains—they sound lovely."

"None of it matters, anyway. I can't leave Najma."

"Take her with you. Take me, for that matter." She winks.

I start to laugh despite myself. "What about all the broken hearts you'll leave behind?"

"I'll find others. Wait, never mind. I won't. I'll stay; I'm not enough of a threat to Solena." She bites her lip. "Your mother would not have wanted this for you."

My smile vanishes. "She didn't want to wind up dead in the Lost, either. No one really gets what they want here, do they? Except Solena." Even as the words leave my mouth, I think of Solena shivering outside my chamber years ago when her mother threw her out.

"She is wasting away more and more every day from the cosmetics," Petra says. "How much longer can she last? She might go even faster if you were to make some slight adjustments. I've been thinking that her eyes could use a bit more kohl, and I don't think that shade of lip cream works for her at all. You need to make her something much darker." She lays down three Hammers.

I've thought about this myself in the dark hours just before dawn. The amount I've given her should have already killed her, but like me, she's full of poison. The gradual amount over the years has made her immune to the toxins. She'll be as fleshless as the skeleton on the Wall and still ordering me to do her bidding and threatening to hurt those I care about.

Petra's words bring me hope, which is just as dangerous as poison. What if I paid my mother's ransom and fled with Khalen? Surely their entourage would be protection against the Duke's Witch.

Would Solena allow it? Does it even matter anymore?

What about Najma? I think of her hiding with Safiya's poisoned glass of wine. Would Solena force her to take my place as her assassin? I can't leave her here, but would she even agree to leave?

We hear footsteps outside and Petra sweeps the cards into her basket. She kicks it under the table just as the door opens.

"What are you doing here?" Solena demands of Petra.

"I needed something for my headache, My Queen," Petra says, dipping her head. Solena frowns.

"Leave us," she says at last. Petra bows her head and leaves, casting a sidelong glance at me.

"How are you feeling, Diya?" Solena asks. Purple veins snake beneath her pale skin, and the shadows that pool under her eyes are nearly black. "I'm not surprised to see that you are still in bed. I'm told you drank quite a bit last night in a short amount of time."

I swallow, my throat as dry as the desert. "Yes. I should have been more available to you. I understand that Najma was given a task meant for me."

Solena's eyes crinkle at the corners. "She is old enough."

"No. She is not."

Her eyes widen and a smile touches her lips. "Oh, I think it's about time I let my darling sister grow up a bit. As I am her true sister, I think I know what is best for her."

"How can that be what's best for her?" I ask through gritted teeth.

"You've shown that you are less than willing to complete even the simplest of tasks," she hisses, swiveling to face me. "How is it that the Duke of Dorros woke from his death?"

"A miracle," I reply.

"And Safiya? How is it that she requested that her breakfast be sent to her chamber this morning? She should be ill unto death."

Safiya, you fool.

Solena leans in so close that I can smell the coffee and poison on her breath. She taps her nails on the table. One, two, three.

"Do you think me a fool? You've failed me too many times, Diya. I've allowed your little indulgences—they've cost me nothing. But you took my father from me and I do not want you to believe that I've forgotten that."

"How could I ever forget?" I ask. Her mouth tightens and I hold up a placating hand. "I will not fail to follow your orders again, My Queen. Just don't ask Najma to carry them out."

She relaxes, drawing a deep breath. "Good, because I have a more urgent task."

Thoughts tumble through my mind, one after the other. *Khalen. She's going to order me to poison him. How could I have been so careless?*

"Who is it?" I ask, my voice a croak.

"My betrothed. The buffoon, Prince Arlo."

I feel a rush of relief, though it quickly dissipates. "Do we no longer need the security and riches that Tanera has to offer?"

"Wait until after the wedding, once we've signed our agreements. But right after that—I do not plan to consummate this marriage." She shudders. "And I mean kill him, Diya, none of your moral lessons this time. I want him dead."

I tighten my fists, my nails cutting into my palms. "What has he done?"

She paces. "The man is repulsive. The way he eats and drinks as if we are animals in a pen!"

"And that's enough to condemn him to death?"

Solena stops pacing and glares.

"Can't you just refuse to marry him?" I try.

"Security and riches. Remember?"

Damn. Why had I reminded her?

"Sir Khalen warned me that his entourage would not stand by idly should something happen to their Prince."

"Then you will have to be very careful to make it look natural, won't you? No more sloppiness like with the Duke of Dorros."

She strides toward me and I rise, retreating back a step. She follows me, her fists clenched and her pulse throbbing at her throat. "I want him dead, Diya. I am warning you. I know you very well; I can see in your eyes that you are in danger of making another mistake. I would have no choice but to punish you for what you did to the King."

"Then who will do your cosmetics, My Queen?" I snap.

Red veins bulge in her neck and her eyes pop from her face. I wonder if she might finally die right in front of me. But I do not have that kind of fortune.

"Do you not think Najma knows what to do after watching you all these years?" she hisses.

I feel cold to my bones; I have become expendable. "Don't drag her into this."

"I've put it off too long," she says, "I've been too lenient. If you do not comply with this request, you will hang from the Wall in chains."

Her breath is acidic, smelling of hatred. For a long moment we hold each other's gaze, and I swear I can see her pulse in her eyes. She's threatened me for years, but I have never been so fearful of her.

"I can't promise anything," I tell her. "You haven't given me much time."

She opens her eyes again, her face the epitome of serene beauty. "It certainly looked as though you and Khalen were enjoying other's company last night," she says. "I do hope nothing should befall him. Those you love have such bad luck." Without another word, she turns and glides from my chamber.

How am I going to poison poor Prince Arlo? Solena will be watching relentlessly, so I must make his poisoning very convincing, or he will have to die. Either way, it must be gentle, like falling asleep while doing something he loves.

Under the pretense of needing a book on how to remedy a headache caused by too much drinking, I leave the cool refuge of my chamber for the library.

Outside, the remains of the Festival lay scattered across the grass. One corner of the tent has come loose from its pole and flutters in the breeze. Silver stars litter the grass, though now they are nothing more than crumpled paper in the daylight. Leftover streamers that were blown across the grass by the wind are now just garbage waiting to be collected.

The rest of the city lies silent, soporific. I am not the only one who imbibed dangerously the previous night.

Prince Arlo is in the library, as I suspected he would be. He is sprawled in a chair with his boots propped up, head lolling. A light snore escapes him.

A book lies open in his lap for anyone to see and read his heart. He would never survive in Aran, not as a King or as a citizen. I steal to his side and glance at the open pages. *And so, the All-Powerful Princess of the Seas took the hand of the Great King who had been cast from his ship, and led him to the depths of the ocean where they rule over the Sunken Kingdom. The Great Kings and Queens of Mera are all descendants of these original rulers, as are many of its citizens.*

Like me and my mother. Although, as she pointed out, I am far more earth than sea.

"You could poison the pages." The words are hardly louder than a breath. "No one would know. You could dust a powder over the words. He always rubs his eyes after he reads." Najma stands at my shoulder. Has she been spying on him? On me?

Taking her arm, I draw her into the empty Hall. "I don't want you involved in any of this." I don't want her to become poisonous like me.

"You just need enough to slow his heart, as you did with the Duke of Dorros," she says. She holds my gaze for a heartbeat, then pulls away and slips through the door and into the daylight.

Ninety-one silvers and four Moons. My head throbs, the thick smell of leather and paper pressing into it like a vise.

CHAPTER ELEVEN

Within the hour I have returned to my chamber, my knees stained from kneeling in the dirt as I searched for stillbreath. Midmorning is not the ideal time for gathering, so I will have to use much more than usual to convincingly stop Arlo's heart. But Solena has not given me much of a choice.

I glance at the half-finished Stardust gleaming in a vial on the table, waiting for my blood. There is not enough to earn the silver that I need.

If only I could offer the Witch my tears, but they won't fall. She might accept my blood, though. After all the years of ingesting poison, a few drops of either will bring either regret or euphoria, depending on how they're mixed. If they are added to wine, they might infect someone with despair; if they are blended with honey, they can induce clarity.

How much of my blood would she demand?

I push the thought away. Combined with the silver I've collected, it will have to be enough. No matter what happens today, I can't stay in this city any longer.

The air smells as though it's been faintly scorched. I begin chopping and my thoughts drift. A vulture appears at my window. "What would Sir Khalen think of your plan?" it asks.

"Go away," I say as the knife sinks into my finger. I curse as blood that is nearly black with poison oozes from the cut. I hold my finger over an empty vial and allow it to drip inside. I needed to add blood to the stillbreath anyway.

"That's too much," the vulture warns.

"No, it isn't," I reply, but the bird has already flown off. The poison in the wine has weakened my immunity, and now the fumes from the vial are warping my reality. I will have to talk to Najma about the amount of poison she used.

No. Najma will never have to poison anyone again.

I add the stillbreath to my blood and stir it into a paste. Once it dries, I will chop it into a fine powder to brush over the words of a book.

I sit and look out the window while I wait for the paste to dry, pondering Petra's words. Time drifts by as I allow myself to imagine another possibility, one in which I warn Khalen and persuade him to take me with them as they flee Aran instead of poisoning Prince Arlo.

I start to think of the rush of the wind and the waves in Mera, but then I imagine the snow in the mountains. It must be so quiet there, and cool, and so close to the stars.

"If he wanted to take you with him, he wouldn't have vanished before you woke." The vulture is back.

"I didn't ask you," I snap, and it chuckles. But it is right. Besides, I can't leave Najma to be raised by Solena.

The sun has risen higher as I've been lost in my thoughts. I begin grinding the poison into a fine dust, though my vision blurs. When I have filled a vial with the dust, I change my clothes and wash my hair in orange-scented water. Still, the odor hangs about me like a sheen of perspiration, as if something nearby were singed.

The poison glitters scarlet in the vial, just waiting to be brushed onto the pages of Arlo's favorite book. Almost no one has ventured from their chambers, taking refuge from the relentless sun, the sour smell of the previous night's wine, the odor of the meat from the feast, and the cloying smell of perfume.

The library will be empty at this hour; the air is even heavier inside than it is outside. Arlo has surely left his book open on the table beside his favorite chair. He has made this too easy for me; I will simply pinch the powder between my fingertips and brush it over the words.

Then he will run his fingertips over the lines of the book and rub his eyes. Soon he will begin to feel tired. It could take hours, but he should be asleep by the time the dancing begins tonight. His heart will slow enough that even his doctor will think that he is dead.

After half a day's journey into the Lost, he will wake with a terrible headache, but his heart will beat and his lungs will fill with air. It will be a miracle.

All of this will happen if I follow Solena's orders.

Before I can talk myself out of it, I carry the vial to my window and tip it into the wind. For a moment it twists in a poisonous ribbon before being carried off in a hundred directions.

"You've done it now," the vulture chuckles as it glides past once again. My head feels light. I have no choice now but to act.

There is a knock at the door. Perhaps it is the poison, but I think I catch the scent of debts unpaid. I know before she enters that it is Safiya. She slips inside as soon as I answer. Despite the heat, she wears a dark scarf around her head and shoulders.

"Well, I heard you had an interesting night," she says.

I roll my eyes, though it causes my head to pound.

"Ugh, what is that odor? Is something burning?" Her face creases and she pulls her scarf around her nose and mouth. "Oh, you have another victim?" Before I can answer, she thrusts a purse into my hands. "Here, I owe you." It is heavy and something jingles inside.

"What is this?"

"The winnings I took from Solena."

I push the bundle back toward her. "If she finds out that you gave it to me, she'll kill you."

Safiya tilts her head. "Or she'll order you to punish me. So let's pretend that you beat her to it. I will fall ill—deathly ill—and when I recover, I will have lost all my luck. I will never win, at least not when she sees, but when she isn't around, I'll be only too happy to lighten the purses of other fools."

I shake my head. "I don't know if that will work."

"It's worth the risk, isn't it? You know how much I love risks," she says with a wink.

What looks like thirty silver coins gleam up at me from inside the purse. I swallow as I try to slow my heart and control my eagerness. "Why are you giving this to me?"

"Because you could have poisoned me and you didn't. And maybe you'll remember this the next time you're ordered to slip something into my wine." She raises her eyebrows at the bowl from which the fumes furl. "I'm going now, before I breathe in too much of that. Don't worry, I won't tell." She smiles over her shoulder as she slides through the door.

"Wait." But my voice is too weak and she is already gone, leaving me with the purse.

I begin to pace, my thoughts tumbling through my mind. Now I have one hundred and twenty-one silvers and four Moons: enough to free Mother, but not enough for the Duke's Witch or enough to buy a horse that is fast enough to outrun her and escape.

I will bring Najma. We will go to Mera, to freedom. She will never have to make the choices that I was forced to make. I could even warn Arlo before we leave.

Now I just need to convince Najma to come.

I hide Safiya's purse full of silver in a plain clay jar that I keep tucked behind the others on the shelf above my table. It's not the best hiding place, but I will only be gone for a few minutes.

The city is still sleeping even though the sun is high in the sky. Most are still recovering from the festivities of the night before, but there are a few more servants out now. One man holds his head as he rinses the tiles with water. A girl picks up empty glasses from the edge of the fountain. Hopefully neither of them notice that I am going to the stables.

The Master of Horses is also asleep, his head resting on his arms on the table. I touch his arm and he jolts awake, shielding his eyes from the brightness of the day and blinking blearily. When he sees me, his eyes widen and he leans backward, nearly falling from his chair. I hold up my hands. "I'm here for a favor, not to harm you."

He swallows, his body still stiff. "What is it?" he croaks.

"I need your fastest horse left untethered tonight."

"Forgive me, but I didn't think you knew how to ride." It is true. The King ordered that no one teach me because it would give me an opportunity to escape. Desperation will have to keep me in the saddle.

"I need one that can outrun the demons and carry two riders."

"None can do that, at least not with two riders."

"What if one is a child?"

He presses his lips together and runs his hand down his face.

Behind me I hear a slight sound, like a breath or a rustle. Cursing under my breath, I turn, but no one is there. I stride to the door and throw it open, but no one is outside. I close my eyes and take a deep breath. I am imagining things. I must calm myself or risk making mistakes.

The Master of Horses watches me warily from his seat. I pull out my purse and tip the heavy coins that I won from Khalen into my palm. He catches his breath, then regretfully shakes his head. "I can't accept it. How will I explain where I got it?"

"Who has to know? Save it for a time when you truly need it." His eyes are locked on the coins. "So, you say there is no horse that can outrun the demons?"

"There is one," he concedes.

✷

Before I go to Najma's chamber, I stop by the library, only to find it empty. Arlo's favorite book is closed on the table. I take it and slide it onto a shelf behind some other thick tomes, where no one else can find it.

I go to Najma's chamber and enter silently, without knocking, but I find Mina there instead, hanging some of Najma's dresses. She hums a song that I recognize from the previous night. She turns and I see she has not put on her scarf; scars cross her mouth and cheeks, but her former beauty lights her face. I remember the way Theron had gazed at her the night before.

As soon as she sees me, she goes silent, her eyes bloodshot and wary. She lifts her chin and holds my gaze. "What do you want?" Her voice is laced with insolence. I draw a breath. *No matter*, I remind myself. *I will be gone soon.*

"Where is Najma?" I ask.

"With Queen Solena."

I curse silently. There is no way I can approach her with my plan, not right now.

"You had a good time last night," she says as I turn to go. "With Sir Khalen."

"I did, thank you," I say over my shoulder.

"I don't see him now though," she calls as I step through the door. I shut it on her mocking laughter.

Honestly, it is impossible to be good in this place with people like Mina here. *You did scar her*, I remind myself. *And I would be hard-pressed not to do it again.*

Next I go to the guest chamber where Arlo is staying, and knock on the door of the smaller chamber that is adjacent to it. There is no answer. Do I dare leave a message? I decide against it.

I venture to the Dining Hall, where I see Najma sitting at Solena's side. Solena catches my eye and smiles. I exit quickly, on to my next destination.

I try the Gambling Hall, the Wall, and the Dome, but I can't find Khalen or Arlo, and Najma is always at Solena's side.

For the next few hours I search and fret, going over my plan again and again in my head. When night falls I will take Najma to the stables where we will find the horse untethered and the gate unlocked. Outside the city, I will seek out the Witch, pay her with the silver that I've saved, and finally set my mother free. Then Najma and I will ride for Mera.

Doubts rise in my mind as though the vulture is at my ear.

What about the mountains?

I must keep with what I know, especially if I have Najma with me.

What if the Witch goes back on her word?

She won't, not when she sees the silver.

I don't know how to ride a horse.

It won't matter. The horse is swift and will want to escape the demons as fast as it can. All we have to do is hold on.

What if we are caught?

Everyone is far too sluggish from the Festival to pay much attention. Anyone who does pursue us will be loath to enter the Lost, and our horse will far outpace theirs.

Even the Witch?

Yes, I answer myself. Even the Witch.

What about Khalen?

What do I care about Khalen? I answer myself defiantly.

I decide to return to my chamber to count the silvers once more, though I already know exactly how many I have, but it might keep me from obsessing over these endless doubts.

I have barely entered my chamber when the door opens like a whisper. I stiffen at the scent of arsenic and flowers and turn to face Solena. She must have been watching for my return.

"Well," she paces, picking up a jar from the table and setting it down. "You've succeeded."

"Succeeded in what?"

"Ridding the world of Prince Arlo."

"What do you mean?" A smile steals over her face and I know that she caught the hitch in my breath and the panic in my voice. I turn away as nonchalantly as I am able to and fold a scarf that was strewn across my bed. "I haven't been able to do it yet."

"Oh?" Her voice trembles as though she is about to burst into laughter. "That's odd. My sources say that not only is he not breathing, but his heart is not beating, his bowels emptied themselves all over the silk bedcovers, and his eyes are open and rolled all the way back in his head."

How? What did she do? "Is he dead?"

"Most certainly."

I can no longer keep up my façade. I sink onto my bed, the scarf twisting in my hands. Poor foolish Arlo.

Solena is openly smiling now, her teeth white and sharp against her blood-red lips, her dark eyes gleaming. "I knew you wouldn't do it. You've lost your nerve. Perhaps all this happened because I coated my lips with several extra layers of the rouge you give me. It left blisters! But it was worth it to see the look on the fool's face after he kissed me. He actually turned purple." She laughs in a way that is meant to be silvery, but it sounds maniacal.

No.

"You didn't think I actually trusted you to carry out my orders, did you? Especially considering the way you slather all over Sir Khalen." Her voice twists his name mockingly.

"It seems you were right," she continues. "I am now so full of poison that I can kill a man with a simple kiss, with no harm to my health at all!" She cocks her head. "But of course this is all so familiar to you."

She takes a step toward me. "There will be questions, of course. I will insist that I have no idea what happened; perhaps the meat did not agree with him, or the heat, or he did too much carousing during the Festival—he is overweight." She shudders a bit. "You had better think of what you're going to say, for surely Khalen will brow-beat you for answers. It had better be something good."

"What *I'm* going to say?" I choke.

She widens her eyes. "Well, yes. You're the assassin, aren't you? Everyone knows how dangerous it can be to cross you: Mina and the Duke of Dorros. Even though no one says it, there are plenty who suspect you in the King's death as well." She tsks, shaking her head with mock sadness. "Whatever will your Khalen think of you now?" She gives me one more long look, then backs away through the door.

When she is gone I press the heels of my hands into my eyes.

Unrelenting nausea washes over me and I vomit into a bowl full of blueleaf. The sharp odor of the toxin rises from the pile of sick.

Poor Arlo. He had no idea what he was getting into when he came here.

Khalen will surely hate me now.

I must find Najma and go. Now.

I move about the room swiftly. I go to the armoire where a silver goblet is tucked among my tunics; to the bookcase where silver chains and bracelets are hidden among the pages of books; to the tile beneath my bed where I have tucked the purse filled with silver. Next I move to my work table and shove jars and tins full of roots, leaves, and powders haphazardly into the bag Mother carried with her across the Lost. I finally reach for the earthen jar on the shelf above my work table where I hid the silver that Safiya gave me.

I know as soon as I touch the jar that it is too light. The lid falls to the tile and shatters as I plunge my hand inside, scraping my wrist against the rough neck. My grasping fingers only find the dried husk of a dead insect. The silver is gone.

I shriek as I hurl the jar to the ground and it smashes into shards that slice my ankles and feet, but I hardly feel the pain. I fly through the door and out to the gallery. It had to be Solena.

Mina stands at the top of the stairs as if she is waiting for someone. She raises her eyebrows. "What's the matter, Diya?" she asks, her voice honeyed with concern.

"I've been robbed," I choke.

"Oh, no. That's awful." She doesn't even bother to hide her smile.

"What do you know?" I demand. I can barely stop myself from gripping her shoulders and shaking her.

"Oh," she says, examining her nails. "Only that I saw Yadira moving with more purpose than I've seen in a while. She's been trying to borrow silver for some time now." She looks up at me. "It would seem that your evil ways have finally caught up to you."

Yadira is even more desperate than I realized. "She can't pay me with money that she stole from me," I snap. "I won't give her the Stardust."

Mina's eyes narrow. "Who says you are the only person who can make Stardust?" she asks. "Don't you think Najma has learned by now?"

There is no chance I will allow this. I don't bother to ask Mina where Yadira is. Pushing past her, I storm down the gallery to her chamber.

"Watch yourself, Diya!" she calls sharply, but I don't slow.

I pound on her door. "Yadira!" When there is no answer, I try to open it, but unlike my chamber, hers has a lock. I move my face close to the door so that I won't have to shout. "Open this door or you'll never get another flake of Stardust." There is still no answer.

I can hear Solena sobbing inside her chamber. The guards are already rushing to her. Mina has started towards the room as well. I must hide before Solena can accuse me of Arlo's death.

I rush to my garden where I am fairly certain I won't be followed. I pace back and forth, my fists knotted. *What do I do now?*

I could go to the stables and ride away on the horse I bought, but I don't have the money to free Mother, and I can't leave Najma.

I could deny Solena's accusations, but no one in Aran would dare to contradict her.

I could tell Khalen what really happened and beg him to take me with him. But after what's happened to Arlo, he might not want anything to do with me.

Footsteps approach. Someone is coming through the willow door. I race up the steps to the Wall.

The wind has risen and the Bones clatter against the stone.

"You might need to change your plans," they wheeze. Are they laughing at me?

The air goes still as if even the wind is waiting to see what I will do next.

My heart aches for Prince Arlo and for Khalen, but it also aches for the years I spent mixing concoctions into lotions and powders; for the years I spent enduring the disdain and mockery of women and men alike because I was so desperate for their silver, while the venom in my potions numbed my tears and deadened my heart. It's all been for nothing.

But I still have my blood. Mother once told me that there wasn't enough magic in my blood to trade with the Witches, but maybe now it's been filled with enough poison to be of some value. And I always have my tears...

"If only they would fall," the Bones sigh.

"Shut your mouth," I tell them.

"If only I had a mouth to shut."

Enough. I cannot be Solena's puppet, or anyone's puppet, for even one more day. I will take my chances in the Lost with what I have right now.

But can I risk Najma's safety with no horse and not enough silver to bribe the Witches? I am susceptible enough to the ghosts on my own—how can I protect Najma?

"The dead wear silver," the Bones muse.

"I said shut—" My voice dies mid-sentence. There is a gleam of silver in the darkness, on the brow of the effigy of a dead queen.

No. I can't go back there. I remember the dust of the dead on my feet and clothes; the voices speaking to me in the darkness; the thick air that will close my throat.

"Then you'll be joining me on the Wall," the Bones reply to my unspoken thought. "I could use the company." Their wheezy laughter sounds like the wind.

"Damn you, Yadira," I mutter. "Damn you and everyone else in this forsaken city. I hope the curse takes you all with it." Fueled by my anger, I turn and rush down the stairs, trying to outrun my fear.

The heavy doors that lead to the Crypts swing open much more easily than I anticipated, as if someone had pushed them from the other side. Just as I enter, I realize that I've left my knife in my chamber. I can't go back for it now. There is no time.

The lamps throw eerie shadows onto the walls. My heart thunders in my ears. I blink away the dust of the dead as I begin my descent into darkness. One, two, three steps. I stifle a scream as an arm reaches from the wall, but then I realize it is only a shadow cast by the deceptive torchlight.

Four steps. Five steps.

The air grows cooler with each step until I finally reach the bottom. The silence is deep and impenetrable. The effigies lie in the darkness as if they are waiting.

I take a breath and force myself forward. The torchlight catches the eye of a King, the hand of a Queen, and the stone-likeness of a pet curled under the arm of a child. I shudder.

I see the gleam of silver and move toward the Queen Mother. The band crosses her forehead just above her closed eyes. *She's sleeping*, I tell myself. *She won't care. She has no use for it now.*

I take hold of the silver band and pull. It scrapes away from the Queen Mother's forehead. I half expect her to open her eyes and demand to know what I'm doing, but she sleeps on.

The crown is heavy and cool. It will surely be enough.

I turn to flee the Crypts when a hand clamps down on my arm. This time I do scream, the sound echoing from the walls.

"You really are a coward."

The familiar voice sends an arrow of terror down my spine. I whirl to see Khalen at my shoulder. Even in the darkness I can see that his eyes are lined in red.

"It's not enough that you poison others for your own profit. Now you are stealing from the dead as well."

"What are you doing here?" I choke.

"I followed you. I watched as you raced from your chamber. At first I thought it might be out of grief for my Prince, and I was touched. But then I saw you pounding on the door, threatening Lady Yadira. I didn't want to believe that you could have actually played a part in Arlo's death, but I became suspicious, so I followed you. And now," he spreads his hands.

"I'm so, so sorry Khalen. I didn't poison him." I am babbling, my words tumbling over one another.

"Ah, yes. You only gave him enough to make it *seem* like he is dead. We all know that one. Only this time he's actually dead."

"No! I gave him nothing!"

"You expect me to believe you? You haven't been honest since we met!" His voice breaks.

I feel desperate at the injustice. He is right, I haven't been honest, but I didn't poison Arlo. Yet I am the one being blamed anyway. "I'm sorry," I tell him. "What can I do?" The darkness swallows my pathetic words.

"You can listen to what you've truly done."

Shaking my head, I back away, but within a few steps I'm up against the Queen's effigy. He steps closer and closer until we are nearly touching. "You owe me that, at the very least. You owe it to Arlo." I can feel the grief radiating from him. I turn my head, but he speaks anyway. "I was very arrogant growing up. I was raised to believe that the world, and everyone in it, was here to do my bidding. My father did his best to teach me to be noble, and he never gave up on me." His hand tightens into a fist.

"One evening there was a report of bandits just outside the city where the Lost began. My father insisted that I come with him, but I hated the desert—I secretly feared it. So I refused and pouted like a child even though I was nearly grown. My father tried to reason with me, even threatened me, but in the end he left without me. It was the last time we spoke.

"My father's bodyguard and the son of one of the guards went with him instead. They returned injured and incoherent, but my father did not." He rubs the back of his neck. "We were never sure whether Arlo dreamed it or if his shock made him see things that weren't really there."

His words hang in the air. "Wait, you said Arlo." I wonder if he is confused in his grief.

"Yes," he says. "Arlo." I catch my breath and Khalen continues. "Arlo said that when he stepped into the sand, hands reached up and grabbed my father's legs, dragging him in up to his knees, his waist, and then his chest. Then a Witch appeared, sensing a bargain. Arlo hacked at the hands to no avail. He offered the Witch jewels and gold, sure that my father would pay whatever price. But she wanted none of it."

"Silver," I murmur. "They like silver."

"By now only my father's head was above the sand. In desperation, Arlo said that he would trade places with my father and let the demons take him instead. Because—" his voice cracks, "because my father was a noble king and deserved to be spared, and Arlo was only his humble knight."

He rubs his fist against the wall and I see a layer of skin peel away. "The Witch said that the most noble would be spared. My father was sucked beneath the surface and Arlo lived."

Khalen falls silent, lost in thought, and I think of slipping past him. He holds up an arm to block me.

"I knew that what the Witch said was true, that Arlo was the most noble of us all. So I, the prince by blood, stepped aside and allowed the prince in character to take my place." In the torchlight his eyes are like dark pools full of despair and fury like a demon's.

"And now, Badriya, you've killed the best man that I know. Your mistake, and the Queen's, was that you should have killed me instead. Now I must make things right for the man who tried to save my father and died in my place."

He moves closer and I try backing away, but the unyielding wall of the Crypts stops me from going further. He steps closer and closer.

"Solena anticipated what you would do, but luckily so did I. I'm not the only one with tells."

I swallow. I have to sound brave—he can't know how afraid I am. "Oh, really? And what is my tell?"

"You don't blink, like a snake; it's unnerving. It's how I knew how terrified you are of the Crypts."

I think of how hard I've worked to keep my face still and expressionless, without even blinking. I curse. I'm such a fool. "Are you going to lock me in here and let me die?" I try to sound indifferent but my voice trembles.

The torchlight catches the redness in his eyes. "Actually, I mean to strike a bargain with you."

I groan. No more bargains.

"You can bring justice to Solena."

I give a short, harsh laugh. "How? Shall I tell her she is under arrest? You could do that better than I could."

"I want you to assassinate her."

"Oh, certainly. That's no problem at all. Don't you think I would have done that already?"

"Even if I were to lock you in these Crypts, which I ought to, what do you think Solena will do to you if you are caught?"

She would lock me away as well; she knows that it's one of my greatest fears. No. She would have me hung from the Wall, but not until I regained consciousness so that I could feel the birds tearing at my flesh. The Bones and I could entertain one another for all eternity. I nearly laugh, my head spinning with the madness. Najma could come visit me and ask for advice.

Najma. What would become of her now?

"With Solena gone, Najma will be Queen," Khalen says, as if he's read my thoughts.

"She is thirteen," I protest.

"As we've already discussed, some of the greatest monarchs have also been the youngest. Najma shows great promise as a ruler, despite her youth. And she will no longer be under Solena's shadow or her influence."

I think of the way her eyes gleamed when we spoke of the possibility of her ruling Aran, and the signs of her shrewdness. With Solena gone, perhaps she could have a chance at happiness.

"You want to control her," I realize, "so that you can take advantage of Aran. With a child on the throne, it would be so easy."

"Aran has much to offer," Khalen says. "Under Solena's rule, and her father's before her, it has been difficult to form an alliance. This… situation…offers a unique opportunity, but I give you my word that we will treat Najma and the citizens of Aran fairly."

His voice softens. "Najma is her own person," he says. "She is stronger than you think, and much more capable than you give her credit for." It is too dark to read his expression.

I mull over his words. Have I been thinking of Najma as myself? All I know is that I want her to travel a different path than the one I have.

"I promise you on my father's memory that I will help her," he says it so quietly that I almost don't hear him.

This is yet another deceit. Isn't it?

If I do nothing and refuse, Najma will gradually be poisoned by Solena until she becomes just like her, I will end up either in the Crypts or on the Wall, and my mother will be doomed to dance forever in the Lost at the whim of the Witch.

"How am I to do it?"

"That is for you to decide."

The only way I know how to kill someone is with poison, but after years of wearing the cosmetics almost nothing can end her, at least not quickly enough. I've thought about this a lot through the years. I shake my head. "If poison could kill her, she would be dead by now."

"Then you'll have to find another way."

I think of my mother's knife that I carelessly left upstairs in a pile of half-cut petals. Could I actually plunge it into her chest enough to kill her? I've imagined it many times, but now, confronted with the reality, I feel sick.

"If I do this, then what?" I ask.

"The kingdom of Tanera supports Queen Najma and the city of Aran. We will become allies and you will not be arrested for the attempted murder of Prince Arlo."

My throat is as dry as sand. Once I'm inside the city, I can slip into my chamber and collect the hidden silver so that I can pay the Witch and free my mother. But then what?

"You must take me to Mera," I tell him.

Khalen sighs. "How will that look if we harbor the murderer of our Prince and carry her to safety rather than seek justice? Not to mention that you are Queen Solena's assassin."

"I will not do it." The words are all bravado, and the tremor in my voice betrays me. We both know I have to do it, but he reminds me anyway.

"Then I will leave you here with your ghosts, demons, and Witches," he says, his voice turning harsh. "You will either be abandoned in the Lost, hung from the Wall, or locked in the Crypts."

He wouldn't—he knows this is my greatest fear. But then again, he blames me for the death of his Prince and his best friend.

He catches my wrist, his fingertips jabbing at the scars there. "Is this better?" he asks. "Do you truly believe that it is better to keep using your own blood in exchange for silver to keep Solena in power? Soon you'll be nothing more than a ghost and nothing will have changed. You will have helped no one, not your mother and certainly not Najma. But if that's what you choose, then I will leave you here among the dead."

I tear my arm away and stumble against the stone. By the time I get to my feet, he is already striding away. I can hear his footsteps against the dust and stone, and I see his shadowed shape moving swiftly to the steps. I am only halfway up the stairs when I hear the door scrape shut and seal.

I sink to the steps, the dust of the dead filling my throat. I am not sure I can draw another breath. Yet I continue drawing in one breath after another until my heart slows and my head clears.

He'll return. He has to. He needs me to assassinate Solena. He wouldn't leave me here. Would he?

Then a voice speaks to me, the same one from all those years ago when Solena and her friends first locked me in the Crypts. It is filled with dust and hoarse with disuse, but I can hear the words clearly.

"There is a way, child. Why have you given up so easily?"

A woman dressed in a shroud appears in the lamplight, standing next to her effigy: the Queen Mother. I press the heels of my hands into my eyes. Damn this poison.

"I'm sorry I almost took your crown. I was desperate," I say into my hands.

She speaks again, her voice like a breath. "Do you feel the breeze?"

A draft of air circles my ankles, fluttering the fabric of my trousers.

"You're dead, but not dead," she says.

"Dead, but not dead," I repeat. Isn't that what everyone believes of me? I am half-dead, aren't I? A shell, a ghost? The Bones and the ghosts in the Lost speak to me, and now this ghost in the Crypts.

"Follow the breeze," she says.

The Queen Mother points a long, white finger to a shadow on the wall that disappears and then reappears in the flickering torchlight. It takes me a moment to realize that it is not a shadow but a crack that is barely wide enough for me to fit through.

"I can't," I murmur, panic stabbing cold needles into my heart. I can't go into that cramped darkness where I might become trapped, where my breath might stop. My bones might turn to dust, and then no one would ever find me.

Another warm, gentle gust of air wafts from the crack.

Where does it lead? Perhaps out into the Lost, or straight into the teeth of a demon.

"Would you rather stay here?" she asks.

I eye the crack doubtfully. "I won't fit."

"You are hardly more than bones yourself," the ghost sighs.

I glance at her, then back to the crack. Why would she help me when I am about to steal her crown, when her daughter and granddaughter both hate me?

"Solena is lost, but Najma is not," she says, as though she's read my thoughts. "Help my granddaughter. She will restore Aran to the place it is meant to be."

For several long heartbeats the ghost and I hold one another's gaze. She might be real or she might be a vision from the poison. Either way, I know the words are true. "I'll help her," I promise.

I take a deep breath and put my arm into the crack. When nothing grabs or bites it, I cautiously put my leg inside. I realize that the ghost is right: the years of poison must have eaten away at me because I can fit my whole body inside the crack.

I take a deep breath of the thick air in the Crypts, perhaps my last, and slide into the crack.

The smell is terrible. I cover my nose and mouth with my scarf to keep from gagging, but there are times when I can't breathe at all. The ground beneath me is rocky and unstable, and at times the walls press in so much that I fear I will become caught. When I finally push past them, the stones tear at my clothes and flesh and I imagine myself leaving smears of blood along the wall. The darkness is as thick as a blanket, and the roof overhead lowers so much that I unexpectedly crack my head against it hard enough that lights flash behind my eyes and I must pause a moment to let the world steady. By now I can no longer see the light from the entrance behind me, so there is nothing to do but push forward.

Sometimes I hear whispers and laughter as though there is someone at my shoulder, but there isn't enough room to turn and look. At one point I stumble on something that feels like sticks beneath my feet—bones of some other fool who got themselves trapped in here, I wonder?

Once I am sure that I feel a hand on my neck. I can't help but scream, the sound strangled and swallowed in the dense lightless air. I move as fast as I can, heedless of the stones tearing at my flesh.

And then I see a light ahead, dim and amber, but after the darkness and terror of the tunnel it beams like the sun. Scrambling forward, I reach for it, but only one hand pokes through. It is a porthole that is only big enough for one of my arms and a shoulder to fit.

My breath echoes against my ears as I pull away and press my face to it. I see silk curtains, empty tables, and the stone effigy of the Queen, her smile cold and forever frozen. It's the Dining Hall.

Through the hole, I hear the sound of a lute strumming a mournful tune. Suddenly the music stops, and I hear footsteps. A face peers down at me, running a hand over the too-long hair that Mina is so fond of stroking. Theron.

I know it is hopeless, but what choice do I have? "Help me. Please?" My voice is a ragged whisper. I don't know who else is with him, but I hope it's not Mina. She will surely raise the alarm.

He looks over his shoulder, then back to me. He sets aside his lute and squares his shoulders, then puts his shoulder to something and grunts. There is a great scraping sound. He pauses, shakes his shoulder, then grunts again. The crack widens a bit and cool air rushes in. I breathe it in gratefully and add my shoulder to his, pushing with him. Suddenly I tumble from the crack and onto the floor of the Dining Hall.

I roll over and look up into the eyes of the King, who is laughing down at me. Theron stands panting beside the great urn that was placed in front of the crack to hide the place where my mother had once stood.

I scramble to my feet. "Thank you," I tell him breathlessly. "Thank you for helping me."

He does not answer, just puts a shoulder to the urn again, grunting as he shoves it back into place. The King beams down on us as if sharing a joke. I join Theron, adding my weight, and the urn slides a bit more quickly until it covers most of the hole once more. We are both panting.

I wait for him to ask me what I'm doing, but he says nothing. "Please, don't tell," I begin.

He shakes his head. "I won't. You're not the first person to emerge from there with that request."

"What?" I sputter. This city is even more mad than I thought.

He jerks his head over his shoulder. "You better hurry—Mina will be here any moment."

"Thank you," I tell him again.

He does not meet my eye. "I never repaid you."

"For what?"

Now he looks at me, his long lashes wet. "You were supposed to kill her, weren't you? You could have even taken her voice."

"Her face…"

"I don't care about that, and she will learn not to as well."

I am speechless. I thought everyone hated me and blamed me for what I'd done, thinking that I had acted out of cruelty. He turns away and begins to shove the effigy back into place. "Go," he grunts, and I rush for the door. I risk a quick glance behind me and see him re-seated and strumming the same melancholy song of love on his lute.

CHAPTER TWELVE

Night has fallen like a dark curtain. I wonder about the best way to assassinate Solena as I make my way along the Wall. The night is hushed, and the courtiers and servants speak quietly to one another. By now everyone has learned of Prince Arlo's death. The Bat wheels overhead.

If I could slip into her chamber, perhaps I could force a sleeping draught down her throat while she sleeps. It will have to be powerful though since she is already so full of poison.

I may have to use my mother's knife, though the thought of using it for murder, even Solena's murder, sickens me.

There is movement on the path, and I press myself into the shadows against the wall of the Great Hall. It's one of the many guards on the lookout for Prince Arlo's assassin. There is no doubt that Solena has already told everyone that I acted out of envy, that I am uncontrollable like my mother, who will take whatever she wants with no thought for others. I peer around the city and see guards everywhere: watching from the Wall, pacing in front of the Gambling Hall, and patrolling the Rooms of the Favorites.

Then a song that makes my heart ache fills the night sky. There aren't any words, but the melody tells of loss and love that can never be recovered. All of the guards move toward it as if drawn toward it like a siren's song. Several guards stand atop the Wall stare as if they are mesmerized.

They can see my mother.

I am pulled toward her just as surely as the guards. If only I could see her, then I would feel so much braver about what I have to do. I imagine her spinning with her arms over her head and her eyes closed, the moon above and the Snake coiled nearby. I think of her smiling the way she had in Mera as she danced with Cayo.

Go. The voice is like a breath, but it's hers all the same. For a moment I hesitate, reluctant to leave her. I want to dance with her as we had in Mera before the night of the Blood Moon.

Go. I hear her voice again as if she is standing right next to me, even though she is on the other side of the Wall. I move like a ghost along the edge of the city while the guards are too spellbound by Mother's voice to notice me.

A couple sits on the edge of the fountain, locked in an embrace, looking toward the Wall. They don't turn as I hurry up the stairs to my chamber.

As soon as I enter, I see my knife waiting on top of the acheroot I'd been chopping. I grab the bag I'd packed earlier and turn to go.

The room flares with light. Solena is standing in the center of my chamber holding a candle. Deep shadows have pooled beneath her bloodshot eyes and her cheeks are sunken.

"I wondered if you'd return," she says. "But I suppose the temptation to assassinate me was too great. What did he offer you? What did he threaten you with? Imprisonment? Prolonged torture? Death in the Lost? I can't imagine he'd be merciful now that he knows the horrible things you're capable of."

My eyes dart around the room, my heart pounding; my knife winks at me from the table and I curse. Why hadn't I grabbed it first? I step toward it, but Solena moves in front of it. "One scream," she says. "And Darien will be here in an instant, and that will be the end of you." She laughs. "You've got nowhere to go now, do you? You should have jumped from the Wall like your mother. You could do it now. Go on. I won't stop you."

Why hasn't she summoned her guards already? The answer comes a moment later as the door opens behind me. I whirl to see Najma, who draws in a breath when she sees me. "Badriya."

"Close the door, darling," Solena says, and Najma obeys.

"I got your message," Najma says. "I came as quickly as I could. I brought your favorite wine." Crossing to her, Najma hands her the goblet.

"Sweet girl." Solena traces her finger down Najma's cheek and drapes an arm around her shoulders, toying with her hair as she drinks from the goblet. Najma looks at me with a blank expression on her face.

"Look, Najma. Diya has returned. She's didn't scuttle away after all. Perhaps she can tell you stories again. I have a story I'd wager she's never told you."

She takes another drink from the goblet. "After our mother died, our father was never the same. He loved his wine, to be sure, but once Mother was gone there was no one to protect him. The enchantress was already gone, but her daughter still remained. She made sure that he drank a bit too much and that he was always a bit confused and off-balance."

"That's not true!" I burst out.

Solena raises her eyebrows. "Then you tell her, Diya. Tell her how her father died." She takes another drink.

I feel light-headed, like I'm standing atop the Wall on a windy night. But if I tell the story, Solena will no longer be able to hold it over me. I draw a breath and begin.

"The King was grieving."

"He was bewitched," Solena says sharply. "You bewitched him as surely as your mother did."

I shake my head. "No. He was heartbroken. The only thing that bewitched him was grief and the wine that he drank to soften it."

"He loved Mother," Najma says, her voice uncertain.

I suddenly realize that she is nearly my height and that her brown eyes are much lighter than Solena's. How had I never noticed before? "He did. He loved your mother very much. But he also loved someone else."

"Your mother," Najma says softly.

I bow my head. "Yes. It broke your mother's heart, and I'm sorry for that, and so was my mother. She never meant to hurt anyone."

Solena snorts. "But she did, didn't she?"

She did, just as I did. I never meant to hurt anyone—not Yadira, or Khalen, or Arlo, or Rumin, not even Solena—but here we are.

"The King was never the same. He drank too much and was confused. He forgot things."

"So it became all too easy for Diya to take advantage of him," Solena interjects.

"No, Little Crocodile. No. I would never do that." My throat tightens. I did take advantage of him, but not in the way Solena means.

"Tell her," Solena snaps.

Drawing in another breath, I speak. "He followed me into the garden—he had indulged a little too much and thought I was my mother—and then he died." I knot and unknot my hands, unable to look at her.

Solena's silvery laugh sounds nearly hysterical. "Really, Diya? Is that really all? He kissed you and then he died, purely by accident?"

Mother's song fills the silence as tears fill Najma's eyes and pour down her cheeks. I envy her ability to cry.

I force myself to look at her. "He did kiss me, and all the poison that I'd taken and the wine he'd been drinking must have been too much. It was an accident," I tell both her and Solena. "It was an accident."

Najma goes very still, her face unreadable. Solena watches her with shining eyes. Then Najma turns and rushes into Solena's arms.

"There, there," Solena murmurs. She turns her face to me in triumph as my ribs tighten around my heart. I hold out my hands but Najma presses closer to Solena and kisses her cheek.

It happens in an instant. The goblet clatters to the floor as Solena's eyes widen. She clutches her throat. Najma turns to face me, her cheeks as pale as bone, but her voice is calm as she speaks. "When someone is already full of poison, it takes only a taste of the wrong thing for their life to end. A terrible accident, isn't that right, Diya?"

"Najma," I whisper, but my lips are too numb to say more.

"I knew Solena would never suspect me of poisoning her wine, just as my father didn't expect to die after he kissed you. But was it the wine that killed her, or am I poisonous enough on my own?" she continues. "All those years stealing tiny bits of poison until I became immune and poisonous like you, and now I'm even more poisonous than her cosmetics. Didn't you notice?"

Solena falls to the floor and lies there twitching.

"Of course, I wasn't born with magic like you. I've learned a lot, but not quite enough. So I had to borrow some of your blood—the extra that you kept in a vial where anyone could find it. Remember?"

I feel sick, remembering the night I'd accidentally cut myself and saved the blood because I hadn't wanted to waste it.

After all my efforts to shield her, this is what I've brought her to. I've failed utterly and horribly. I step toward her, but she moves away. "Get out of here. I never want to see you again. Never. Leave here and never return." She looks like her father, her face thunderous.

"Badriya." Her voice, low and measured, brings me out of my stupor. "You killed my sister and my father. You must flee now and go as far away as you can. Do you understand?"

Little Najma. In her face I see etched lines of the King and Solena; she will be strong like them—stronger than I could ever be.

I suddenly realize what she must have wished for the night I washed her hair with the tuberose rinse, though I doubt that the rinse actually granted her wish—it was her own will.

I know now that she will not leave with me, and she never would have.

Her voice softens. "The spell is fading, but Aran is still a beautiful place. Please, Badriya." She sounds like a child again. "Please. I can save Aran, but everyone has to believe it was you who killed Solena."

I see Solena's determination and her father's optimism in her eyes, but none of their cruelty. Khalen is right—she will make a good leader.

I cannot speak so I nod. Her face crumples and I reach for her, wrapping her in my arms. Her poison won't affect me because I am even more toxic than Solena. She allows me to hold her one last time before pushing me away. "Take this," she says, holding out the crown that I had tried to steal from the Crypts. My mouth falls open as I remember Theron's words: *You're not the first person to emerge from there with that request.*

"I can't take this."

"She has no use for it."

I reach for the crown and take it. The Witch will surely be satisfied with it. "Najma," I begin, my throat full, but she speaks over me.

"And take your knife." I rush to the table and grab my knife, its edge scarlet from the poisons. "Now go," she says as I turn, her face like stone.

My eyes burn as I stumble through the door and close it on Najma, who is standing over Solena's body.

Someone is waiting on the other side of the door. I nearly scream until I recognize Petra's voice. "Somehow the Queen's fastest mare has been left untethered," she murmurs. "How strange."

I clutch at her. "Come with me."

Petra gives a short laugh. "What will I do by the sea? I can't swim. I hate water. And I love ghosts." She lifts her chin and I suddenly wonder if she sees ghosts over the Wall. How have I never asked?

As if she were reading my thoughts, she gives me a small smile. "You've always been preoccupied with your own problems."

"Petra, I—"

"No." She holds up a hand. "If I wanted to talk about them, I would have. Just go. But maybe leave me some lip rouge?"

I laugh, though the sound is choked. "You know you can always make it yourself. I've offered to show you a hundred times."

"It's not the same and you know it."

"Najma can show you."

"That's true." She swipes at her face with the back of her hand. "That color makes you look too pale, and you have bags under your eyes."

"And you…" The insult curdles in my mouth. When I am able to speak, I tell her, "You are beautiful, with Stardust and without. You are brave, and loyal, and strong—stronger than I could ever hope to be."

"In one minute I must find Solena's body, so be quick." She pulls me into a tight embrace.

"Take care of Najma," I beg.

Her arms tighten around me. "Of course. And you take care of yourself as well." She shoves me away roughly.

I turn and flee before she can reply and before I can see her lovely, freckled face crease with grief.

I nearly collide with Mina on the stairs. She isn't wearing her scarf again; perhaps she has decided not to wear it anymore. Her scars are like dark shadows in the dim light, yet she is still beautiful. Fear flickers across her face for an instant before her expression hardens.

"I knew it," she breathes. "I knew you'd come back." Her eyes fall on the crown in my hand. "What did you do?" she whispers. She looks up the stairs and into the gallery, then takes the stairs two at a time.

I turn and race toward the stables, shoving past servants and courtiers with solemn faces. As I pass, they draw away and some even hiss accusations. But I have no time for this.

The mare has been left untethered, just as Petra said. She's not the fastest in the stable, but she's quicker than I could ever be on foot. I fear she will not allow me to mount her, but she only nickers crossly as I clamber into her saddle. I hang on desperately as she rushes from her stall. A groomsman rushes in front of us, arms raised and shouting, but he dives out of the way as the mare barrels toward him.

We are quickly through the gate and out into the Lost. The wind rises around us immediately, howling and tossing sand.

Shouts rise in the still air, drowning out my mother's song. I listen for the pounding of hoofbeats, waiting for the guards to ride out after me and drag me back to the city. I'll be hung from the Wall alongside the bones of the guard and forced to face the spirits I'd failed endlessly as the birds nibble at my remains.

I risk glancing back and see the Bones gazing sightlessly down on me as the crows circle above. "Faster," they wheeze, though I might have imagined this.

Suddenly the King is standing before me. My mare shies away from him, and the world is a blur of sound and color as I fly through the air and land in the sand, the breath knocked from me. I struggle to stand as invisible hands below the surface of the sand lock onto my ankles. The wind laughs in my ears as the terrified horse disappears into the distance.

"The Bat has arrived in the sky," says a voice. "Where is my silver?" It's the Duke's Witch. I try to pull away, but the demons won't release me.

She tugs at a coin in her hair. "Well?" she asks, baring her teeth.

"The silver was stolen," I manage.

"You're lying," Her eyes dart to the pouch where I've hidden the crown.

"I only have enough to free my mother," I tell her, glancing behind me to see that two horses have burst from the gate. They struggle toward us in the sand as their riders shout and curse. The King stands nearby in silence.

"Then you must pay with your blood. It has grown quite potent over the years." Stepping closer, she makes a show of sniffing me, and I flinch away. "I can smell it," she says with relish.

I pull the knife from my belt and it thrums in my hand, ready to fight even though I can barely stand. Mother's song fills my ears.

The Witch is at my side in an instant, as if she's flown toward me. She snatches the knife from my hand and holds it to my throat.

I close my eyes and brace myself for the pain. *It will all be worth it,* I tell myself. Mother will be safe, Najma will be Queen, and Solena can't hurt any of us. The knife cuts deep and I smother a cry. My eyes burn and tears pour down my face as I wait for the fatal slice. In my final moments I can cry again. *It will all be worth it…*

"Stop! She is mine." Through my tears I see the First Witch, the one who holds my mother hostage. She stands with her hands on her hips as her gown whips in the wind. Mother's hair is still wound in a plait around her neck.

The Duke's Witch snarls as she turns to face her. "She owes me and says she has no silver." The knife presses into my throat again. The wind howls and the sand stings my face. I close my eyes.

"Give her the silver," the First Witch says.

I am sobbing now, tears dripping from my face. "Then how will I pay you?" I wait for her to tell me that she will take my blood instead.

"Give her the silver," the Witch says again.

I look up at the Duke's Witch and her lip curls. She finally shoves me away into the sand and holds out her hand. "Well?"

I reach into my belt for the crown and hand it to her.

Her eyes light as she snatches it from me and slides it onto her forehead. She begins prancing around. "Look at me!" she trills. "I am the Queen! Everyone bow to the Queen!"

"Stop this nonsense," says the First Witch.

The Duke's Witch glares at me. "Never let me catch you in the Lost again," she says, and vanishes in a cloud of sand.

"Now I have nothing but my blood to offer," I tell the First Witch. Tears spill down my face once again.

"I've never liked blood," she says with a shiver. She flicks her fingers and the demons release me. The approaching horses disappear behind a wall of sand.

She turns back to me. "My mentor would have preferred the jewelry, but you have something even more valuable." She pulls a vial from her belt. "I don't have time for this. They're drying."

"What?"

"Your tears." She steps closer and holds the vial beneath my chin. A fat tear drops into it, then another. "There is true despair and heartbreak in these tears," she says. "And a good deal of poison. They will be very useful."

"What will you do with them?" I ask.

"Don't stop crying," she says sharply. "After all, you'll never see Najma again, and Khalen will likely never forgive you, even though it wasn't your fault."

Her words cause my heart to wrench and more tears spill from my eyes. I am wracked with sobs as she collects them.

"Yes," she says at last, stepping away. "These are a powerful talisman indeed." She tucks the vial back into her belt. "My colleague is too greedy and stupid to notice," she says, her mouth twisting as she looks at the spot where the Duke's Witch disappeared.

She unwinds the hair from her neck and holds it out to me: Mother's dark hair, threaded with red, gold, and a few strands of white. My throat catches for a moment as I remember its scent: salty with a hint of rain.

Mother appears. She smiles at me as she sings. The King stares raptly at her.

"You can go to Cayo now, Mother," I whisper. I tuck the knife into my belt and begin unwinding her hair, casting it into the air where it floats away in different directions.

Mother's song fades to an echo, a murmur, and then a whisper.

"Goodbye," I whisper.

Goodbye, she breathes, her fingers trailing against my cheek. *Goodbye, my brave girl. My Badriya. Return to the living now.* Then she is gone, followed soon after by the King.

My face feels hot and wet, and my vision is blurry. Now that I have begun crying again, it seems that I cannot stop.

The Witch holds the vial to the light, studying my tears. "Tears are much better than blood," she muses. "I've never liked blood, not since my father traded me. He changed his mind at the last moment and the Witch was not pleased."

I wipe my eyes and take a deep breath as I stare at her fine gown. Her dark eyes are very much like the King's and Najma's. "You're her—the Lost Princess."

The Witch rolls her eyes. "Princess," she spits. "I much prefer being a Witch."

"What happened to the first one?" I ask. "The one you were sold to?"

"We don't live forever, you know," she huffs.

Apparently they do live for centuries, though.

"The story always made me out to be the victim," she continues. "Saying that I was traded against my will, but the truth is that I volunteered."

"Why?" I can't help asking.

"In exchange for my sacrifice, she offered to lengthen my life." She taps her chin, pretending to think. "Centuries of freedom or a short life as a pawn—which would you choose?"

If the original Witch is truly gone, perhaps she will help. "Will you save Aran?" I ask.

She narrows her eyes. "What do you care, anyway? You were miserable there. And it's full of horrible people."

"There are good people inside, like my sister, Najma. She will be a good leader."

"She's not your sister."

"She is." As much as anyone could have ever been. "She is the one who told me about you. She will make a bargain with you. She loves Aran."

She regards me with her head tilted for what seems like an eternity. At last, she sighs.

"Very well. I will see what bargain this young Queen is willing to make for Aran." She holds up the vial again. "Seek me out again if you have more reason to cry," she says. "Your tears are very valuable indeed." With that she vanishes.

Now that the Witch is gone, the sand wall falls and the sound of hoofbeats and voices grow closer. Behind me a voice shouts, "Over there!" It's only a matter of time until I am caught, if not by the guards, then by the demons.

I turn and begin to run through the sand, though with every step forward I slide back. Already my lungs burn and my legs ache. The hands of demons skitter at my feet just inches below the sand. I realize that I have no wine for the demons or poison to dull the pain of what is to come when the guards capture me, as they surely will. If they don't catch me, the demons will, and then they will tear me apart as they pull me under the sand. Then I will carry that pain with me as a ghost, doomed to wander the Lost for eternity.

But Najma will be alright, and my mother is free. These are the thoughts that I cling to as I prepare to escape one last, desperate time.

I hear the muted whisper of footsteps and see the streak of a shadow, and suddenly Khalen is beside me, swinging down from his horse.

"Badriya, take my horse. She will do anything she can to get out of the Lost. All you have to do is hang on." Before I can find my words, he boosts me into the saddle. The horse tosses its head, pulling against the reins. Khalen holds her steady, murmuring into her ear and soothing her.

I find my voice. "I'm sorry about Arlo."

His jaw tightens. "Najma will be Queen," he says. "I promise."

"She will be a good Queen," I tell him. "And the Witch will help."

His face creases, but I don't have time to explain. There are so many more things that I want to tell him, but there is no more time.

"Just look to the place you want to go," he says. "And she'll follow."

From beneath the sand there is a groan and the horse breaks away. All I can do is hold on. The wind is hot against my ears, but we are moving too fast for me to hear its taunts. A bony hand reaches from a dune to snatch at us, but the horse easily dodges it as its hooves fly over the surface of the sand.

When I dare to look behind me, I see Khalen's silhouette as he turns to face the riders from Aran. I catch only a glimpse before I am forced to turn back around in the saddle.

I have no silver, but in my bag are cuttings from all of my roots, leaves, and blossoms. There is enough here to mix potions for the lovelorn, for those who fear aging, and for those who are plagued with nightmares. Many people in Mera will pay well for these.

I also have my blood and my tears, which still fall freely from my eyes and down my cheeks, nearly blinding me.

Above the wind my mother's song rises in my ears as if she were right beside me, never really gone at all.

The air is electric tonight. I am almost positive that if I look in the right place, I will see the Lights of Mera. But I do not ride toward Mera. Instead I look toward the mountains where the air is cold and new and I can be close to the stars.

The Bat wheels overhead, but I can only spare a glance, for I must keep my eyes trained on the mountains and urge the horse onward, leaving the ghosts behind.

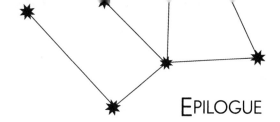

EPILOGUE

It is as cool and clean here as Khalen said it would be. I sleep as night falls, and don't wake again until clear sunlight pours in through the window.

Each morning I work in the garden that I've planted on the side of my tiny house. I've given names to the new roots and plants that grow here: there is sweet stem, which brings good dreams, and one that I named petra because of its cheering effects.

I've traded some salves and sleeping draughts for warm cloaks and trousers to replace the threadbare set that I escaped in.

The scars on my hands and arms are nearly healed, and I hope that I never have to use my blood again. But I know what can happen to hopes.

Khalen's horse brought me here after two days of dodging demons and Witches in the Lost. For a few hours I was sure that the Bat spoke to me from the sky.

Finally, the air grew cooler and the ground became greener as we climbed a steep path up into the mountains. Trees grew around us, their branches whispering in the soft wind.

We reached a small village that was perched high on a cliff. People stopped what they were doing as the horse finally stopped at its center and I slid from its back.

My legs were so chafed and sore that they couldn't hold me anymore, and I hadn't eaten in what felt like days. A man and woman took me into their home; they fed me and allowed me to sleep on a soft bed that smelled of pine.

When I woke, the woman offered me a salve that cooled the pain in my legs. "What is this?" I asked.

"A cream that I make from lowleaf," she replied.

I asked her to show me where it grows, and she led me to a wild garden. I sucked in my breath at the sight of the riot of plants, vines, and blossoms, all with purposes that were waiting to be discovered.

The people here are kind. The couple who took me in, Brynn and Jordy, allow me to stay in a tiny cottage that they own in exchange for Khalen's horse and the salves and tinctures that I create. The other villagers are distant, but friendly enough, and that suits me.

Late one afternoon I am gathering lowleaf to make into a cream for Brynn in exchange for a pie. Overhead the wind blows and pine needles rain down as I hum a song from Mera. I am thinking of the sea when I hear his voice.

"Badriya."

My heart leaps as I slowly stand and turn toward him. His cheeks are burned, and his clothes are dusty, but his smile is the same bright flash.

I want to run to him, but instead I bow my head. "Sir Khalen."

His smile fades and he bows in turn. "Lady Badriya."

"What are you doing here?" I ask, wondering if he plans to drag me back to Tanera to face charges for Arlo's death.

"I came for my horse," he says.

"Well, there she is," I tell him, gesturing to the pasture where his horse grazes happily.

"What have you done to her?" he asks in dismay.

"She's happy."

"She's fat!" He strides over to the horse, running his hand down her neck, but the horse hardly looks up from her meal.

I walk over to his side. "I'm very glad I found you," he says, looking at the horse. "It was a long journey across the Lost. If I hadn't found you here, well, I wasn't looking forward to a trip to Mera."

My heart gives another leap. A retort forms on my tongue, but I say something different altogether. "I'm glad you found me as well."

In that moment he's not a prince and I'm not a poisoner. We are no one as he takes me into his arms.

We spend three days in my little house in the clouds. We wander the mountainside and I cook for him—Brynn has taught me to make a delicious soup. I show him the village and in the evenings we talk after dinner.

"How is Najma?" I ask.

"She is as strong a ruler as you hoped," he says. "A few missteps, but nothing that couldn't be corrected. She hopes that you will send her a tincture for love."

"No," I say immediately, and he is already laughing. "Who is it?" I demand.

"Don't worry," he says. "She listens to Petra, and Petra is very practical."

"Hardly," I mutter, but this is just for show. I feel a rush of relief. Of course Petra is taking care of her.

He takes my hand, running his finger over the scars there. Leaning over, I kiss his lips, no longer afraid of poisoning him. I lead him to my bed.

"You've bewitched me," he breathes, brushing his lips over my temple. His mouth travels across my cheek to my neck, my mouth, and my collarbone until I can't catch my breath enough to deny his words.

On his last night we sit outside and look up at the sky. The stars are scattered across the sky like the jewels from the Festival of the Full Moon. The Crocodile is in the sky—it is the time to watch and see.

When Khalen leaves, tears fall from my eyes. "I can stay," he tells me, but I shake my head. He must rule Tanera and help Najma in Aran.

"I'll be back when the Moth rises," he promises.

I don't send Najma the love tincture, but I do send her sweet stem, and for Petra a balm to make her lips bright and full. For Khalen I send bluewort, to help him make wise decisions.

When he kisses me goodbye there is no poison, only sadness and promise. I wait until I can't see him anymore, then I return to the garden. There is cloudflower to be gathered, and needleroot and hopeseed. For wishes granted.

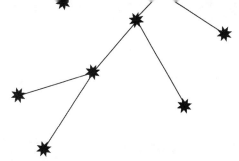

About the Author

Kristin Burchell writes primarily for middle-grade and young adult readers, including her book, *The Witches of Proposal Rock*, but *Court of Venom* is her first adult fantasy novel. She has won recognition from Willamette Writers and the Northwest Institute of Literary Arts for her novels. She currently lives in the Pacific Northwest—the perfect place for her to dream up her stories. When she's not writing or teaching, you'll find her reading, stargazing, and hiking with her husky in the Columbia River Gorge.

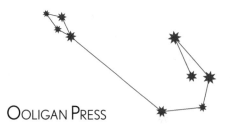

OOLIGAN PRESS

Ooligan Press is a student-run publishing house rooted in the rich literary culture of the Pacific Northwest. Founded in 2001 as part of Portland State University's Department of English, Ooligan is dedicated to the art and craft of publishing. Students pursuing master's degrees in book publishing staff the press in an apprenticeship program under the guidance of a core faculty of publishing professionals.

Project Managers
Wren Haines
Bailey Potter

Editing
Rachel Howe
Erica Wright

Design
Katherine Flitsch
Morgan Ramsey

Digital
Amanda Hines
Chris Leal

Marketing
Sarah Moffatt
Hannah Boettcher

Publicity
Emma St. John
Alexandria Gonzales

Social Media
Riley Robert
Alix Martinez

Book Production
Alexandra Burns
Alexandra Magel
Amanda Fink

Claire Plaster
Eily McIlvain
Elaine Schumacher
Emma St. John
Frances Fragela
John Huston
Katherine Flitsch
Kelly Zatlin
Megan Jessop
Megan Vader Bongolan
Phoebe Whittington
Rachael Renz
Rachel Adams
Rachel Lantz
Rebecca Gordon
Rosina Miranda
Sarah Moffatt
Sophie Concannon
Stephanie Johnson Lawson
Kyndall Tiller
Kelly Morrison
Alena Rivas
Alexander Halbrook
Elliot Bailey
Jenna Amundson
Alexa Schmidt
Ashley Lockard
Anna Wehmeier Giol